Scandinavian Music

Scandinavian Music

Finland & Sweden

Antony Hodgson

RUTHERFORD ● MADISON ● TEANECK
Fairleigh Dickinson University Press

LONDON
Associated University Presses

© 1984 by Associated University Presses, Inc.

Associated University Presses
440 Forsgate Drive
Cranbury, NJ 08512

Associated University Presses
25 Sicilian Avenue
London WC1A 2QH, England

Associated University Presses
2133 Royal Windsor Drive
Unit 1
Mississauga, Ontario
Canada L5J 1K5

Library of Congress Cataloging in Publication Data

Hodgson, Antony.
  Scandinavian music.

  Bibliography: p.
  Includes index.
  1. Music—Finland—History and criticism. 2. Music—
Sweden—History and criticism. I. Title.
ML269.H6 1984   781.74897   84-47547
ISBN 0-8386-2346-8

PRINTED IN THE UNITED STATES OF AMERICA

781.74897
Hod

Contents

Acknowledgements

My thanks are due to the following for their help and encouragement in preparing this book: Henrik Antell of the Finnish Embassy, London; Terry Carlbom of the Swedish Embassy, London; Kristofer Gräsbeck of the Ministry for Foreign Affairs, Helsinki; Bo Hyttner of Sterling Records, Stockholm; to Robert Dearling for his skill and thoroughness in assembling the discographical information; and to Eric Hughes of the British Institute of recorded sound for providing material to which I should not otherwise have had access.

Part 1

Introduction

The cultures of Finland and Sweden have for long been closely linked. In 1582 Finland became a Swedish grand duchy and remained so until 1809.

The overlapping nature of the two countries' early musical history is exemplified by the career of Bernhard Henrik Crusell (1775-1838). Finnish-born he moved to Stockholm at the age of sixteen in order to continue his studies, later going to Berlin and Paris to gain further experience; he never performed in Finland after 1801.

The cosmopolitan nature of the careers of Finnish and Swedish composers of the pre-romantic era parallels the spread of Bohemian influence in southern Europe. If, in the eighteenth century, one wished to hear outstanding music by Czech composers, one could scarcely do better than go to the court of the Elector, Karl Theodore von der Pfalz, at Mannheim. The influence of central Europe was pervasive; small wonder, therefore, that the music of Crusell and of the Czech composer Antonín Reicha have, superficially at least, a great deal in common, especially with regard to their Beethoven-like use of the orchestra.

This period of common culture between Finland and Sweden seems less obvious when viewed from a twentieth-century standpoint, since the independent nature of Finnish artistic progress, based on revolutionary changes of outlook at the end of the nineteenth century, is now seen with hindsight. The adoption of, and considerable pride in, the Finnish language influenced all the arts in a dramatic way and it is difficult to look back to a time when this was not so. By 1900 Swedish music had been progressing for almost a century during which time Finland had become an independent duchy of Russia though she could not entirely forget her Swedish cultural roots. Sweden, since separation from Finland, had continued in her mainstream of cultural thought. This did include some central European ideas but, by the time Finland had finally changed artistic direction, a specifically Swedish culture had emerged.

To chart the growth of the two musical cultures it is interesting to go back to the thirteenth century.

Songs played a vital role in the early development of Swedish and Finnish music. The traditional songs of Scandinavia were often bound together by references to events of common knowledge such as the wars between the kings. For example, the murder of the Danish King Erik Klipping in 1286 (cousin to King Erik of Norway) is well documented in song and even the visiting German Minnesingers are known to have written verses in his praise and to lament his death—we have accounts of such performances during their Scandinavian tours. It is, therefore, not entirely surprising that a late thirteenth-century ballad should relate the adventures of the two daughters of chancellor Stig, (who was popularly supposed to have plotted the murder of Erik Klipping,) driven from the Danish court, they sought refuge first in Sweden (without success) and eventually found a home at the court of the more sympathetic King of Norway.

The first example of song notation is the Codex Runicus. The notation describing the weaving of gold and silver, is given at the end of the manuscript in runic characters. The date is somewhere between 1296 and 1319.

ᚠᚱᛆᛘᚠᛏ: ᛘᛁᛕ: ᛏ ᚱ: ᚠᚱᛆᛘ: ᛁ:
D R Ø M D Æ   M I K   Æ N   D R Ø M   I

ᛏ ᛁ ᛏ: ᚩ ᛘ ᛋᛁᛚᚴᛁ: ᛆ ᚴ: ᛏ ᚱᚠᛁᚴ:
N A T   U M   S I L K I   O K   Æ R L I K

ᚴ ᛏ ᚠ
P Æ L . . .

This text lacks the obligatory *omkvaed* or chorus ending which simply summarised the essence of what had gone before. The Codex Runicus also inscribes the musical notation above the text. An English translation by Pamela Vaughan adds a suitable *omkvaed*.

> In a dream at night I've seen the finest of silken weave,
> Gold cloth and fine attire, riches I'll never own,
> Silk and gold I've seen in a dream.

It was not until the late sixteenth century that the written compilation of songs hitherto verbally handed down became more customary, with courtiers of the time often responsible for such collections. Also in the late sixteenth century the culture of Sweden emerged from that of the rest of Scandinavia with an individuality of its own. Central to the development of these cultures were the early choir schools such as those established by Laurentius Petri during the reign of Johan III (1560-92) under whose rule the linking of Finland and Sweden came about. The most famous of these schools was at Turku (Åbo), where Theodoric Peter of Nyland compiled his great collection of songs, *Piae cantiones*.

For a country to nurture the development of its music in parallel with that of its other individualistic works, a stable artistic background is needed. Until Gustav Vasa came to power in 1523, therefore, Sweden's musical-artistic threads are crossed by those of neighbouring countries and almost another century passed before a musical monarch, Gustav II Adolf, made it possible for a musical establishment to be founded at the court of Sweden.

With the seventeenth century, distinctions between Swedish and Finnish music became blurred and it was not until the cessation of Swedish rule in Finland that the true contrast emerged. Swedish music moved in parallel with the individualistic development of other works, setting it apart from central European thought in its avoidance of heavy sentimental romanticism, while Finnish music awaited the development of Finnish literature.

Mainly as a result of the political alliance of Sweden and Finland, Finnish culture is thought to be Scandinavian and outside Scandinavia there is little attempt to make a distinction. The true contrast really becomes clear however, when regard is paid to the individuality of the Finnish language. In order to trace any continuous line of Finnish musical tradition before the seventeenth century, however, it is necessary to turn to folk music and to the *kantele*.

The first thorough account of Finnish poetry and music comes from the writings of Joseph Acerbi whose travels through Sweden, Finland, and Lapland published in 1802 gives something of an organised account of Finnish music-making and the appendix which collects Finnish kantele melodies, provides a valuable link. Because of the *kantele* and the inherently Finnish nature of the folk poetry set for this instrument, the humble folk aspect of Finnish music was the essence of the preservation of Finnish Art.* When in 1835, Elias Lönnrot published *Kalevala,* the epic poems of which it is comprised proved to be the very material handed down over the years through the settings for the kantele. Lönnrot also collected other lyrical poetry which he called *kanteletar.*

In the realm of artistic rather than folk poetry, the notable Finnish poets such as Creutz and Kellgren had used the Swedish language. So the preservation of the Finnish epics and continuation of the folk music tradition was not central to the artistic progress of the Swedish-Finnish empire of the eighteenth century but had its parallel outside the courts and was certainly free from central European thinking.

Finland's musical development was influenced by the Reformation, though the effect was more concerned with a widened appreciation of music than any inherent change in the music of the time. Lutheranism made it possible for Gregorian chant to be used in the Finnish language. Whilst Christianity had originally come to Finland in the twelfth century, the Swedish Christian influence dates back to the ninth, nevertheless the Reformation was scarcely less influential in Sweden than in Finland.

Although the characteristic differences which have emerged over the past two centuries between Finnish and Swedish music can be discussed in terms of the different political routes taken by the two countries, this is no more than a pointer to the differences of environment which in turn altered the influences on the composers themselves. A dramatic change of artistic direction will have an overwhelming influence upon the precise nature of the music written after its manifestation, though such an event is not essential to progress.

A parallel to the huge change of direction brought about by Lönnrot's publication of *Kalevala* is the rise of the eighteenth-century Sturm und Drang movement in Germany. Goethe, Herder Hamann, and later Schiller, were closely associated with this literary movement, which drew its name from a tragedy by Frederick Maximilian von Klinger (1752-1831). By the standards of that day the passions of the characters portrayed were extravagant in the extreme: the onlooker was no longer permitted to sit back and allow the drama to unfold, rather he was caught up in it, forced to identify with a character of a philosophy, and kept in a state of tension until the dénouement. This feeling spilled over into the music and Joseph Haydn's marked alteration of style around the beginning of the 1770s is usually thought to stem from the feeling behind this literary movement.

---

*The Finnish painter, Akseli Gallen-Kallela (1865-1931) was a contemporary and friend of Sibelius and holds as remarkable a position in the field of visual arts in Finland as Sibelius holds in the field of music. Gallen-Kallela is best known for his powerful illustrations of the Finnish national epic, the *Kalevala*. (See Plate in Finnish section)

Kantele player: Jaako Kullu from Suojärvi (East Karelia).
Traditional type hollowed out of wood.
(Photo: A.O. Väisänen, Museovirasta, Finland)

There is good evidence to suggest that at this time Haydn's music, and particularly his symphonies, took on a tense insistent nature, gripping the listeners by the closely-argued development and the original use of progressive harmonies, delaying the resolution to the tonic key until the last possible moment, so parallelling the taut discipline and delayed dénouement of the plays of the period.

It is by no means far-fetched to move forward over half a century to Lönnrot's publication of *Kalevala* in 1835* in order to see a similar pattern emerging. Here the literary influence of the Finnish lore which, though already in existence, had never previously been collated, affected artistic thought enormously. Whilst the Sturm und Drang movement permeated English and French literature and thought, the inspiration of the *Kalevala* was specifically national. Finland, though not at that time wildly alive with thoughts of independence since the relationship with Russia had been relatively amicable, was nevertheless awakened to an important part of its heritage which had hitherto lain dormant, preserved mainly by the passing from mouth to mouth of the old tales. † Because the tales were often told through recitation where one folklorist would take over from another, some moments had to be devoted to the assembling of the narrator's thoughts. A constant feature of the poetry therefore, is repetition, the alternative formulation of a single statement, as illustrated in the following six lines taken from W.F. Kirby's translation:

> Vietyä vetoperänsä
> maajyväset maksettua
> rekehensä reutoaikse
> kohennaikse korjahansa,
> Alkoi kulkea kotihin,
> matkata omille maille

> When he now paid the taxes
> And had also paid the land dues
> In his sledge he quickly bounded
> And upon his sledge he mounted
> And began the journey homeward
> And to travel to his country.

The renaissance of a partially forgotten folk art was taken up in the mid nineteenth century by many writers. Further impetus was added because of the imposing reappearance, in an artistic context, of the Finnish language after general subjugation—a subjugation brought about more

---

*The first edition of some 12,000 verses was published at this time and the second edition of just under 24,000 verses was published in 1849.

†The entirely individual style of the verse in *Kalevala* is related closely to the semi-improvisatory nature of the story-telling.

Jouhikko player: Juho Vaittinen from Impilahti (East Karelia).
(Photo: A.O. Väisänen, Museovirasta, Finland)

Fiddler: Kustaa Laitala from Keski-Pohjanmaa (Central Ostrobothnia)
(Photo: Kansanmusiikki-instituuti, Kaustinen, Finland)

from inattention and the convenience of Swedish than from conscious discussion or counter-nationalism. (The deep effect which this dawning of new Finnish consciousness had upon Kajanus and Sibelius is discussed later.) A similar event occurred in Norway as the new national awareness typified by Rikard Nordraak fired Grieg with his visionary enthusiasm and became a strong factor in guiding the development of his music.

Although Sweden's music did not undergo a dramatic change of direction, its development was no less sure. Indeed by the mid nineteenth century Berwald, then at his best and most industrious, had taken Swedish music along lines in the orchestral and instrumental field, which could stand proudly alongside the notably musical countries of Europe. Sweden could not boast the sheer quantity of fine composers active in Germany, but here, in a fallow period for Germany's constant rival Bohemia, Sweden could offer forward-looking music.

It seems reasonable at this point to take an example, in earlier times, of Swedish development without specific impetus—a sort of negative parallel to Sturm und Drang. It appears that the eighteenth century shows a number of examples in music but in order to keep comparisons close, let us return to Haydn who was refining and developing the art of the symphony in leaps and bounds. At Eszterhazá, in the remote Hungarian countryside, orchestral music was being first changed and then established. Not surprisingly, reflections of this remarkable phenomenon were not too far in arrear in neighbouring regions: Vienna was fairly well aware of such developments and Prague had some musicians in the Haydn mould, but just because these influences were not to be found in certain other areas, it did not mean that the development of symphonic art ceased. It developed miraculously in parallel, despite the complete lack of direct influence.

To take one far-flung area which Haydn's influence could scarcely have reached, it is worth considering the court of Don Carlos, Prince of the Asturias, (later King Carlos IV of Spain,) which, for virtually the whole of the latter part of the eighteenth century, housed Gaetano Brunetti (*c.* 1743-1808). This composer's exact title was never defined but he was certainly court composer, leading violinist, and probably Kapellmeister. His compositions were frequently noted as being for the sole use of the Prince of the Asturias (and occasionally in similar vein, for the use of the Duke of Alba: Brunetti's other patron).

Through the extensive series of symphonies written by Brunetti, shut off as he was from the rest of Europe and its influence, a powerful symphonic pattern was soon discernible. The symphony under Brunetti achieved a regular form, similar to what is regarded as classical form but no such criterion existed at the time. Brunetti's third movements are in dance form, but not necessarily minuets. The Gavotte appealed to him more, but the convention of the trio section was still employed. Sonata movements would more often have three subjects than two (a Bohemian trait) and the recapitulation section might not be confined to the conventional place but be fragmented about the latter half of the movement.

The differences between the characteristics of a Brunetti symphony and the standard symphonic form are small. Symphonic form as developed around the late 1760s to 1770s is very close to Brunetti's philosophy, yet Brunetti did not have to develop in this way, indeed he could have held to the baroque-influenced style of the Italian school of the 1750s. Instead, alone, enclosed in a court in Spain with only Boccherini of similar culture for company (and the enmity of Boccherini, who came to Spain later than Brunetti as musician to the Infanta Don Luigi, is legendary) Brunetti developed as complex an art form as did Haydn, or indeed Mozart, or any of the Mannheim school.

So too, the steady, ostensibly undramatic progress of Swedish art, relatively removed from central Europe but with strong, Germanic teachings reaching deep into the theoretical skills of its exponents, had a parallel to the development of the music of other countries in the eighteenth century.

It was not until the time of Sibelius that Finnish music became noticeably Finnish whilst Stenhammar and his contemporaries are reached before Swedish music can be seen to be moving firmly away from central European influence. Sweden may not have had quite Finland's nationalistic motivation but the individuality of Swedish music began to develop subtly yet with a certain inevitability until the generation of composers active in the first half of this century made so individual an impact that influences other than internal ones may scarcely be detected. To be hypercritical one could take an important work such as *Forklädd Gud* by Lars-Erik Larsson and cite the powerful influence of Carl Nielsen (one which Larsson would be unlikely to deny) but this would merely assert the closeness of Scandinavian thought in the 1930s. Indeed why should a Swede not write music which reflects certain characteristics of a near-contemporary Dane? It would have been far stranger if some of the musical fingerprints of Sibelius had been incorporated.

Finnish musical thought is as dissimilar to Swedish thought as the difference in language between the two nations. Common ground is concerned with respect for musical logic, an affinity for symphonic structure and a very cautious view of atonality, twelve-tone music and similar twentieth century offshoots from mainstream thinking. In these aspects, Finland and Sweden are very similar, in others, contemporary composers travel along different lines of thought. Whereas in the nineteenth century it is not very much more than the accident of Finnish birth that places the Swedish and German influenced Crusell in the Finnish section of this book, phenomena such as the totally Finnish upsurge of opera in the 1970s or the entirely Swedish predilection for truly creative electronic composition, make the line of demarcation very positive indeed.

The impact in Finland of the Savonlinna Festival - centred upon opera—is hugely significant. The festival was first held in 1967 and it has grown ever since. The only danger is the temptation to suppose that since so many musical miracles have been worked, they will inevitably continue. It is not for this book to try to place Finnish feet too firmly upon the ground in this respect except to add that the overwhelming success of the art itself overcame any lack of organizational or financial support and swept officialdom along in its wake.

Prior to the recent artistic blossoming, only two attempts had been made this century to exploit the natural beauty of Savonlinna, both were by the soprano Aino Ackté and neither succeeded. It was left to Yrjö Kilpinen to rejuvenate an idea abandoned finally by Aino Ackté in 1930. Savonlinna was at first simply a centre for musical master-classes but in 1967 the Finnish President attended the première of *Fidelio* at Savonlinna and the opportunity to capture public imagination had arrived. In 1970 the revival of Merikanto's *Juha* began to reawaken enthusiasm for national opera and, protected by an efficient, carefully designed awning across the courtyard of Olavinlinna Castle, spectacular and spacious effects could be created culminating in the vast battle scenes of Panula's *Jaakko Ilkka*.

To be cynical one could point out that the National Opera House in Helsinki seats only about 500 people and so something revolutionary had to be created. On the other hand without remarkable music, the project could not have succeeded and artistry has, encouragingly enough, triumphed where mere political expediency would never have sufficed. Finnish composers now write operas, a new and successful opera festival exists and consequently the application of the term *opera* has broadened. For example Kalevi Aho, one of the most exciting young symphonists of recent times, has written *The Key* - a one act, one man soliloquy. This work is described as an opera and if effort is not made to give a broad view of Finnish music to foreign audiences, there is the danger that music lovers will decide for themselves that this is either an example of Spartan economy or alternatively that the calculated extravagance of Jorma Panula's gigantic *Jaakko Ilkka* is typical of the new Finnish direction. It seems that the real route lies somewhere along an average of the two, but it remains encouraging that the range is so wide.

Even less is the average music lover aware of the details of the domestic Finnish musical scene; that is to say the output of composers not widely known outside Finland. A good example of contemporary music which has not crossed the borders whilst yet showing skill and preserving the traditional values of composition is that of Erik Fordell (b. 1917) whose half-century of symphonies is fast approaching and whose music, largely symphonic, more often achieves radio performance than public acclaim, yet there is more than mere worthiness in Erik Fordell's gifts. Just as the average enthusiast for music of the eighteenth century need not feel that there is a huge gap in his knowledge if he cannot claim to have heard the music of the Polish composer Jan Wánski (1762-*c*.1800) or the Slovak composer Anton Zimmerman, it does not prevent revelatory beauty being encountered when a work by such relatively neglected composers is, on rare occasions, performed or recorded. So too Erik Fordell appears to enjoy a position in Finland slightly better in terms of familiarity than that which Havergal Brian had in Great Britain for the greater part of his career before belated recognition arrived.

Meanwhile the Finnish Finnlevy company (using the label Finlandia for its exports), is also beginning to make inroads abroad for the cause of Finnish music. Overseas appreciation has been helped by a sudden surprising awareness during the 1970s and early 1980s of many important events taking place in Finnish musical life, events including the Helsinki Festival in its newly increased scope, the impressive developments of the Helsinki Philharmonic Orchestra, and the awareness of the importance of Savonlinna. Admittedly this last is due largely to the popularity of Talvela as an artist, for his name is so well known that his tenure as artistic director from 1973 to 1979 itself made news and this tended to understate the meritorious fact that his enormous enthusiasm helped the whole artistic conception of Finnish opera to progress admirably in those years.

Finnish music lovers may be surprised at the reasons for the flowering of foreign appreciation, but if it is realised that, inevitably, outside knowledge will be led more positively by the recorded availability of music in countries other than Finland than by any amount of internal critical acclaim then an understanding of sympathy from abroad may dawn. This strangely biased reflection on Finnish musical life may also serve to show that a sense of responsibility in what is published on internationally sold recordings becomes important. In Great Britain there is an encouraging nucleus of those who appreciate Finnish music but because its members may never have had the opportunity to visit a Finnish festival, their appreciation may not be entirely current.

The latest developments in Swedish music bear no relation to the Finnish turn of events. Where in Finland, the operatic revolution looks set to increase the relative importance of the music of a country whose roots lie in symphony rather than drama, the Swedish musical establishment succeeds with solid progress through democratic, usually government-supported channels. To most countries in Europe (and particularly to the music lovers of Great Britain) dependence on government intervention and support is something akin to an artistic kiss of death. In Sweden, despite the risk of supporting dross along with worthwhile and original music, the progress of musical culture continues apace. The decentralisation of musical schooling can only be beneficial. The attempts to create an overall uniformity in methods of music teaching throughout Sweden suggest the kind of threatened disaster which might befall any well-intentioned streamlining of methods. Fortunately Swedish music seems so healthily varied and independent that it is likely to throw off such organisational shackles before they threaten to stultify creativity.

The continuing anthology of Swedish music on records promoted by the Institute for National Concerts (Rikskonserter) is proceeding steadily and many a country may envy so brave a centrally financed project. Perhaps no less exciting however, is the enthusiasm of several fairly small Swedish record companies—supported only by their own know-how and business acumen—for the promotion of Swedish music. If in England there is an uncomfortable feeling of undue chauvinism at recording English music, Sweden has no such inhibitions and in the last few years the European catalogues have benefitted enormously from the diversity of Swedish material being offered. Composers, though not given indiscriminate support, appear at least to have their names and nature made readily available to interested music-lovers, so that the only real danger in terms of outside recognition appears to be that because of the diversity of the considerable musical talent in Sweden at the present, the very plethora of significant names may confuse those not moving within specifically Swedish circles.

From differing yet overlapping cultures, the music of Finland and of Sweden has progressed to a point where an extraordinary difference of outlook is apparent to outside eyes. Sweden is now the progressive country, teeming with musical talent, home of the avant-garde, the brilliant experimenters and traditionalists who do not hesitate to break their own rules if it suits them, yet alone of Scandinavian countries Sweden boasts no national composer of such a stature as to spring immediately to the lips of musical foreigners. Sweden is surely the obverse of the Eastern Scandinavian coin, a nationalistic design, worked with craftsmanship and taste: a musical democracy rather than a kingdom. On the other side of the same coin in Finland: no need to suggest whose head is metaphorically represented there and scarcely any need to explain the Finnish musical situation. A new tradition puts the modern Finnish composer in an unenviable position, if he chooses, for example, to employ the effect of continued ostinato then he is open to the charge of imitating Sibelius, if he does not use ostinato then he is deemed to be deliberately avoiding Sibelian style.

These simplifications are not too far removed from current opinion about Finnish and Swedish music, the real truth lies in the individuality and variety of the music of both countries. In Finland the composer-performer is more frequently encountered and music is on the whole written for large forces, while the modern diversity of instrumentation on the smaller scale so beloved of Germany, France, and England is given more attention by Sweden (and by Finns of Swedish persuasion). One might suggest that there is nothing more to this than Swedish astuteness in realising the enhanced possibility of performance when fewer instruments are employed, but the characteristic of economical, analytical scoring in Swedish music goes further than mere commercial expediency. Lars-Erik Larsson, one of Sweden's most famous composers, is of a stature which does not necessitate commercial considerations, but his considerable output includes quantities of music suitable for chamber ensembles.

Most musical appreciation tends to run along traditional lines and one of the unwritten conventions is the demand to have important artistic names for admiration—"great" composers who are the pride of their nation. Finland boasts one stunning example in Jean Sibelius, Sweden does not. In substitution, foreign appreciation chooses its heroes illogically. Hugo Alfvén caught the imagination with *Midsommarvaka* but in addition a cheapened, café band arrangement of only its first tune brought enormous further popularity in the mid 1950s. Would the composer have been better-off without such spurious popularity or is it good that his name should be known to those who might otherwise never have heard it, nor indeed listened to any of his music?

Karl-Birger Blomdahl composed the first "space-opera", but can one be sure that the enthusiastic musical recognition which ensued was due to an appreciation of his exceptional compositional orginality, or was it merely a result of the novelty of the conception?

The most recent composer to benefit from quasi-musical ideas rather than simple attraction to his music is Allan Pettersson. There has been much inconclusive discussion on the meaning behind his more dramatic works. Probably some conclusions have been drawn about Pettersson's philosophies which, though interesting and even controversial were not central to the music of this remarkable man. Then again he fought courageously both with the deprived circumstances of his upbringing and with the daunting ill health which dogged him in his last years. It is easy to allow these well-publicised non-musical discussions to take precedence over the music itself. It does seem however that any reason to interest the public in so keen a musical mind may show the end to be justified by the means.

In the last resort, time justifies all. Pettersson will be remembered by the quality of his music, not the circumstances of his life, just as Alfvén's most popular piece will serve to remind the listener of the special regard which the composer felt for Swedish folk origins. After over a century it is apt that Berwald is regarded as an important composer of orchestral music. The unusual combination of this with more prosaic occupations, once a talking point, has ceased to matter in today's musical atmosphere where a joint career in broadcasting and composition is so common as to excite no comment. Sweden is at last emerging from her position of mystery, hitherto compounded by the unfamiliarity of foreign audiences with the most important names, but talent seems now to be given something like its due.

In Finland a different but genuine awareness is taking place, the shadow cast by Sibelius is fading gradually. A new appreciation of those composers who, not seeking to avoid Sibelian influence, have long been regarded as mere disciples, however, is now overdue. If Sweden deserves improved recognition for her exciting wealth of contemporary musical talent, Finland merits recognition of the music of the recent past in order to complete a balanced view.

Finland

By convention Fredrik Pacius (1809-91) is regarded as the Father of Finnish Music, although it would probably be more accurate to say that the patriotic aspect in Pacius was one of the elements from which arose the nationalistic development of Finnish music during the nineteenth century. Pacius set to music one of the poems of J.L. Runeberg (1804-77) taken from *Fänrik Ståls Sägner*. The poem, drawn from the beginning of that epic, was written in Swedish (the poet's language of the day) and showed concern over the assertion by Russia of rights upon Finland. Pacius did much more for Finnish nationalism, however, beyond the setting of Runeberg's famous anthem, *Vårt land*: during his term as lecturer at Helsinki University he transcribed traditional music for student choral organisations and collected Finnish folk songs (kanteletar). Although his work was never published as a single organised collection of folk music (its later collation was the work of Krohn, Launis, and Väisänen at the start of the twentieth century), the nature of Pacius's research can reasonably be compared to that of Bartók in Hungary.

The one element, however, which sets him apart from other artists with Finnish traditions at heart, and makes the title Father of Finnish Music strangely incongruous, is his birthplace (Hamburg) and his German musical education. His studies under Ludwig Spohr at Kassel stood him in good stead as a notable violinist, while composition was taught him by Hauptmann. His considerable output included the first Finnish opera, *Kaarle-Kuninkaan metsästys* [King Charles's Hunt], to a text by Topelius.

It is certainly true that Pacius, through his enthusiasm for and dedication to the Finnish musical cause, encouraged the expansion of essentially local, Finnish thinking during his lifetime but too much concentration on this focal point of nineteenth-century musical life obscures the importance of earlier Finnish composers. For Finnish musical tradition, although not necessarily so well organised, goes back rather further than Fredrik Pacius.

The tragedy of the remarkable classicist Erik Tulindberg (1761-1814) is the loss of so many of his manuscripts. Tulindberg was an excellent violinist and cellist (playing both instruments in orchestras during his student days) and later he became a member of the Stockholm Academy of Music; his profession, however, was that of a civil servant, an accountant, auditor, and Head of Finance from 1794 until the end of Swedish rule in 1809. Born in 1761 at Vähäkyro, Tulindberg studied at the Turku Academy from 1776 and gained a master's degree in 1782. In 1783 he wrote the first large-scale Finnish composition—a Violin Concerto—but it is not known whether a performance of either this or the succeeding concerto, op. 2, ever took place during his lifetime. Only the First Violin Concerto has survived and its Haydnesque nature is at once apparent. The scoring is for two oboes (or flutes), two horns, strings and continuo. More developed and rather more mature in its harmonic content is the set of six string quartets, marked variously on the manuscript parts as op. 1 and op. 2 (notwithstanding the fact that Tulindberg had referred to his Violin Concerti by the same numbers when dedicating them to Baron Olof Alström, the founder of the Stockholm Academy). In many ways the set of quartets is more unified than the famous group of the Six Quartets op. 3, attributed (amid numerous dissenting voices) to Joseph Haydn. Even Tulindberg's fantasia-like slow movements are consistent within themselves, and the sonata form and minuets show a Haydnesque organisation. It is a matter of some regret that the original second violin part has never been found, although the omission has since been righted by Toivo Haapanen and John Rosas.

The remaining Finnish composer of note from the generation before Pacius is Bernhard Henrik Crusell (1775-1838). Although the most important Finnish musical organisation in his time was the Musical Society at Turku, which provided for orchestral, choral and chamber concerts, Crusell travelled much throughout Europe after his musical education in Stockholm in the 1790s. Initially he was a clarinettist and his interest in the instrument remained throughout his life. When in Stockholm, he played in the Court Orchestra and had a career as a soloist, whilst also being director of both Bands of the Royal Guards. His most frequently performed works are those for clarinet, including the Concertante for Clarinet, Bassoon and Orchestra, the three Concerti and the three Clarinet Quartets. *

When in the 1820s ill health began to take its toll, leading to his premature retirement from European appointments in 1830, Crusell turned to literary work for the theatre and was responsible for translations of the great operas, including Beethoven's *Fidelio,* Rossini's *Il barbiere di Siviglia* [*Barberan i Sevilla*], Mozart's *Le nozze di Figaro* (which translates particularly charmingly as *Figaros bröllop*) and works by Adam, Auber, Boeldieu, Meyerbeer, and Spohr.

A most revealing book about Crusell, including over a hundred close-printed pages of transcriptions from his diaries, was published in Swedish by the Royal Musical Academy in Stockholm in 1977.† His remarkable talents reflect upon Finnish musical history through the prism of a central European culture, stemming from his sojourns in Sweden and Germany and his use of Swedish as a first tongue. This effectively puts the abilities of this remarkable man outside the scope of Finnish musical development from a nationalist standpoint.

The influence of the organised mind of Pacius was, in the best sense of the word, academic, for here was an admired figure who methodically gathered together the important elements of a culture which had fragmented for political reasons. His son-in-law, Karl Collán (1828-71), a writer rather than a composer, had great sympathy for his father's philosophies and composed many songs to German and Finnish texts. Although a minor figure in Finnish music, Collán was nevertheless part of the mainstream and can be considered the last of the Finnish classicists.

By the time the earliest of the Romantic school of composers, Filip von Schantz (1834-65), had begun his work, the climate of artistic feeling in Finland had changed course through Lönnrot's publication of *Kalevala* in 1835. Through the use of Finnish as the epic's language, poetry and nationalism became inseparable. The literary change became evident only

---

*Finnish Radio have a score of the Concertante for Two Clarinets and Wind Ensemble. The Royal Academy in Stockholm has copies of the Concertino for Bassoon and the extensive Singspiel *Pieni orjatar* [The Small Bondwoman], which dates from 1824. Crusell's later songs, based on traditional Norse Sagas, are not all published but Müller of Stockholm has printed the most substantial contributions to this literature: notably, the cycle of ten songs composed in 1822, the group of seven from 1824 and, perhaps best known of all, *Ten Songs from Frithiofs Saga.*

†*Bernhard Crusell. Tonsätare Klarinetvirtuos.* Stockholm: Kungl. Musikaliska Akadamiens Skriftserre 21, 1977.

gradually: Runeberg (1804-77) and Topelius (1818-98) were certainly nationalist poets, but Aleksis Kivi (1834-72) was the first to use the Finnish language to this end in original poetry; the first opera in the Finnish language (*Pohjan neiti* by Oskar Merikanto) was not composed until 1899. It was within this atmosphere of change that Richard Faltin (1835-1918) developed his musical skills. He was probably the true heir of Pacius–also German-born, he had a talent for choral and organ music, and he did valuable work on liturgical texts–although he was more skilled artist than revolutionary. His skill as a choral and orchestral conductor won him fame alongside his publication of arrangements of Finnish folk songs. Always the professional, he reflected the Russo-Finnish alliance of the time in both his Russian folk songs to Swedish and Finnish texts (with orchestra) and *Czar Alexander's Cantata* (1894). Faltin's only major work to use the Finnish language was *Promootio kantaatti* [Graduation Cantata].

Ernst Fabritius (1842-99) shared a similarly progressive romantic outlook and his fame as a concert violinist placed him at the centre of Finnish musical life, but, although he too composed music for specifically Finnish poems, his best known vocal works were his German songs (with orchestra) and his Violin Concerto. Fabritius composed no major work during the last twenty years of his life.

The focal point of the Finnish musical awakening was, characteristically, centred on a famous Finn whose artistic upbringing was grounded far more in the German tradition than the Finnish. This central figure, Robert Kajanus (1856-1933), was, towards the end of the nineteenth century, to become the catalyst in Finland's marked change of musical direction. Kajanus originally studied theory with Faltin in Helsinki and the violin with Niemann and Leander. He continued his studies at Leipzig under Hans Richter and Heinrich Carsten Reinecke, his cosmopolitan education was completed in Paris and Dresden. Whilst in Paris he had the opportunity to work with Svendsen and, on his return to Finland, Kajanus laid the foundations for a notable conducting career. In 1882 Helsinki's musical life took two important strides forward: Martin Wegelius (1846-1906), whose training had also been in Leipzig, formed the Helsinki Conservatory of Music, and in the same year Kajanus formed the orchestra of the Helsinki Orchestral Society—now known as the Helsinki Philharmonic Orchestra [Helsingin Kaupunginorkesteri]. This was the first permanent orchestra to be formed in a Nordic country, a development from the court orchestras which had given many European countries (but not Finland) a tradition of orchestral performance. Realising the absence of such a tradition, Kajanus also established an orchestral school again maintained by the Helsinki Orchestral Society—which in 1895 became the Helsinki Philharmonic Society [Helsingin Filharmoniseksi Seuraksi].

Despite a successful and busy concert career, Kajanus regularly found the opportunity to compose. His works were rarely extensive (the longest

is probably his twenty-five-minute Sinfonietta in B flat, published by
Breitkopf & Härtel of Wiesbaden in 1915) but his most famous work
stands exactly at the crossroads of Finnish musical culture: this is the *Aino*
Symphony, quoted in most books of reference but not normally encountered even by those students who have read of its historical significance and
applied this to subsequent trends in Finnish music. The large orchestra
and choir are used in a romantic style and the work is strongly, if darkly,
scored. There is considerable personality in the writing, yet it clearly
shows a Germanic background and musical philosophy. Lisztian overtones
are also obvious but the lapses into banality of which the Hungarian master
was occasionally guilty are avoided by Kajanus. The final peroration, in
which the affirmative use of chorus is underpinned by an orchestral passage
of logical unity summing up the existing thematic material, has the stamp
of the best German masters and is somewhat reminiscent of the close of
Mendelssohn's choral masterpiece, *Die Erste Walpurgisnacht*. The work's
relatively short time-span (approximately a quarter-of-an-hour) does not
prevent the inclusion of a wide-ranging selection of symphonic elements.
Aino dates from 1885 and in German circles made a considerable impression. The importance attributed to it in the history of Finnish music is,
however, only partly due to the nature of the composition itself.

   Whilst the young Kajanus was going from strength to strenth as an
interpreter and all-round musician, conducting some of Europe's greatest
orchestras while still in his twenties, the young Johan Julius Christian
Sibelius, nine years Kajanus's junior, was moving through a brilliant
musical studenthood. Born of a Swedish-speaking family at Hämeenlinna
in 1865 the young Sibelius—known as Janne to his family and later, in his
student years, by the French form Jean—was orphaned before the age of
three and spent much of his early life under the influence of his maternal
grandmother in Hämeenlinna, his paternal grandmother in Loviisa and his
uncle Pehr, a successful amateur musician in Turku. Despite his passion
for composition—the chamber works of Sibelius's teens were performed
with his brother and sister at home—his education led to his studying law at
the University of Helsinki. This did not, however, prevent his becoming a
musical student at the conservatoire (albeit part-time) and he made
immense progress under the tutorship of Martin Wegelius. A close friend-
ship sprang up between tutor and pupil, so that during vacations Janne
Sibelius found himself invited to Wegelius's house where his youthful
compositions for chamber ensembles were performed.

   Sibelius's outgoing nature enabled him to expand important encounters into genuine friendships. This occurred when Busoni took up a
professorship at the academy, whilst the piano accompaniment of
Wegelius and Faltin, whose stature was at its greatest during these years,
was an encouragement to Sibelius in his violin performances. At this time
Sibelius also became friendly with the Järnefelt family and in 1889,

encouraged by the distinguished musicians who had shown faith in his abilities and having won a state scholarship which enabled him to further his musical studies, he set off for Germany. (Evidence of Janne Sibelius's progress as a full-time law student peters out as his musical activities become all embracing.) The enormous wealth of music to be heard in Berlin provided a supplement to his thoroughly disciplined studies under Albert Becker, as well as a widening of his musical spectrum that could not have been envisaged within the confines of Helsinki (which, though a thriving city artistically, was by no means among the most important of Europe's musical centres in the late nineteenth century).

At this time there occurred one of the most important and significant events in Finnish musical history—and, as with most historic encounters, the kernel of the event lay in a mere coincidence. During the season of 1889 Sibelius went to hear a concert given by the Berlin Philharmonic Orchestra under the direction of his compatriot Robert Kajanus. One of the new pieces featured in this season was *Aino,* which naturally was conducted by the composer. The reasons for Sibelius's immediate attraction to so impressive a work were obvious: the Germanic craftsmanship which at that time was new and immensely exciting to him, combined with the Finnish philosphy of the text. It was not, therefore, mere nationalism which drew Sibelius to the work so much as his appreciation of its overall significance and technical mastery. It must have shown him that any step taken which might incorporate the use of Finnish texts in a purely Finnish way was, although bold, merely an obvious continuation of Kajanus's beautifully constructed hybrid of Finnish literary thought and German musical flow; within seven years Sibelius himself had taken that step.

Sibelius was above all, a symphonist and within his symphonies and symphonic poems subconscious and consistent deference is paid to Finnish folk literature. It is not too surprising that the first symphony which he composed was the *Kullervo* Symphony of 1892. The previous year had found him returning from Vienna, much stimulated by the musical atmosphere there; in Helsinki he was friendly with a number of noted writers, including Arvid Järnefelt whose nationalistic views were well known. It was in this fruitful period of his development, therefore, that the influences of his environment led Sibelius to compose *Kullervo,* an orchestral and vocal symphony, including solo and choral parts, based on scenes from *Kalevala.*

Finland's music did not, as far as the rest of Europe was concerned, have any of the accepted roots of musical tradition, yet here was a work welded with extraordinary naturalness to strange but unarguably powerful words. The very rhythms of the purely orchestral movements are built from those of the Finnish language itself. It is strange, therefore, that, despite the success of early performances and the significance of *Kullervo* in the evolution of Sibelius as a Finnish composer, the work was not thought by its creator to be of sufficient merit to be published—more extraordinarily still, no performance of this early masterpiece took place between initial presentations and some years after the composer's death. Whilst it would be unreasonable to suggest that *Kullervo* has the concentration of the later symphonies or symphonic poems, Sibelius's ability to state his musical invention in direct terms is never in question, the orchestral first movement being particularly remarkable for its cogency.

Sibelius starts with an air of suppressed mystery. Later, partway through the Finale of his Second Symphony a similarly shaped theme was to appear. The intention is different in the Second Symphony a somewhat dark respite; with *Kullervo* it is a deliberately imposed darkness which seems bound to turn in due course to light. Bruckner would have used *tremolando* strings; Sibelius uses the theme itself. In either case, portent rather than content is the essence of the passage. More significantly still, the music has a Finnish contour, equating with the shape of the Finnish language: the themes are bereft of any suggestion of a Viennese or German upbeat; there is no *Luftpause*. Sibelius begins, as does every word of the Finnish language, firmly on the downbeat. Thus, with seemingly insignificant technical differences of stress and minor detail, Finnish music begins to emerge with a recognisable character of its own, although it is very unlikely that the composer himself would have been aware of it. Just as an English listener is scarcely aware that the rhythms and metres of Elgar's music are linked to the rise, fall, and stress of the English language, so there is no reason to suppose that the new, though still not outrageously different style of Sibelius, immediately made a specifically nationalistic impact on Finnish audiences.

The influence of Finnish folklore on Sibelius can perhaps be seen more clearly in a work where no specific programme or literary inspiration is expressed. This is *En Saga,* the work requested by Kajanus after the success of *Kullervo*. Although Sibelius revised the work in 1901—and it is this revision which is current today—the first performance actually took place early in 1893 under the direction of Kajanus. A symphonically constructed tone poem, *En Saga,* contrasts a dark, brooding melancholy with threatening *ostinati* and triumphant full-throated splendour (of a Sibelian kind, inasmuch as the key is loth to move away from the minor). Sibelius never divulged which saga had inspired this composition but there can be very little doubt when one considers the rhythm of the subsidiary subject which heralds the striding, *tutti* culmination of the opening thematic sequence:

The poetic metre of this example seems so close to the rhythm of the *Kalevela* that coincidence seems unavoidable.

> Suihki sukkula piossa,
> Käämi käessä kää per öitsi
> Niiet vaskiset vatisi
> Hopeinen pirta piukki
> Neien kangasta kutoissa
> Hopeista huolittaissa.
> (The shuttle flew swiftly beneath her hand,
> The reel was turning within her hands,
> The copper rods clattered and
> The silver comb rang as the maiden
> Wove the fabric, interweaving it with silver.)*

The Finnish words are remarkably close to the gait of Sibelius's music. The

---

*It is interesting that the Maiden of Pohjola, clad all in white, should be weaving golden fabric interwoven with silver. Such a recurring reference, subconsciously absorbed by all listeners, becomes a passing feature of the main drama. Cloth of silver and gold frequently recurs: for example, Runo XIV finds Mielikki spreading out the finest flax with glittering gold and shining silver beneath it, and in Runo XVIII Ilmarinen's finest flax shirt is girt with a gold-embroidered belt. Even in the climactic scene of Sibelius's *Kullervo*–drawn from Runo XXXV–the hero adorns his sister with gold-embroidered stockings and silver girdles. There seems little doubt that the extraordinary and individual rhythm of the poetry of the *Kalevala* provided the entire basis for Longfellow's "Song of Hiawatha." If one reads Schiefner's German translation of the *Kalevala* the source of the inspiration becomes even clearer, with some of Longfellow's lines seeming to be direct English translations of the German version of the Finnish. "Hiawatha" is not without merit as a work of English literature but it is surely impossible for an English-speaking Finn not to find the elements of plagiarism somewhat uncomfortable.

above quotation is from Runo VIII of the *Kalevala,* but almost any similar passage would have done.

One of the most perceptive analyses of *En Saga,* written by Robert Layton, takes the *Kalevala ostinato* sequence and affords it especial importance. Indeed, it is the key to the symphonic logic of Sibelius's thinking. Like several of the greatest symphonists (Beethoven, Bruckner, Dvořák, Mahler, Schubert, Vaughan Williams), Sibelius really wrote nine symphonies: *Kullervo, The Four Legends* and the First to the Seventh Symphony. The Seventh is a special case, a symphony in one movement; the margin between this and *En Saga* is small, but it is reasonable to say that op. 105 is a symphony and op. 9 a tone poem. The symphonic aspect of *En Saga,* however, is not to be denied and Layton hits the nail firmly on the head when he says, about *En Saga,* "An exciting ostinato heralds the re-entry of the first theme. It is characteristic of Sibelius's economy of means that the ostinato should be a subsidiary idea, which had already appeared as a foil to the fourth theme at its first appearance. This kind of creative thinking is typical of the symphonic writer."*

Quite apart from the newly-found flood of inspiration stemming from national traditions, Finnish music, by the time Sibelius began to be accepted as a successful composer, was also changing in structure. In the days of Crusell, the forms of Beethoven, Weber, and Mendelssohn had been adopted without question; by the time of Kajanus, Liszt's tone poems, together with those even more expansive tone poems with vocal and choral parts which we call Wagner Operas, had widened and altered basic forms whilst still respecting the structural philosophy of the Classical masters. Finnish music had entirely followed these trends and the German musical education of many nineteenth-century Finnish composers had certainly been a factor in keeping Finland in line with the thought processes of central Europe. Fabritius, Faltin, Floden, Genetz, Greve, Järnefelt, Kajanus, Kotilainen, Krohn, Linsén, Merikanto, Pacius, Palmgren, and Wasenius—every single one of them had studied in Germany. In fact, Erkki Melartin (1875-1937) was the only notable exception in this respect. Small wonder, then, that the entirely original and obviously Finnish-based style of Sibelius made such an impact. Here was not merely a new language but a national language, and it seemed inevitable that everything Sibelius wrote would be accepted as typically Nordic in nature.

That Nordic music began to be accepted with enthusiasm outside its immediate environment was a huge step forward in itself and, whilst Sibelius was a little embarrassed by the overwhelming popularity of *Finlandia* (since there was other music which he, and indeed the critics, considered more worthy), there can be no doubt that the enhancement of

---

*Robert Layton, *Sibelius* (London: Dent, 1978), p. 63

his reputation was not unconnected with this single example of Finland's gradual disenchantment with the rule of Tsarist Russia—a rule which hitherto had, both culturally and politically, been far more amicable than the relationship of Grand Duchy to a ruling state would normally portend. The year 1899 was critical, for then the autonomy enjoyed by Finland for ninety years suddenly ended. The story of the rallying point which *Finlandia* represented, the attempts to ban its performance and, untypically, Sibelius's lack of wisdom in selling its copyright, is familiar enough; other traditional views of early Sibelius, however, bear looking at more closely.

Finlandia has been described unfavourably, accusations of banality being common and its very popularity being held against it. The First Symphony is also sometimes held in less than high regard, the richness of the themes deemed (quite fairly) as Tchaikovskian; rather less fair, however, is the suggestion that a "modern" composer of the stature of Sibelius was failing to develop merely because his First Symphony did not take great strides forward in comparison to those works of his contemporaries. Should it have been expected to? Bruckner's Ninth, Mahler's First and Tchaikovsky's Sixth seem to be the focal points of previous years. *Kullervo, En Saga* and even *Rakastava* in its gentle, subdued way had already advanced Sibelius's individualism.

The well-known English composer Robert Simpson has said that, if one cannot come to terms with Sibelius's Seventh Symphony, one does not understand Sibelius, yet the developed nature of that late masterpiece can be the more easily understood by an appreciation of Sibelius's early style. The works of the 1890s were not inchoate attempts to achieve the capable, lucid writing of the 1920s; rather, they flow continuously and with logical progress from the composer's mind. To commence with a recognisable Finnish tradition and then to create another so individual as to bear only passing resemblance to contemporary Late Romantic style, and then further to throw aside even that small resemblance after composing only one or two symphonies, surely represents a remarkable, even revolutionary, achievement.

Sibelius's stark and beautiful modulations, often leading to a hushed, broad passage for strings alone, are a characteristic fingerprint. Such a moment occurs in the opening movement of the First Symphony, but the entry of the elegant, infinitely sad, second subject of the Seventh Symphony is part of the same philosophy. The techniques have not changed; only the context differs.

Sibelius's contours, even when he is at his most expansive, are also far more classical in structure than those of the average nineteenth-century romanticist. The second subject of the Finale of the First Symphony sweeps unflinchingly forward, the 4/2 Andante Assai being metronomically identical to the preceding 2/2 Allegro. In the first movement the lengthening of note-values by perhaps four times the basic unit of the existing pulse (for example, the tense trumpet-led third subject) never impedes the forward flow. Sibelius either underpins such a transition with an ostinato figure or imprints such a rhythm so firmly upon the listener's mind that the ostinato still seems to exist beneath the progress of the music.

It is rare indeed for critics of Sibelius performances to take exception to chosen tempi. Was there ever a Seventh Symphony too slow, a Fourth Symphony too fast, a dragged *Pohjola's Daughter* or a rushed *En Saga*?* Sibelius did not use metronome markings as a rule (of his symphonies only the First has any such indications and those were put there by the publisher) nor did he feel that a specific approach to tempo had to be consistent, provided that the outcome made musical sense. When Koussevitzky asked the composer to approve a proposed change of tempo on one of his symphonies, Sibelius simply sent him a telegram saying, "Play it as you feel it."

Sibelius was one of the few composers whose life spanned both the era of Late Romanticism in music and continued into that of the long-playing record; he even lived to the time of the stereophonic record, although the equipment at Järvenpää indicates that he probably never had the opportunity to hear that particular advance in high-fidelity reproduction. For a composer born in the time of Rossini and Berlioz to have had the opportunity of studying performances of his life's work reproduced with adequate fidelity at home must have been an exciting advantage in his years of retirement. Whereas Bartók, through his precise indications of the time-lengths of his pieces, stressed that his music needed to be performed virtually as written, Sibelius (with the advantage of improved recording techniques to aid his judgement) seemed to conclude that any interpretation of his music which was technically competent and logically structured was a valid representation of the work concerned. Viewed in this light, Sibelius's kindly and encouraging appreciation of the work of various conductors, and his disinclination to offer any comment other than praise in varying degrees, seems less eccentric than one might have supposed.

The development of Sibelius's style, the interweaving of folk tradition and vocal influences into orchestral conceptions—in short, the entire forty-year span of Sibelius's active musical career—is also the story of the rise of Finnish music. Without Sibelius, Europe would have been far less likely to underrate Merikanto, Palmgren, or Kuula so grossly; yet without Sibelius it would have been difficult to imagine Finnish music achieving

---

*Even the fastest *En Saga* on record (conducted by Herbert von Karajan) received no comment about its tempo. One might raise an eyebrow or two at the extreme intensity which results (although this writer does not disapprove) but the tempo is no less effective than with conventionally broader interpretations.

the individuality that it can boast today. Sibelius's influence has been immensely powerful and a challenge to the individuality of his contemporaries, yet it has never been less than beneficial.

It was first in Germany, and later perhaps with greater permanence elsewhere, that Sibelius became appreciated. It was not difficult to comprehend the course of his genius: his development from the style of the 1890s to the slightly more severe, but thought-provoking, works of twenty years later made excellent sense to the non-Finnish listener. It was almost too easy because, apart from the over-exposed *Finlandia* and the amazing popularity of one trifle from *Kuolema (Valse Triste)*, Europe and eventually America usually heard Sibelius through his largest and most significant compositions, the symphonies and the tone poems.

By viewing Sibelius only from the point-of-view of works of epic proportion, something of the essence of his progress can be overlooked. For example, *Rakastava*, in the version for strings, timpani, and triangle which was made in 1911, is a distillation of Sibelius at his most tender—an inspiration growing from the twin roots of the Finnish heritage, Lönnrot's *Kanteletar*, and Sibelius's own clear-headed romanticism. *Rakastava* was originally conceived in 1893 as a choral setting of some of the *Kanteletar;* five years later, string parts were added. By 1911 Sibelius realised the true essence of his creation and a vocal work was transformed into a purely instrumental composition. Only the strange titles to each movement remind one of its origins. It would not be too far-fetched to suggest that *Rakastava* is, in microcosm, representative of all Sibelius's non-vocal music. The stages of its creation are set out before the observer in this case but, even without such guidance, the inspiration behind *Kullervo* and the *Legends* is no less obvious and the later, more complex thoughts of the Fourth Symphony and *Tapiola* seem inspired by similar philosophies.

Sibelius is thought of as the great writer for the orchestra - a symphonist, a composer who wrote songs and some choral pieces but no operas.* The literary inspiration lies more beneath the surface of much of his music, like the threatening ostinati which he so often used in order to create tension. Sibelius the symphonist is probably as much in evidence in *En Saga* as in the less tightly-knit *Kullervo* Symphony. The *Four Legends* are *Kalevala*-inspired and are mainly concerned with Lemminkäinen. The famous *Swan of Tuonela* was the Prelude to the unfinished opera *Veenen luominen* and, even after being incorporated into the suite, it underwent further revision in 1900. The four movements have the titles:

Lemminkäinen ja Saaren neidot [Lemminkäinen and the Maidens of Saari]
Lemminkäinen Tuonelassa [Lemminkäinen in Tuonela]

Jungfrun i tornet [The Maiden in the Tower], a one-act opera from 1896, was never published and *Veenen luominen* [The Building of the Boat] was abandoned.

Tuonelan joutsen [The Swan of Tuonela]
Lemminkäinen Paluu [Lemminkäinen's Homeward Journey]

The most representative date for the creation of the music is 1895, although the first two were revised in 1897, with further (though not far-reaching) revisions in 1939. * In 1898 the melodious *Kuningas Kristian II—Sarja* [King Christian II-Suite], drawn from the music to the play of that name, showed Sibelius's continuing interest in historical subjects, and its popularity never dimmed. In 1899 *Finlandia* aroused even greater enthusiasm. More recently it has become fashionable to look down upon this brief tone poem, perhaps because of the simple, unvarnished boldness of its themes. There is little that is complex here, but it would be unfair to suggest that Sibelius's powers were any less acute at this time (it was, after all, the year of the First Symphony). Posterity has also chosen to ignore certain other works: the Overture in A minor of 1902, for example; the music to *Kuolema* (1903), other than the *Valse Triste*; and even, to a large extent, other early concert suites such as *Belshazzar's Feast* (1906) and *Swanwhite* (1908).

The intensity of Sibelius's output never flagged. As his career progressed its peaks were represented by the symphonies, and the Second Symphony of 1902 certainly settled any doubts about Sibelius's ability to challenge the great symphonists of the past whilst still bringing his own individual style to bear. This work is the last to show traces of the previous century and to contain a full-scale, life-affirming peroration. Even the symphonic poems avoid affirmative apotheoses, yet in the Second Symphony the music blossoms out from its comforting, if bare, opening bars into a cool and beautiful landscape. In strong contrast is the nocturnal character of the slow movement, with its threatening *pizzicati* and menacing timpani. Throughout the work the timpani are used with imagination, more often as a separate voice than for pedal-points. In *crescendi,* of which there are several supported by timpani in the first two movements, the drums break the surface of the texture as the climax is reached. The Scherzo, swift and straightforward, makes an excellent contrast, whilst the Trio–a delight for the analysts because it begins with the same note stated nine times–brings a hint of the comforting warmth of the Finale, into which flows the reprise of the Scherzo and Trio. This powerful final movement is, subtly, not unfolded in continuous, march-like triumph but

---

*These later revisions were published in 1954 by Breitkopf & Härtel but comparison of the excellent 1952 recording (by Thomas Jensen and the Danish State Radio Symphony Orchestra) with any of the more recent recordings reveals no startling changes to a critical ear unaided by a score. On the occasion of Jensen's recording (1952) Sibelius was asked to give a ruling on the order of the four pieces. Hitherto *The Swan of Tuonela* had sometimes appeared first and sometimes third. Sibelius, however, recommended that it should be placed second, with *Lemminkäinen in Tuonela* third. This order has become the accepted convention, although in his notable recording Okko Kamu reverts to the earlier order shown above.

rather is interspersed with hushed, nostalgic passages. But to what does such nostalgia refer? To nothing earlier, in fact, than the appearances in the same movement, generally on trombones, of

However, as the Nordic forests twice close around this nostalgic mood, the theme which is destined to provide the final climactic triumph climbs slowly from silence, first to establish a mood of optimism and then to crown the symphony.

In some performances, the last three notes of the theme are echoed *staccato* by the timpani—a feature not in the Breitkopf & Härtel edition of the score, yet introduced by a number of eminent Sibelius conductors, notably Serge Koussevitzky, Anthony Collins, Hans Schmidt-Isserstedt, and Malcolm Sargent. The origins of this emendation are obscure and Sibelius's reaction to it is not known, although it seems certain that he must have heard it. The most likely explanation is that Koussevitzky was the originator. *

In 1904 Sibelius moved to Järvenpää and his life-style changed a little. Here he had innately Finnish surroundings in which to work and a certain amount of security. Whether or not these matters directly influenced his style, it is quite clear that after this date the last traces of nineteenth-century Romanticism ebbed from his music.

After the long development, the rediscovery of folk influences, the assimilation of nationalistic elements and the literary, graphic, and musical surroundings had done their work. Finnish music, led by Sibelius now strode forward with complete individuality. Kajanus was a most important figure in this respect: influential in Finnish musical circles, a fervent champion of Sibelius and, judged by the recordings which he left as a legacy of his skill, the most authoritative of his interpreters. Not surprisingly, even Kajanus's compositional style changed, Sibelius's influence—or

*There are hiatuses when, at the end of each phrase, the music rests on long chords prior to each new statement of the figure; these leave the melody in some need of underpinning with rhythmic emphasis. It is interesting to note, therefore, that Paavo Berglund contrives to do this in his recording by accenting the start of each timpani roll. In this way he achieves emphases similar to (though admittedly a little less spectacular than) those of the popular "revision".

at least the influence to which both men had responded—became apparent. The nature of the romantic *Aino* Symphony of 1885 and that of the Sinfonietta in B flat published in 1915 by Breitkopf & Härtel show the change clearly.*

Naturally Sibelius was the leader in the newly accepted stylistic revolution. An element of drama and driving pulse began to lie beneath all that purported to be dramatic. Other composers were less prompt in shedding nineteenth-century influence but as Finland moved towards the significant years of full independence its musical life was certainly in a state of utmost good health.

Selim Palmgren (1878-1951) was probably the Finnish composer of the period to win the widest international recognition. This may have had something to do with Palmgren's early tendencies towards an individual impressionism. By the 1920s he had moved to America and taught composition at the Eastman School of Music, where his style altered quite noticeably becoming more forthright and less consonant. Even though his later works tended to collate his styles, adding a further element of firmer tonality which turned its back on the angularity of the 1920s, the suggestions of impressionism foisted upon him early in his career—when such critical comment merited some justification—were never really renounced. Had the critics ceased to listen? His most important works were probably his five piano concerti and the styles of his first (1903) and last (1939-41) essays in this form are vastly different yet somehow the enormous development of this highly original composer, whose music sounds Finnish without wearing the mantle of Sibelian style, seems to have been overlooked. Palmgren worked in the very field which concerned Sibelius least, that of the piano, and for that reason his characteristics developed along other lines. Hardly less important are his choral compositions—about a hundred of which are for male choir with another thirty or so for mixed chorus. Here, and in the songs, Palmgren and Sibelius have a greater degree of common ground.

Toivo Kuula (1883-1918) is known largely as a choral composer with strong sympathies for chamber music. His orchestral works seem unfairly overlooked (his two Ostrobothnian Suites for example) but the usual description of Kuula as an "impressionist" is probably more appropriate than with Palmgren. Kuula was a pupil of Sibelius, but the modal influences and choral leanings have rather more in common with Vaughan Williams. In particular that English master of twentieth-century choral tradition is recalled in one of Kuula's least-neglected large-scale works, *Orjanpoika,* [The Son of the Slave] more usually performed in the cantata version, op. 14 no. 1. The briefer symphonic poem op. 14 no. 2 of the same

---

*The revival of at least some of Kajanus's music is long overdue and a recorded coupling of the two works mentioned would surely give a revealing view of the composer.

title is less favoured. That Sibelius's pupil should be working along similarly progressive lines without being a mere replica of his all-powerful tutor was a sign of strength in Finnish Music, therefore Kuula's untimely death in 1918 during the war of independence was a sad blow.

Leevi Madetoja (1887-1947) was also the pupil of Sibelius. His development was less precocious than Kuula's but his importance is considerable. Madetoja was the first to be taken seriously as a composer of Finnish Opera. He is also noted for the composition of three powerful symphonies which are excitingly different from those of Sibelius. His style combines lucid, spare scoring with a romantic, melodic flair notable for its lightness of touch. Madetoja does not build with the dramatic power of Sibelius, rather his themes are allowed to flower and expand, tending to remain in a combination of fragments after the music has fully developed. Madetoja has his own adaptation of classical form. His melodies are added to until they have run their full course. Somehow the conventional development section is rendered superfluous since his is replaced by a scheme of continuous thematic generation.

Madetoja's background was Bothnian—he was born in Oulu—and whilst the Bothnian folk elements are not easily discerned by the average European listener, the reflective spaciousness is certainly indicative of the mood of that area. Of the three symphonies the Second has the most obvious leanings towards this tender sadness. The Third, though often thoughtful is laid out with firm structure. Its Adagio is especially touching—Madetoja's musical landscape seems somehow to contain people, albeit viewed from afar, in much the same way as those of Vaughan Williams or Nielsen. Only in the Scherzo does the folk element impinge and then with a quiet yet mercurial gait reminiscent of Stenhammar.

The three symphonies were written 1915-16, 1917-18, 1925-26 respectively. His *Comedy* Overture (1923) is the most often performed of his remaining orchestral works but his output in this field is concentrated in the earlier part of his career including a symphonic suite, his Little Suite, the symphonic poem *Kullervo,* and another *Kalevala*-inspired work *Sammon ryöstö* [Robbing the Sampo], all dating from before the First Symphony. Madetoja's Third Symphony may reasonably be considered his last major orchestral composition. Later life found him composing less in this genre although the 1930s saw a certain amount of film and theatre music but the following decade shows only the incidental music to *Anthony and Cleopatra* (1944) which is currently unpublished.

The other side of Madetoja's talent concerns his ability as composer of songs, cantatas and above all opera. Madetoja is a relatively important if perhaps underrated figure in Finnish music, but his modest standing should not be allowed to cloud his influence on the later development of Finnish nationalist philosophy in music. There is little doubt that from the time of the first performance of *Pohjalaisia* on the 26 May 1925—two years after its completion—it was regarded as the archetypal Finnish opera. Although the subject matter concerns the problems of the peasant community in Finnish Bothnia* it is quite clear that the underlying philosophy concerns freedom in all its aspects. This point would hardly have gone unappreciated by audiences in a Finland which had been fully independent for only a few years. Jarviluoma's text presents a small community overseen by a repressive sheriff. The struggle to assert freedom and individuality includes ill-advised and hasty actions which inevitably lead to tragedy. Madetoja, at the height of his powers, (at the point before he was about to embark on his third and most remarkable symphony,) welded the whole story together with a symphonic logic which would place him high in the list of Finnish composers regardless of his other works. This naturally lyrical musician not only adapted his style to support tragic drama but even contrived to interpolate an element of *leitmotiv* - for example there can never be any mistake about the presence of the sheriff

or of the hero Jussi

The choral writing is less complex than the interwoven action accorded the soloists. Within the drama there are other elements, a synthesis of traditional Finnish problems. The element of strong Christian faith is portrayed but so too is that aspect which drives the simple folk beyond joy in their faith until mere pietism replaces it. The farmer's daughter Maija seems a sad, lonely figure as she disapproves of most aspects of life from drink right through to pleasant dreams. Inevitably there is a drunken scene, a clever piece of writing and a most suitable point of light relief towards the end of Act I. The text portrays Maija's narrow pietism as being the threatening element which drives her companions to act carelessly. As the sheriff's authority is challenged so she is the first to be shocked that the law—however unfair or unreasonable—should be challenged.

Within the confines of one relatively simple story, all manner of familiar problems are raised and no wonder that the opera took on the mantle of national representation. Not until Joonas Kokkonnen wrote

---

*That is to say East Bothnia, hence the cumbersome translation of the title *Pohjalaisia* into English as *The Ostrobothnians.*

Viimeiset kiusaukset was the meaning of Finnish lifestyle of the past and its residual effect on today's thinking again explored so thoroughly. Madetoja's *Pohjalaisia* therefore, was a central representation and probably the only Finnish opera generally accepted until Merikanto's *Juha* was first performed as late as 1957—even though it was contemporary with *Pohjalaisia*.

Aare Merikanto (1893-1958), although so closely contemporary with Madetoja had clearly a more modernistic outlook by comparison. There seems little doubt that in the 1920s Merikanto must have seemed very advanced and difficult, probably this is why *Juha* had to wait for forty-two years before being performed. Because of the impact of this masterpiece critical opinion tends nowadays to look upon Merikanto as an operatic composer but in fact his grounding is as firmly in the world of the orchestra as was the case with Madetoja or Sibelius.

Merikanto's studies were Leipzig-based, Max Reger being his teacher. Continuation in Moscow awakened in the young composer an appreciation of the individual style of Skriabin. Such apparently conflicting influences joined together within the creative talent of this Finnish composer and the result was a highly original style, less tonal than was generally acceptable in the earlier part of this century whilst also less acceptable in that it seemed unrelated to the exciting pioneering paths travelled by Sibelius. Polytonality rather than atonality seems the most suitable description of Merikanto's work. Early in his career, Merikanto numbered some major works among his output, of which the First Piano Concerto (1903) falls well outside the "polytonality" label, harking back almost to Rubinstein, but the exotic colours of Skriabin are already bursting from the orchestra. It is hardly surprising therefore that it achieved enormous success in Russia and that subsequent exposure to the Skriabin-influenced musical atmosphere should have led Merikanto further along those paths.

For the decade which followed, Merikanto progressed firmly towards a personal brand of modernism. His rethinking was somewhat radical. For example he revised his First Symphony (1914) a few years later, applying his new ideas to the old material and the public—the same Russian public that had taken the work to its heart on its first performance—was now much cooler and indeed this work is symptomatic of the alienation of the musical world as Merikanto's career proceeded through the 1920s. It is quite clear that Merikanto followed his own line regardless of this cooling of appreciation. The direction in which he was aiming became a matter for conjecture, for, as the 1920s progressed, his creativity became less intense and he wrote very few works. When in later years his inspiration returned, he admitted a little more of a compromise in his style: the excellent Second Piano Concerto of 1937 has a modernistic flavour but a lyrical undercurrent. As time went on, Merikanto was less interested in the nationalistic aspects of music but postwar Finland began to take a renewed interest in his earlier, strictly tonal works and revived many of them. This in turn seemed to release the composer's creative power and in his last years he composed some larger scale works in contrast to the 1940s where he was largely content to toy with miniatures. Between 1953 and 1955 he composed the Third Symphony, the Fourth Violin Concerto, and the Third Piano Concerto. The style here shows tendencies to revert to rich harmonies and colourful scoring.

Merikanto's masterpiece is undoubtedly *Juha*. This was written in 1922 at the end of the first of the three easily-defined periods of the composer's life. Merikanto had only once before attempted operatic composition—this was in 1912 and in that year his Helena was performed. It seems that that work (not fully scored, the first performance was to piano accompaniment) was destroyed and therefore *Juha* stands as sole monument to Aare Merikanto's operatic art and it was not until its first performance in 1967 on the occasion of the fiftieth anniversary celebrations of Finland's independence that it was realised that an opera in the grand national tradition had been lying unheard except for a radio performance in parts in 1957 and the Lahti Opera Association production in 1963. It is difficult to understand why Merikanto had seemingly taken no further interest in the work after laying it aside in 1922 having taken since 1919 to complete it. Could it be that he was moving so quickly into what Finnish writers have called his "radical period" that he could no longer feel satisfied with extended stretches of lyricism? To be sure, *Juha* is not lyrical by early twentieth-century-standards for the broken orchestral rhythms are very much geared to the accurate portrayal of the words—the fashion of long, lyrical arias was obviously well into the past, instead the themes adapt themselves to the metre of the language—very much in the way that Menotti achieves clarity of diction through open, spare-harmonied writing which flexes itself in line with the needs of the literary content.

The libretto is from Juhani Aho, adapted from his novel *Juha* written in 1912. Aino Ackté* the operatic soprano saw great potential for an operatic libretto and made the adaptation herself. It would be unfair not to give the greater part of the credit for the *Juha* libretto to Aho however since Ackté's transcription is by and large a fairly literal borrowing, but she deserves praise for her perception in observing the operatic possibilities and she even managed to interest Sibelius who kept the libretto for a couple of years before deciding that he did not feel that he could commit himself to writing the opera.

Merikanto's interest in the libretto proved fruitful, it seems highly fortunate that his style was caught in the very midst of its transition and on

---

*Aino Ackté was founder of Helsinki opera house in conjunction with the publishers Fazer and also dedicatee of Sibelius's *Luonnotar*

examination *Juha* seems to present a quite individual side to his art. It is musically an opera full of motifs, but not in the *leitmotiv* style of Wagner (or less obviously Madetoja). Merikanto's motifs are often a matter of reference to rhythmic pattern and they tend to apply to situations between characters as they occur and recur rather than portraying the characters themselves. For example, Juha, the clumsy, but honest central figure and his young wife Marja have their intensely dramatic encounters regularly underpinned by this rhythmic triplet figure:

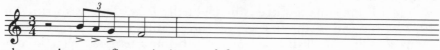

whereas the same figure in inverted form

appears when Marja's attentions are concerned with Shemeikka the salesman from Karelia. Just why Merikanto's *Juha* belatedly caught the public imagination is hard to tell. *Pohjalaisia* had been such an accepted part of life from the time it was written that it is a matter for some amazement that Madetoja's setting of the Aho-Ackté libretto to *Juha* (1934) was not taken to the hearts of the people. The usual pattern of the public knowing what it likes and liking what it knows was for once broken so that it now seems unlikely that Merikanto's setting of *Juha** will ever lose its place in the forefront of Finnish folk-based opera.

For a composer of three symphonies, nine concerti, sixty other orchestral pieces, many chamber works, songs and choral pieces, it seems strange that Merikanto's one accepted opera should remain his principal claim to fame, but there seems little doubt that he is now regarded as an important operatic composer on the strength of this single composition. Opinion had treated him in a fickle manner during his life—he lived just long enough to see some reawakening of interest in his music—but surely Merikanto would have been amazed to know that *Juha* had created this undeservedly one-sided reputation for him. He is recorded as having said that he thought opera could be more significant without words and he even suggested that by listening to the separate words of an opera, one loses oneself in their meaning thereby allowing the music to pass by relatively neglected. Merikanto therefore has been forced by circumstances into the role of one of the leading and most influential operatic composers of Finland, ignoring the pattern of his output, and his sceptical view of opera in general. It is almost like referring to Beethoven as a leading operatic

---

*The First Finnish opera to be recorded complete.

composer on the strength of his one (admittedly remarkable) essay in that form.

Palmgren, Madetoja, and Merikanto lived a bare generation later than Sibelius and each seemed to suffer from a mysterious fallow period round about the 1920s. In the case of Palmgren and Merikanto, there is little doubt that their attractions towards a more modern style of expression did not prove particularly fruitful and both composers returned to a more harmonious style in later years. To some extent it may have been simple non-appreciation by audiences during the 1920s. It would be wrong to suggest that merely because Merikanto thought along more modernistic lines, he courted unpopularity. Palmgren's ideas of modernity would have outraged reactionary ears far less, but still he was unable to make a vast impression with his middle-period works.

Perhaps this enigmatic pattern can be viewed in the light of the two operas so far discussed. In the 1920s Finland was ready for an operatic revolution: if the gigantic figure of Sibelius would not lead it, then another would have to be found. Madetoja was selected through *Pohjalaisia,* it could also have been Merikanto's *Juha,* and certainly today's hindsight view of Finnish opera almost brackets the two operas as products of the 1920s. But the revolution never came about—it had to wait nearly half a century before the next generation of composers seized upon this line of development, and, along with the new and powerful genius of such composers as Kokkonen and Sallinen, Merikanto was caught up in the new wave of operatic inspiration and his *Juha,* belatedly, became accepted as part of Finnish operatic heritage.

The creation of the Savonlinna Opera Festival engendered, in the 1970s, a new appetite for national operas to perform. It seemed also to point to the possibility of re-examining those operas which had hitherto been left by the wayside. If so considerable a composer as Merikanto could have had a masterpiece overlooked for so long, what others may have suffered the same fate?

The identical subject matter of Madetoja's *Juha* will probably prevent it ever being accepted as Merikanto's setting has been, but perhaps one should look again at other neglected operas of earlier this century.*

---

*For example Väino Raito (1891-1945) is a sufficiently accepted name in concert circles to merit re-examination as an opera composer. *Jeftan tytär* [The Daughter of Jefta] composed in 1929, *Prinsessa Cecilia* [Princess Cecilia] of 1933, and the brief *Lyydian kuningas* [The King of Lydia] dating from 1937 could surely be re-assessed together with his last opera *Kaksi kuningatarta* [Two Queens] written in 1944. Also Tauno Pylkkänen (b. 1918) is surely sufficiently famous to deserve a re-evaluation of his operas: *Bathsheba Saarenmaalia* [Bathsheba at Saarenmaa] (1940); *Mare ja hänen poikansa* [Mare and her Son] (1943); *Ikaros* (1956-60); *Simo Hurtta* (1948) *Opri ja Oleksi* (1957) or *Tuntmaton sotilas* [The Unknown Soldier] (1967). It would be unfortunate indeed if such works were to be neglected merely because they were written at a time when opera did not happen to be in the ascendant as an art form.

In the significant years leading to Finnish independence, as the friendly relationship with Russia started to go sour and nationalism began to be frowned upon to the point of oppression, Sibelius had remained the shining light. Those composers mentioned in the previous chapter had diversified their talents, they are not actually direct musical descendants of Sibelius for they are too close to his generation and although they were slightly under Sibelius's shadow, very few Sibelian fingerprints are to be found in their music. Perhaps Palmgren shows a few echoes of this nature but they are not central to his lyrical style. His general neglect by performers outside Finland may well be accounted for by his predilection for tuneful melody in a way which implies that he was a man of his time rather than a pioneer.

In the early part of the twentieth century the pioneering aspect of Finnish music continued to lie firmly in the hands of Jean Sibelius, once past the romantic watershed of the Second Symphony, his style remained clear-cut, direct, assertive and utterly individual. Gorgeous though the melodies of the Violin Concerto written between 1903 and 1905 may be, they have much of the granite-like strength of the later symphonic Sibelius, the critical comparison with Tchaikovsky no longer holds water. The Finale is a Polonaise—Tchaikovsky also wrote Polonaises: at this point the comparison ceases, for the threatening ostinato rhythm which is at the base of the Sibelius Finale is rooted in symphonic thinking, a Tchaikovsky Polonaise stems entirely from balletic conceptions. One might have supposed that the growing atmosphere of political protest at this period, would have resulted in outspokenly nationalistic music, but largely this went little further than *Finlandia*. Sibelius's interest, passionate and devoted though it was, concerned itself with the furthering of Finnish art in its musical aspect—political effort, and political change through his art was not part of his philosophy. Similarly although Beethoven glorified the conception of brotherhood by setting Schiller's *An die Freude* he did not imply an attempt at achieving political change through it: nor indeed could a musical masterpiece however towering, effect changes in a world outside its own. Were this possible, Beethoven's *Missa Solemnis* would presumably have wooed audiences to the Roman view of Christianity, or his *Battle* Symphony earned support for all that the Duke of Wellington stood for.

Since political or national opinion can be no more than a statement and the influence cannot be transitive it is hardly surprising that the one remaining nationalistic work of Sibelius from around this time was *Vapautettu Kuningatar* ([The Captive Queen] or alternatively, [The Liberated Queen]—according to which aspect of the text the English commentator wishes to stress). The philosophy is strongly patriotic—with the relationship between Finland and Russia strained to breaking point at this time (1906) there is little doubt as to the representational intention of who represented the Queen and who her captor. Musically the work was not strong enough to stand the test of time (few politically-inspired works pass such strict examination) and it is never heard nowadays.

Vapautettu Kuningatar is an exception among the major works of the period. For a few concentrated years, the development of Finnish music and the development of Sibelius was synonymous. These pre-world-war days saw a number of orchestral masterpieces: *Dryadi* [The Dryad]*Pelleas et Mélisande, Pohjolan tytär* [Pohjola's Daughter], the Third Symphony, *Belshazzar's Feast, Pan and Echo, Öinen ratsastus ja auringonnusu* [Night Ride and Sunrise]. Over the half dozen years which incorporate these works, practical success, increasing fame and powerful musical thought are inter-linked. From 1908 the compositions of Sibelius tended to become more intense and more concentrated still. The development of his most notable contemporaries and/or pupils occurred round about the time of the First World War. Such elements as relate to Sibelian style seem to have been touched by the change of direction obvious in Sibelius's music over about five years from around 1908 to 1913. The writing became more spare, the harmonies more icy and ever darker thoughts occupied the composer's mind in *The Bard, Luonnotar, Kuolema* [Death], and the Fourth Symphony—the forbidding economy of utterance of which earned it the nick-name *Barkbröd* Symphony in some circles.

Commentary on the composer's life at this period cannot avoid chronicling Sibelius's illness around 1908 when a tumour of the throat was diagnosed and a number of operations were necessary for the removal of the tumour. The frightening uncertainty concerning the possible recurrence of the tumour which might have meant that fatal consequences could result, must have taken enormous toll of Sibelius's peace of mind and it seems not at all unreasonable to suggest that this deeply disturbing influence affected the very roots of the nature of his musical composition. Physical misfortune during a relatively short period compared with Sibelius' long life may seem a transitory matter, but even after this black cloud had lifted, his music was indelibly marked by the change of philosophy and since these years found Sibelius, almost alone of his countrymen, achieving stylistic progress, it can reasonably be argued that this event also affected the entire course of Finnish music.

During this period the growing grasp of structure through his very individual eyes had become a strong element in Sibelius's music. Naturally the Third and Fourth symphonies are the focal points which show this aspect and they do so in different ways. The Third Symphony is of the utmost thematic simplicity: what could be more innocent than the opening melody

(*See over*)

Allegro moderato

but the tension is built up so fast that when the climactic held chord is reached, (signalling the affirmation of the first idea,) the power unleashed by the timpani in crescendo through that chord has an uncompromising seriousness. Thus as the textures are changed startlingly within a single fully harmonized note, it becomes clear that Sibelius's affirmations are never again to be so resplendently comforting as they were at the end of the Second Symphony.

The Third Symphony is above all a symphony of growth—be the fragments melodic or rhythmic, they are welded inexorably into shape. The classical ideal of exposition and development is so compressed that the first movement is almost one huge development.

The central movement has a comforting melodic pattern over one which is more rhythmically disturbing and is a rare example in Sibelius's music where extremes of tempo do make a considerable difference to the interpretative effect in performance.*

Even more than hitherto, the Finale of the Third Symphony hurls into the melting pot fragment after fragment and certainly art conceals art in that the overall impression of thematic organisation is gained from the music whilst the symphonic rule book is given scarcely a glance. Even the opening cannot shake off a melodic insistence which refuses to forget the second movement. There are two distinct sections but although loosely speaking, one expounds and the other develops, the second appears at the moment that a viola-coloured swinging melody infiltrates into the textures.

---

*Of outstanding performances the two extremes are best represented by the pioneering long-playing record by Anthony Collins and the much more recent version by Paavo Berglund. Hearing the latter alone, the great, dark, tranquil breadth seems totally convincing yet, despite the less immaculate orchestral execution, Anthony Collins's swift view of this Andantino con moto quasi allegretto accentuates all the disturbed inner elements.

This ruins the normal analytical processes since this secondary theme

ends the work, thus its appearance could be argued as representing the beginning of the coda - or would the analyst prefer to describe the first half of the movement as a quasi-Scherzo and the remainder a Finale? A good compromise seems to be to enjoy the incredible imagination of the whole remarkable conception without attempting to dissect it. This Finale in its transition from eager impulsive drive to large scale confident optimism may seem like a parallel to the tone poem *Öinen ratsastus ja auringonnousu* [Night Ride and Sunrise]. The scheme of things was fitted into a new mould certainly but the idea of driving, eager fragmentary music, ennobled by a great, broad, rhythmically confident theme which filters subtly into the music was evident as far back as *Lemminkäinen's Homeward Journey* from the *Four Legends* and if concession may be made to the suggestion that the *Four Legends* are worthy of symphonic status, the appearance of such a device in the finale is a logical enough procedure. The Finale of the Third Symphony and the generally underrated *Night Ride and Sunrise* were composed in near proximity, when Sibelius's career was at its most triumphant. Although the tone poem first appeared in 1909, its general conception dated from two years earlier, hence it shares a sense of triumph with the Third Symphony because the terrifying shadow of the unknown—in the shape of threatened serious illness—had not yet fallen across the composer's outlook.

The Fourth Symphony of 1911 shows the change in startling fashion, yet the uncompromising nature of the work is in itself exciting. One thing is certain, there is nothing autobiographical about the Fourth Symphony. Whatever the outside reasons may have been that so radically altered the course of increasing optimism in Sibelius's large-scale works, the music is basically symphonic, not a symphonic poem but a symphony. Whatever programmatic allusions Sibelius may have placed upon other works of his, his symphonies were purely abstract in the very best sense. With the notable exception of Anton Bruckner and Johannes Brahms, among great symphonic composers it is hard to think of any who join Sibelius in the attribute of applying no title to any of their symphonies.

The sheer appropriateness of the contrasts within this often forbidding music show that for all that a certain darkness was oppressing him, Sibelius was now even more capable of instilling a clear-cut cogency. The first movement's threatening opening cello melody

(*See over*)

Tempo molto moderato, quasi adagio

serves as a humbly serious basis for a development as taut as that of the previous symphony but this time the first climactic chord is far from being one of affirmative triumph. Rather it is a bleak outcry from the woodwind and the use of uncapped crescendo heightens the despairing tension - especially when the brass have the movement in their icy grip.

The placing of the Scherzo second is a brilliant touch. The tragic first movement has no sooner ended with grave, stoic sadness than the mercurial Scherzo commences with the oboe spinning a line of melody over the hastening strings like an elusive spirit darting through a dark forest, leaving a trail of bright, quickly fading light behind it.

No wonder then that the succeeding slow movement has a mysterious character as if the theme for which Sibelius is looking were for ever evading him. It makes its appearance, but only fragmentarily at first. Gradually the melody evolves and eventually appears in this form

This profoundly sad movement was played, through the composer's prior request, at Sibelius's funeral.

Despite its speed, the music of the Finale does not give too much hope of triumph. The note-for-note repetition of a rising phrase heard in the previous movement on clarinets and bassoons

now transferred to violins shows on the one hand the tautness of structure but on the other a total change of emphasis, for the final version is so different in mood that the allusion seems to be no more than co-incidental—especially as Sibelius chooses not to exploit it and one is reminded of his similar reference at the start of the last movement of the Third Symphony which was thereafter cast aside.

At this period an account of the progress of Finnish music and a chronological description of the works composed by Jean Sibelius become virtually identical. Robert Kajanus continued to be a powerful champion of Sibelius's music and his interpretations could scarcely have been more authentic. At this time however, his compositional activities had almost dried up. No orchestral or orchestrally accompanied work by Kajanus appeared for the first ten years of the twentieth-century although his art was to be revived as time went on, but by then his style had changed radically. Since, as a conductor, Kajanus was soaked in the new direction which Finnish music had taken, it is hardly surprising that his subsequent compositions took a direction which had a strong Sibelian philosophy. Whilst the adoption of a style betraying the influence of a powerful contemporary artist need not reflect uncomplimentarily upon a composer, the fact remains that Kajanus's works are generally neglected although he does have a modest reputation as a composer of songs.

The Sibelian influence continued throughout the First World War and by this time his music had begun to move away from the hints of darkness and introspection which attended so many of his works at the time of uncertainty over his health—indeed over his survival. Not all music of that period showed the bleakness of the Fourth Symphony, but there was always an underlying sobriety. The concert suite *Swanwhite* and the *Scènes Historiques* no. 2 represent the earliest and latest chronological points of this area of inner disturbance. They are not entirely filled with foreboding but shadows lie nonetheless within this ostensibly lighter music.

Whilst a new stream of Finnish thought began taking the existing patterns along a parallel route to that of Sibelius through works such as Palmgren's Second and Third Piano Concerti (1913 and 1915 respectively) Madetoja's Symphonic poem *Kullervo* (1913) and his First Symphony (1915-16), Sibelius concerned himself with a varied cross-section of music, almost as if he were exploring in order to find the most suitable new direction. He wrote several pieces for violin and piano in 1915 during a period of renewed interest in the violin. The period 1912-13 had seen the Two Serenades for Violin and Orchestra which in form, philosophy and duration, are very much akin to Beethoven's two Romances and in 1914 he produced two other brief pieces for violin (or cello) with orchestra. *Aallottaret* [The Oceanides] stretches into areas which are, on the one hand, not uncharacteristic (mysteriousness, tension, alternation of light and shade), but on the other hand these incorporate an element of impressionism and

Finnish Landscape

this is something new in Sibelius. The most down-to-earth, plainly Sibelian, generally untroubled music of this period is contained in the stage music for Scaramouche: composed in 1913 but not published until 1918. It is an hour-long work which, because of its unsuitability for concert performance and the composer's failure to draw concert suites from it, is largely neglected. Stripped of the dialogue it has served as ballet music in choreography by Imre Eck. Jussi Jalas gave the first performance of the new incarnation and has recorded it (see Discography).

Even at so mature a stage of his career Sibelius now wrote a work which did not fully satisfy him at first and which he felt he had to revise. Revisions to previous works had not been a feature apart from *En Saga* and, to a lesser extent, the Violin Concerto. The *Four Legends* is probably more a case of the whole developing with minor adjustments from the sum of individual parts so that by and large Sibelius could be said to be a composer who completed the conception he had had in mind and any changes of thought process were adjusted during composition rather than afterwards.

Where Bruckner tended to be pre-occupied with revision of his masterpieces as he reached later years, Sibelius avoided this tendency despite his long retirement. Only the Fifth Symphony (the score was presented in 1915 with the revision in 1919) seemed to give him any real problem of this nature. Originally the first movement was thought of as two separate pieces as the concert programme for the first performance in December 1915 indicates.

Sibelius was the conductor and he made only a very short break after the "Tempo tranquillo assai". The equivocal nature of the form is indicate by the cumbersome title of the first two movements, "Tempo tranquillo assai quasi attacca aus Allegro cominciando moderato a poco stretto." By December 1916 Sibelius had composed a bridge passage between the two sections. Doubt seems to have been left only in the minds of the listeners. The completed structure had obviously satisfied Sibelius but commentators continued to be concerned by the origins. Cecil Gray thinks of the second section (latterly Allegro Moderato) as being a Scherzo, Simon Parmet feels that the whole movement is indeed a cogent entity describing it as a sonata-form introduction followed by a toccata.

The bricks and mortar of Sibelius's conception are indeed difficult to define but if they are not central from the analyst's point of view, since one hears Sibelian language rather than individual Sibelian words, the immense certainty of direction is the purest Sibelius and from this point onwards, there is never any doubt as to the road which the composer's music will take. This is a fusion of the controlled romanticism of the earlier music and the stark, economical, direct nature of the inward-looking era of the Fourth Symphony. The pivot seems to be *The Oceanides*, no work better demonstrates the elements of Fourth and Fifth Symphonies within a single composition although, in effect, it is one of Sibelius's least symphonic compositions.

The Fifth Symphony is similar in overall shape to the Third and whatever the nature of the preparation behind the composition, the two-part nature of the first movement can be compared with the similar outline of the Finale to the Third. The difference lies however in the freedom of transition from one element to another. Sibelius has a new impetus to his expression, he now welds extremes of movement (and in these terms, *movement* is not synonymous with *tempo*) within a single piece. Was this perhaps part of the struggle when he was fashioning the first movement, first in two parts and then, seamlessly welded together, in one? The opening is a combination of Bruckner and Wagner, except that perhaps neither of those composers would have permitted the timpani pedal roll to shift upwards in so enquiring a manner. Nor is it characteristic of the nineteenth century that as many as eight thematic ideas should be used to build this wide-spanning movement. Despite all this formal rule-breaking, these elements do appear in something very close to sonata form (the first movement of the Fourth was virtually a strict example of this, while the Fifth Symphony permits itself to telescope the development and the recapitulation together). In between these events, there appears a Scherzo-like section, centred on an ever-shifting tonal base. The trumpet which calls mysteriously across this tonal void is concerned with a rising theme which then falls back with ease.

In a totally different setting giving a contrasting effect is the sombre opening wherein the theme, though not concerned with the same notes, is certainly very similar in shape

Sibelius's Fifth Symphony boasts a first movement of enormous coherence and intense organisation. Its coda encapsulates the opening theme with inner reference to others (notably the related trumpet melody) and so taut is the structure that it is only on account of the acceleration over the final pages that the nature of a coda is exemplified. Thematically the ear would be satisfied with all that the composer has offered but symphonically the stretto device is essential in order to give finalization to the themes, but this could not have been achieved except that the whole movement is one colossal transition from slow to fast, so constructed that only these particular themes, arranged in this very order, could possibly have achieved that effect. Therefore, the final acceleration grows naturally from the music and is certainly not a tailpiece added for effect. Its thematic material is contained very firmly in the strings to which the winds provide chordal support of magnificent richness*.

If the first movement is a transformation of material from slow to fast, the second is similar except that it employs organic transition where tempo is not the focal point. The form is not unusual—fragments marked by strong rhythm flower glowingly into long-breathed melodies. But, virtually hidden within the later developments of this eloquent movement—more sombre and less playful than the equivalent in the Third Symphony—is a ringing, strongly rhythmic alternation of notes which, whilst seeming logical enough on its appearance, does not seem to belong thematically to the foregoing music.

The explanation becomes clear only after the Finale has started its majestic progress. The thematic elements start with a theme hewn out with an intensity similar to that of the Finale of the Fourth with flying strings hammering grouped notes to represent one broader melody. This movement has much of the originality of structure of the first but instead of being a study in acceleration it is virtually the converse and when the great, swinging, bell-like theme takes over partway through, the brilliance of Sibelius's internal symphonic organisation becomes manifest. It also explains the various hints of this facility given hitherto. The breadth which overtakes the Finale of the Third partway through is a good example. The transition of tempo is another fingerprint and again thematic allusion is a foremost part, for the seemingly unrelated item which grew from the slow movement, turns out to be a distinct prophesy of the broad, culminating rhythmic figure of the Finale. As this element begins to grip the music and the shorter-breathed elements are phased out, the form of the Fifth Symphony is apparently palindromic for where broad, explicit melody at the outset became intensified and rapid, so the fury of the opening of the Finale progresses towards simplicity. The palindrome is complete but, as in the first movement, a coda, or at least a finishing touch, is required. Sibelius solves this by asking first for a small increase of tempo and then finishes the work with six massive, unevenly spaced chords. Their very asymmetry is, however, minutely calculated. There is

---

*One conductor, Herbert von Karajan, who has paid especial attention to this work used, in the 1950s, to exaggerate the brass chordal sequences to the detriment of the important figuration in the strings. As time has passed, these accompanying sections have been placed in proper proportion. Karajan's modification of his concert-hall approach is paralleled by the conductor's several recordings, culminating in the most commendable Karajan interpretation where the heavy demands placed upon the strings as set against the massive wind onslaught are met as effectively as possible.

surely, for all its angularity, no more final passage in all music*.

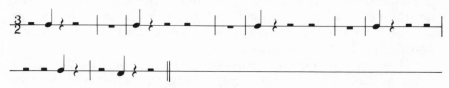

At this high point in Sibelius's career he had fully succeeded in bringing within a single framework, all the elements on which his workmanship had been based: the folklore element, the rugged complex harmonic patterns, the plangent orchestration and, above all, the utterly logical construction which in the Fifth Symphony had advanced to new heights of organisation.

The exciting thing about this period of his life is the refined state of art to which he had brought music in Finland. This mature style had far-reaching effects on many of the important Finnish composers who followed. It is possible to see the immense logic of Sibelius's construction in many later works - even those which are not directly symphonic. As late as 1975 Joonas Kokkonen completed an opera in which an important theme awaits its employment as an apotheosis, just as in the Fifth Symphony and subsequent works of Sibelius, finalizing affirmation waits to be brought forth by hinting at themes until they are on the point of bursting forth†.

There is something innately Finnish about this construction. Although the opera is five times as long as the symphony, its sense of structural inevitability remains and from about 1920 onwards, Finnish composers have shown the ability through control of structural tensions, to give a similar impression whenever they write music of a nature which

---

*The effect of this spacing of chords is dependent upon the conductor's interpretation of "un pocchetino stretto", marked seven bars before the final page of the score as shown above. Some conductors, including Herbert von Karajan, tend to carry the increase in tempo through the spaced chords. If one thinks of the beat as continuously accelerating, the sequence more or less works (unfortunately Karajan's rest-lengths are not always consistent from performance to performance). Other conductors, notably Eugene Ormandy and John Barbirolli, have completed the tempo increase well before the chords, holding them strictly in tempo - surely the only real way of making sense of Sibelius's careful calculations. It would perhaps be presumptuous to suggest that some conductors get this sequence "wrong", but when wild advantage is taken of the previous "Un pocchetino stretto", it is difficult to assimilate the intention in respect of the last nine bars. The most positive effect is achieved by adopting an increased tempo at the marking and holding it firmly. The school of thought which reads this as meaning continuous acceleration certainly makes it difficult for the ear to cope with the resultant rhythmic instability.

†The chorale which supports the hymn, "Sinuhun turvaan, Jumala,/mua häpeästa säästä" ("My Lord my God in all distress, my hope is whole in Thee") at the close of the opera *Viimeiset Kiusaukset* [The Last Temptations]

Drawings by Timothy Hodgson

Bernhard Crusell

Jean Sibelius

Aarre Merikanto

Joonas Kokkonen

respects the older forms. It is a quality less relevant to Latin musical compositions and only slightly in evidence in more recent works of Teutonic origin (although Finland's disinclination to follow the popular anarchic trends in approach to musical architecture makes it less surprising).

The 1920s saw the rise of Madetoja's art and in terms of large-scale composition, his was the alternative muse to that of Sibelius in Finnish culture. Among his works were a number of songs with orchestra - a form favoured by many composers and certainly Sibelius's contribution to this genre can be seen in a sprinkling of such pieces throughout his career. The Six Flower Songs, *Kuusi Kukkalaulua* (1917), are probably the most important of such compositions. Sibelius did however concern himself more with orchestral and choral works at this time and the tradition of large-scale song tended to remain in the hands of Yrjö Kilpinen (1892-1959) whose output is almost entirely concerned with solo vocal music—he composed between six and seven hundred songs. A considerable number were published in orchestral arrangements and the inspiration was drawn from many different sources. The German texts adhere quite closely to the patterns expected from a Lied and Swedish poets also feature in his settings to a considerable extent. Kilpinen is not strictly part of the nationalist group of composers seeking to draw art from traditions inspired by the Finnish language yet when he did choose to set Finnish texts he would often base his ideas on a folk melody and then extend it to become part of his own art. Sometimes his ideas are subtly drawn between folk song and vocal art so that it is not always possible to tell between original folk tune and folk-line melody created entirely by Kilpinen for his text. Kilpinen's most memorable work was done in the 1920s and it is interesting that a public which found it difficult to support the efforts of Aare Merikanto who was making positive efforts to seek new methods of expression, was content to embrace the undoubted beauty of Kilpinen, certainly a poet among composers but one who did not attempt to explore beyond the excellent pattern of lyrical originality which served him so well in his beautifully constructed, if always brief, compositions. Among the most powerful is his group of Morgenstern settings: *Lieder um den Tod* (1928), in which the orchestral parts are original and not arrangements from the keyboard.

The early 1920s saw Sibelius temporarily less concerned with large-scale orchestral writing. *Suite Mignonne* and *Suite Champêtre* (1921) and the five-minute *Suite Caractéristique* (1922) seeming to represent a drawing in of breath before the final onslaught of orchestral originality featuring the last two symphonies and *Tapiola*. There was even a return to composition for Sibelius's least favourite instrument, the piano, although he largely confined himself to miniatures. The works of this period were generally slight: the six Humoresques for Violin and Orchestra op.87 and op.89

(1917); three brief cantatas (*Oma maa, Jordens sång and Maan virsi*); *Valse Lyrique*; Six Pieces for Piano (1919); Six Bagatelles (1920) and Eight Pieces (1922). Where were the powerful techniques of the Fifth Symphony?

The answer came in 1924 with the appearance of the Sixth Symphony, a work of greatness. Comparable in economy and depth of perception to the Fourth Symphony, but without the underlying tragic blackness, similar to the Fifth Symphony, but without the triumphant outbursts, the Sixth is the work which arouses admiration in Sibelius enthusiasts yet somehow they are not always able to bring themselves to love it. Constant Lambert in *Music Ho* put his finger on the essence of this strange contradiction, suggesting that perhaps listeners found it "overshadowed by the grandeur of No. 5" but he felt that "commentators may find its intimate quality more indicative of the true Sibelius, just as many of us feel that Beethoven's Fourth and Eighth Symphonies are more echt-Beethoven than the popular 'odd-number' symphonies".

The orchestration is subtle. Giving the impression of light scoring (though including harp and bass clarinet for added colour), the coolness of his music, with its flow of similar tempo and its sparing use of the climactic moment, represents an exceptionally pure distillation of Sibelian spirit which some audiences may have found less immediately impressive. When beginning a major symphony one might expect a full fledged tune (though composers have eschewed such an easy way out from time to time ever since Beethoven's Ninth Symphony). The opening is powerfully misty with the fullest of harmonies *mezzo forte*. All the elements are here, but what will Sibelius do with them?

The two most important ingredients (to say "themes" would be to preempt the question) are to be found in the first two and the last three bars of the example. Whilst this is not the place to analyse a specific symphony it is worth indicating that there is no typical Sibelius method of construction except in general terms. These themes—announced as developments of the bases shown above—are manipulated in a manner more subtle than hitherto. Where oboes had announced the first fragment it becomes almost a faded memory until the ear is made to recognise it in a viola phrase:

Before this cross-reference however, the second of the "fragments" has already been toyed with after its first announcement on flutes. The violins touch upon it, then seize it at greater length, next the flutes treat it in altered style, then the oboes grasp it. Mention an idea often enough and the elements begin to weld themselves together.

It is interesting in Sibelius to note thematic similarity between elements in various works, probably it was sub-conscious and there is always a danger of overstating the importance of such co-incidences.

Ever since Sibelius's music was first discussed, thematic similarities have disturbed commentators. Sibelius's strength was in the expansion of the initial fragments, whether those of a symphonic poem or of a symphony (sometimes the two forms are amazingly close). The Finales of the Third and Fourth symphonies have thematic sequences in common as has the Scherzo of the Fourth Symphony and the first movement of the Fifth. Even so devoted a Sibelius scholar as Cecil Gray in his book, *Musical Pilgrim,* of 1935 on the Sibelius symphonies, goes to the considerable trouble of thanking Constant Lambert for pointing out the close resemblance between a passage at the end of the Seventh Symphony and a progression from *Valse Triste.*

It has always seemed however that this similarity was so glaringly obvious and yet at the same time so irrelevant as to be scarcely worth mentioning. The first time it occurred to the present writer, he simply put the notion aside as seeming an unworthy thought to have crossed a listener's mind when contemplating a great masterpiece! Thematic familiarity as a method of construction rather than mere co-incidence is, however, a basis of the composition of the Sixth Symphony. It is possible to hear a Sibelius work and catch on to a familiar phrase ("now, in which other work did I hear that?") but in the Sixth Symphony this element captures the attention by jogging the memory with events as close as the end and the beginning of the same movement.

The "woodland" central section of the second movement—Allegretto moderato—of the Sixth Symphony is a strange departure from normal form, otherwise this graceful, withdrawn movement is logical in terms of development and the main theme, announced by first and second violins in alternation, after an extensive chordal woodwind introduction, is later extended: more a lengthening of an already expansive melody than a typical symphonic development.

Even the Scherzo (as it seems reasonable to describe the Poco vivace) though withdrawn, pastel-shaded and elusive, uses these patterns and this Scherzo seems not to have a Trio section either: more a development and recapitulation. The fairy-like delicacy is not allowed to rule fully however and some brass outbursts establish its essential purpose as a more solid interval between the ephemeral Allegretto moderato and the Finale. The main Scherzo theme - announced mezzo forte - has at least a good solid feel to it

The Finale of the Sixth Symphony starts firmly and grandly on violins

but thereafter Sibelius reverts to the subtle use of fragments an approach which had typified the construction of the first movement. The whole of the Finale is geared towards the serenity of the final pages. By this time Sibelius has halved the speed, yet one might scarcely have known at which point this occurred, so accomplished is the composer's manipulation of note lengths. This is not, however, a winding down of tension, rather it is an expansive apotheosis. Simply because it is quiet and without tension or foreboding it does not mean that this is other than a superb culmination of a work which teems with ideas. Just as the Fifth Symphony indicated a new direction in composition which was reflected in later years by composers whose style owed little to Sibelius, so the new direction of Sibelius's Sixth Symphony (seen also, in slightly different terms, in the Seventh) had its later influences. The Sixth Symphony represents the purest essence of Sibelius. This composer was many-sided and audiences tend not to remember the more inward aspects, but the philosophy of the Sixth Symphony was adopted—not necessarily as a result of its influence, perhaps more as an act of parallel thinking—by other Finnish composers, notably Uuno Klami. When Ralph Wood described the work as "Sibelius's greatest Symphony" he was not being esoteric in championing a composition which the public find difficult, there is little doubt that this work, given the right type of performance offers musical rewards which are not always fully appreciated*.

The Seventh Symphony appeared only one year later. It caused the composer some trouble in the fashioning and a little doubt as to how to describe it. There is only one movement (albeit with clearly definable sections incorporated) yet there is no work more symphonic in Sibelius's whole output and any other title than *Symphony* would surely have been a misnomer.

Hints of revision processes have been implied by Sibelius's comments on various works and certainly this includes his Seventh Symphony which, when the notion of composing it came to him as far back as 1918, he planned as being "In three movements, the last an Hellenic Rondo". But there is no reason to suppose that the composer did more than wrestle with the elements of construction before committing them to the final manuscript. Simon Parmet in *The Symphonies of Sibelius* has gone so far as to suggest that Sibelius may have been describing the form of his Eighth Symphony rather than his Seventh.

Sometimes "revision" is no more than the alteration of the style of moulding of themes at the times of composition. Most composers do not set pen to paper with the final outcome of the development of their themes firmly in their heads.

It is the structure of Sibelius's Seventh Symphony which differentiates it from any of his symphonic poems. Several themes are each developed within a specific area of the work rather than relying on a single theme which, though developed, remains the essence of the piece. True, there is a unifying element: the trombone chorale which appears at moments of structural (although not necessarily emotional) climax

sonore

Without daring to presume to equate the form of the Seventh Symphony to normal symphonic structure, Cecil Gray, in an entirely brilliant analysis of the work, insinuates symphonic turns of phrase, "corresponding to the exposition section of the classical symphonic form", "this section has been

---

*It was once the fashion to perform Sibelius's Sixth Symphony in a withdrawn, understated, mysterious manner, commercial recordings did little to redress this problem. Even Anthony Collins, noted in British circles for his gripping, forthright approach to Sibelius, failed to stress the forceful elements which lie very close to the surface of this work and should certainly be allowed to burst forth from time to time. In recent times, Paavo Berglund has shown the streak of iron within the impressionistic exterior of this work and some of this element is captured in his recording although his concert-hall renderings have seemed more spontaneous and forceful, there is something a little calculated about the disc. Nevertheless it represents a mature and ideally strong view of perhaps the most elusive of all Sibelius's major compositions.

compared to the development section of the ordinary symphonic movement", "Scherzo-like section" and so on. Allusion rather than comparison is the secret: to have compared the various sections to conventional symphonic form would have been to force the music into an analytical procrustean bed.

The philosophy is none too far removed from that of the Sixth Symphony. A wealth of thematic ideas, placed together, miraculously form a whole. Two early ideas are worked into a complex, forward-moving section which, once set in motion has irrepressible momentum.

This analysis cannot possibly explain the feeling of tranquillity achieved when the opening statements cease and a hushed, multi-part string statement proceeds with a confident beauty which goes beyond mere technical description. The "Scherzo" section exploits a theme, not really Scherzo-like, but certainly faster and more lively:

The whole essence of the Seventh Symphony is its sense of inevitability. In Karl Ekman's *Jean Sibelius: en konstnärs liv och personlighet* (1935 and revisions) Sibelius is quoted as saying "The directly symphonic is the compelling vein that goes through the whole. This in contrast to the depicting"*.

The thrice-stated trombone theme is the key to the unity of this symphony. If the opening paragraphs are considered in symphonic terms, the sheer quantity of music is staggering. In terms of bar lengths the first thematic episode is longer than the gigantic theme which commences Bruckner's Seventh Symphony. Is it any wonder then, that the most brilliant elements of contraction are applied by Sibelius so that the whole symphony is completed within the time span of only the first of Bruckner's four movements? In a famous and oft-quoted conversation with Mahler (again Ekman is the source) Sibelius referred to his "compulsion to achieve an inner connection between all the motifs". At the time the conversation took place he could never have known that he would embark upon a conception as demanding as the Seventh Symphony but there his compulsion has been justified. Had commentators of the time chosen to do a comprehensive survey of Sibelius's life and work they might, on the evidence, have concluded that with the Seventh Symphony, a fully rounded lifetime's work had been achieved. Of course no writer would have dared publish such an opinion since Sibelius, a mere sixty years of age

---

*From the English translation *Jean Sibelius: his life and personality* (1936 and revisions).

and now in excellent health was in a position to launch forth into further creations. The immense achievements to date were remarkable enough, but what did the future portend? Already, other composers had sufficient signposts to enable them to pursue their own paths. The nationalistic stance had been established and Sibelius, having achieved the ultimate in his compositional aims, had provided Finnish music with the impetus which it had required. Only genius could have provided it and Sibelius had that genius. With young composers showing promise and the existing generation working assiduously (if to some extent unrecognisedly) the climate of Finnish music was surely at its most promising at the point at which Sibelius's Seventh Symphony was published.

The direction—including its changes of course, in which Finnish music was guided because of Sibelius's career—is mapped out with remarkable clarity through the focal points of the symphonies. Although to foreign ears a snatch or two of Sibelius can be located in Finnish contemporaries if it is sought for, the Sibelian sonority was not generally imitated. On the other hand the move from the romantic nobility of the earlier works, through the more cerebral and serious middle period, to the power and concentration of the later works formed a pattern similar to that of the sum of all his contemporaries. Since it is a Nordic trait, Sibelius need not be given the entire credit for creating economy of utterance but this essential feature stayed with him throughout his compositional life and it is rare for any of his successors to be guilty of prolixity.

The final masterpieces: *Tapiola* and *The Tempest*, were published in 1926. The windswept scenes of the former work are very close in construction to the storm scene of the latter. Since however, Sibelius was writing for the theatre and the greatness of *Tapiola* has never been in doubt, it is reasonable to accept that a master of "storm-writing" should be permitted to use a particular technique on more than one occasion. *Tapiola* evokes the forest lands with uncanny realism, not with deliberate bar-by-bar literal description but by a sustained sweeping atmosphere. The forests remain dark, windswept, barely penetrable right down to the tree-lined shores of the icy lakes. Sibelius had always used pedal points with skill and imagination, but here this device is at its most powerful—especially when harmonized with the interval of a second.

The Prelude to *The Tempest* is a powerful work. Performers tend not to use it in conjunction with the incidental music (which Sibelius fashioned into two orchestral suites of about twenty minutes each) probably the reason is that the storm section of the Prelude is simply repeated at the end of Suite no.1—a simple abbreviation of part of the Prelude but with a different ending. *The Tempest* is brilliantly imaginative, that its component parts are sometimes extraordinarily brief is not to its detriment. Sometimes the more obvious movements—for example that which represents Caliban—are strangely uncharacteristic sounding a good deal more like the

March Past of the Kitchen Utensils from Vaughan Williams' *The Wasps,* than anything of Sibelius. The Dance of the Nymphs is most improbably Berliozian too, but the atmosphere of the delicate and soulful movements is extraordinarily Finnish.

Sibelius in *Tapiola* and *The Tempest* was clearly a figure of towering creative ability so where next was his mature ability to turn? There was the Masonic Ritual Music for voices, piano, and organ—naturally this was not heard by the general public—and some brief pieces for violin and piano. Then there was the announcement of the Sibelius Society in which HMV planned many exciting recordings in its six-Album set of Sibelius's works. One of these pieces was to be the Eighth Symphony which was to be performed by Koussevitsky at the close of the concert season of the Boston Symphony Orchestra. This did not happen. Indeed nothing further happened, but this did not stem the musical world's impatience to hear the Eighth Symphony. Between 1932 and 1933 Sibelius promised to submit the score to his publishers and all the time public interest remained—especially in England where Kajanus and Schneevoigt in the concert hall and Cecil Gray's persuasive written championship had caught the imagination. In the USA too, Sibelius was played extensively—especially in Boston and New York. For all this, no Eighth Symphony, indeed no further music, appeared. Reputedly the Symphony was completed around 1932 (some sources say 1929) and in 1945 Sibelius wrote to his "Dear Old Friend" Basil Cameron saying, "my eighth symphony has been 'finished' many times but I am not yet contented with it. When the time arrives, it will be a pleasure to me to give it into your hands". To date no commentator has committed himself to a full explanation of the mystery of the Eighth Symphony although there are theories of its destruction through its creator's dissatisfaction, its non-release after Sibelius's death and even its possible non-existence (it is difficult to accept that it never existed and even now, still not entirely safe to assert that it does not). It seems that music-lovers have been able to accept the general overall "silence from Järvenpää" yet have not quite forgiven the non-appearance of the Eighth Symphony. Whilst not a fully satisfying explanation, Sibelius did give a helpful summary of his feelings on the subject to Ekman for his biography and it is perhaps not fair to attempt to read any more into the situation than is implied by the words written by the composer himself in about 1935, "Composition has always given my life substance and it still does. My work has as much fascination for me now as it did when I was young, a thrill connected with the difficulties of the task. May nobody believe that creating music comes more easily to an old composer if he is serious about his art. Your demands on yourself grow with the years. Your increased skill makes you more eager than ever before to reject solutions that follow the law of least resistance. You are faced with new problems. What has given me most pleasure is that I have been able to reject. Perhaps I have devoted most of my efforts to works never completed."

If the contemporaries of Sibelius approached composition from a parallel but different viewpoint, constructing their music in a different way and quite likely seeking to avoid fingerprints too akin to those of the greatest living Finnish composer, and if the most modern composers have apparently evolved a new Finnish style which is drawn from a living tradition of which Sibelius, though important, represents only one element, who was the true heir to Sibelius? Who links 1926 to the years after the Second World War? One figure seems to fit this description: Uuno Klami (1900-61). His relative neglect and his lack of circulation in Europe and the United States should blind no-one to his extraordinary imagination and skill. Klami's compositional career started at the time of Sibelius's cessation of output. His literary inspriations were often similar and he was responsible for several *Kalevala*-inspired pieces. His *Sea Pictures* for piano and orchestra show vivid imagination and his First Piano Concerto (1925) which is very much a work of its period, even including saxophones, are notable examples of early promise and the *Karelian* Rhapsody (1927) was probably the first link with Sibelian philosophy. The turning point in his career however has a feeling of history repeating itself, for Robert Kajanus encouraged Klami to compose a *Kalevala*-based work. In 1933 the result appeared: a five-moment *Kalevala* Suite. This work became subject to revision and in 1943 reached the form in which it is known today. One of the movements (Lemminkäinen) had been withdrawn from the Suite and published separately in 1934 leaving a four-movement work of remarkable individuality—probably Klami's best known composition outside Finland. His output was impressive however and included three symphonies (four, if one includes the unnumbered early *Symphonie enfantine* of 1928) two Piano Concerti, the Overture and incidental music to *King Lear,* two notable cello works—the *Cheremissian* Fantasy and the Theme and Variations—three concert overtures, and a longish piece for piano and strings called *Hommage a Haendel.*

The remarkably varied style of Klami's music does not by any means reveal his whole background. His most notable teacher was Ravel in Paris and if one can imagine a composer able to employ the subtle orchestral effects general with impressionistic composers moulded into the firm outlines achieved by Sibelius, something of Klami's style can be imagined. That this combination should sometimes have a Stravinskian flavour is perhaps not surprising but the depth of Finnish influence remains and it is not a difficult task to align the opening of the Finale of the *Kalevala* Suite with its subject matter simply from the sound. There is no reason to be apologetic for the aura of Sibelius being instilled into these moments, for the creation of this episode took place in the early 1930s and it includes all the essence of the mature Sibelius. Had that master composed this passage himself at that time it would have been accepted as part of his musical growth. Of course, Sibelius would have written an entirely Sibelian piece whereas Klami shows that influence only momentarily but it is such a magnificent moment that the influence of Sibelius is shown to be liberating rather than inhibiting.

Traditional values are also represented by Klami's contemporary Helvi Lemmiki Leiviska (b. 1902), who is Finland's most important woman composer. A pupil of Melartin and later of Willner, Madetoja and Funtek, she has followed a full career as teacher, and critic and was librarian at the Sibelius Academy for a third of a century. Meanwhile she has added a substantial corpus of works to the repertoire, employing a style which still shows traces of German Romanticism behind the clear-cut Finnish national features. This national characteristic can be said to embrace a leaning towards formal and classical design since the most frequently performed works seem to be the three symphonies (1947, 1954, and 1971). The basis of Leiviska's output lies in some twenty orchestral compositions although there are a number of chamber and piano works, two cantatas and a number of songs, she was also attracted to the traditional story of Julia, writing, in 1937, the music for the film of that name.

By extraordinary coincidence chronological discussion of composers of this period brings Heidi Sundblad-Halme (1903-73) to attention. Here is yet another example of a woman composer nurtured in German tradition (Musikinstitut Berlin) and she shared with Leiviska the tutelage of Leo Funtek. Less the Romanticist in style, perhaps through the influence of Väino Raitio, although not ashamed of programmatic titles, Sundblad-Halme wrote almost exclusively for orchestra or for orchestra with solo voices and her compositions were largely descriptive. No compositions later than 1956 have been catalogued.

Nils-Eric Fougstedt (1910-61), perhaps best known outside Finland as a conductor, wrote a relatively small number of works which are of interest in that some continue to reflect the late romanticism which influenced Sibelius—notably the Piano Trio (1933) and the First Symphony (1938)—whereas others have more aggressive harmonies in mid-European style (for example the Second Symphony of 1949) whilst yet others such as Trittico Sinfonico (1959) extend into the twelve-note system.

Of the more senior contemporary composers, Erik Bergman (b. 1911) steps firmly out of period, falling within the progressive school of thought. His studies moved from Finland to Germany but continued even into the 1950s. His steady output of substantial works did not commence until 1938 with his Suite for String Orchestra. The Second World War is virtually a total dividing line between his romantic-influenced earlier works and his progressive later thinking which commenced with the use of serialism but later incorporated its intentions without slavish adherence to its technical methods. His choral output is considerable and his less frequent excursions into chamber music are opportunities to exploit individual instrumental sonorities in an often experimental manner, as for example in a duo for flute and guitar the former achieves pizzicato effects and the latter is sometimes struck rather than plucked. Only the cognoscenti would venture to discuss whether Bergman's current output places him among current avant-garde composers such as Erkki Jokinen or Hermann Rechberger, (both thirty years his junior,) but in this field Bergman bids fair to be regarded as Finland's youngest older composer.

Bergman's style, though not his characteristic type of sonority, is paralleled to some extent by Bengt Johansson (b. 1914) whose choral experience is similar, his Missa Sacra was his first and one of his most notable of choral compositions together with his Requiem. The chordal sequences familiar in choral music are largely evident too in his orchestral music.

Einar Englund (b. 1916) continues the mainstream of Finnish music, not so much in his reliance on traditional sounds (he is too thoroughly "modern" for such a description to apply) but because, however exploratory his melodic instinct, he has a symphonic outlook supported by a philosophy of rhythmic impulse. This element, rare in contemporary composers who retain large-scale thought, is shared by all too few symphonists but those who do fall within this bracket tend also to come from Nordic countries. Englund's symphonies—of which the second is perhaps held highest in esteem—have an inner cogency based on light, dancing harmonic lines and a determined sense of progress. A certain intensity of violin ostinato recalls the driving nature of Martinů - a notion supported by clear orchestral methods with the characteristic intrusion of the piano into the textures. Englund's studies led him from Finland through Germany to the U.S.A. and the dance element (together with the use of piano) seems to show the influence of the last of these three stages when Aaron Copland was his tutor. More recently Englund's sense of structure has tended to impel him to write more briefly (each successive symphony is approximately three minutes shorter than its immediate predecessor) and the use of piano does not occur after the Third Symphony, although the Fourth and Fifth retain celesta.

Finnish opera, the phenomenon of the 1970s, did not show the expected steady progress from the 1920s when Madetoja and Merikanto were concerned with the genre. To put it at its most basic, opera in Finland waited for nearly half a century and then flared up quite unexpectedly. Three composers are closely involved in this movement: two of them Joonas Kokkonen (b. 1921) and Aulis Sallinen (b. 1935) have fired public enthusiasm yet curiously Tauno Pylkkänen (b. 1918) whose output in this field is rather greater, has been less favoured. His output includes several operas, and in addition he composed *Suden morsian* [The Wolf's Bride], 1940, a radio opera which won the International Grand Prix; *Varjo* [The Shadow] in 1952, and *Vangit* [The Prisoners] in 1964.

Whether the growth of opera gave rise to, or was promoted by the creation of the Savonlinna Festival is a moot point but the phenomenon occurred and its influence is powerful. From it have arisen the twin pillars of contemporary operatic composition Aulis Sallinen and Joonas Kokkonen.

Sallinen's *Ratsumies* [The Horseman] can claim to be the first opera to capture the Finnish imagination since the works of the 1920s. It certainly reflects the sonic differences between the 1920s and the 1970s and the libretto by Paavo Haavikko demands from the listener a philosophical and enquiring mind. The music is so closely welded to the rise and fall of the words that despite its modernity, the essentially vocal nature of the musical invention is never taxing to the listener. The mood of the opera itself remains tragic and inflections of meaning in the text are quickly reflected by Sallinen. When the mysterious Horseman relates his experiences to the superstitious peasants in the middle of Act II every succeeding moment seems to darken the situation as each threatening vocal phrase is echoed in the lower register of the clarinet. Haaviko presents his thought provoking philosophies but chooses not to explain them. At the end of Act I the Horseman is confused between the living and the dead. The situation is represented by a random sequence of murmuring voices, the use of amplified voices over quasi-electronic effects takes the listener into this equivocal world, the same character does not necessarily have his voice reproduced with the same quality for each sentence of this long recitative-dialogue. From this moment, the listener is never quite permitted to leave the dream-world which librettist and composer have created jointly. Even the meaning of the words *sleep* and *dreams* become ill-defined until eventually, after the inevitably tragic conclusion, the audience is left to muse over the unexplained significance of the final non-vocal action as hundreds of "strange rat-chewed candles" are lit to reveal the aftermath of the battle. The lighting of candles was foreshadowed in Act I scene 3. Has the true portent been overlooked? Should one have been more attentive to the libretto? The answer is to hear this imaginative opera again, it is surely not intended to reveal itself at one hearing.

The well known Finnish writer and correspondent Erkki Arni has suggested in an English language article that Joonas Kokkonen's *Viimeiset kiusaukset* [The Last Temptations] has supplanted Madetoja's *Pohjalaisia* as "The Great National Opera" and cites over a hundred performances in the four years after its première at Savonlinna in 1975. The libretto is drawn from a play by the composer's cousin Lauri Kokkonen, which was written in 1958. The historical importance of the central character: Paavo Ruotsalainen probably makes him Finland's most popular operatic hero and true to the tradition of *Kalevala*, this hero has many human weaknesses underlying his visionary character. No wonder therefore, that the real and very important figure of Ruotsalainen has somehow been swept up in the nationalistic fervour which has driven purely Finnish literature to a position of eminence. Cultural tradition can encompass the legendary, the fictional, and the actual all at the same time*.

The British idea of a non-conformist preacher is not necessarily close to the character of Paavo Ruotsalainen, whose passion for spreading the gospel frequently overrode his responsibility to support his family. Ruotsalainen's revivalist ideals are however so strong that he takes every opportunity to challenge the inflexible teachings of the established church. History supports the persuasive power of this virtually unlettered peasant whose coarse exterior appealed to the countryfolk with whom he was in such sympathy—he preached pure Christianity to the farming community, frequently he drank with them, sometimes he shocked them with devastating condemnations of their narrow religious outlook.

Some appreciation of the nature of the central character is essential to the understanding of *Viimeiset kiusaukset* and Kokkonen's transparent scoring and subtle changes of mood make for a gripping atmosphere.

Sallinen's *The Red Line*, premièred in 1978, is based on a work by Ilmari Kianto (1874-1970). The opera is traditional in philosophy in that it takes appealing Finnish themes - one could almost describe it as an amalgam of *Juha* (Topi the crofter blusters and rants and threatens to kill the bear that threatens his livestock but everyone knows he is incapable of doing so) and *Pohjalaisia* (The community is downtrodden by the oppressive rule of Tsarist Russia). This work has certain elements of harmonic bitterness which Kokkonen would never employ. It is not so much an advance upon Sallinen's *Ratsumies,* but more a rationalisation. There is no oblique symbolism in the story, it is merely a tragedy of peasant life. Accordingly Sallinen is thoroughly direct and forceful. The protest and the anger—especially in Act I scene 4—occupies him fully, a parallel to the mysticism of *Ratsumies.*

The enormous upsurge of opera in Finland has certainly done much for the reputation of both Aulis Sallinen and Joonas Kokkonen, but this explanation of public approval of two remarkable composers whose popularity has been richly deserved should not blind the observer to the contribution that both have made to the orchestral field.

Kokkonen's output is modest in quantity and clearly he considers with deliberation everything he composes: *Viimeiset kiusaukset* took fifteen

---

*At the première the enormously taxing part of the great preacher Paavo Ruotsalainen (1777-1852) was taken by the bass Martti Talvela. It has been suggested that Talvela's immersion in the character of Paavo Ruotsalainen has, for many people, resulted in a kind of artistic confusion; somehow Martti Talvela *is* Paavo Ruotsalainen whereas the other noted exponent of the part, Martti Wallén, is regarded more coolly as an excellent singer who gives a magnificent account of a challenging characterisation. It is not surprising therefore that the rumour has arisen that through playing this part, Talvela has been caused to re-examine carefully his own religious outlook.

The Red Line, *Usko Viitanen*

years in gestation. Kokkonen is a remarkable exception among composers in that he is self-taught. He now has a reputation as a teacher but was never a student of composition.* His first compositions were confined to chamber works and not until 1957 when he was thirty-six years of age, is an orchestral piece listed: this was Music for String Orchestra. The first of his symphonies dates from 1960 (a parallel with Brahms in his late approach to the supreme musical art-form). Even so, Kokkonen's symphonic style has been consistent: always terse and to the point—each of his four symphonies (five if one includes his Sinfonia da Camera of 1962) takes around twenty minutes and his chamber works, especially string quartets, have the same classical respect for form. Although as time has passed, Kokkonen has kept even more closely to essentials—the economical composer personified—the public has warmed to his compositions as his career has progressed. Atonality is simply not part of his philosophy whilst structure and its logical processes are supremely important, as the clarity of his writing proves. His interest in the science of architecture is hardly surprising in the circumstances, indeed one might almost deduce this from the evidence of his compositions.

The innately symphonic nature of *The Last Temptations* also grows logically from the direction in which Kokkonen has moved. His music places him among the group of notable names deserving of the description *symphonist*. Used thoughtfully this term does not necessarily demand that the composer concerns himself particularly with symphonic form (although Kokkonen has in fact done so) but in any event, this side of Kokkonen's art qualifies him to be considered one of the heirs of Sibelius.

Aulis Sallinen, although fourteen years Kokkonen's junior, is in the strange position of having come to public notice not much later than the older composer, his career seeming to run on contemporary lines. His liberal approach to tonality does not now stretch as far as atonality and he is not the only Finnish composer to have dabbled briefly with dodecaphony only to abandon it.†

His orchestral output commenced at much the same time as that of Kokkonen with whom he studied, together with Merikanto, in Helsinki. Sallinen's first large-scale work was his *Two Mythical Scenes* (for orchestra 1956), but the first work to draw public attention was his powerful and supremely dramatic *Mauermusik*: effectively a devastating criticism of the regime which seeks to imprison German subjects behind the Eastern side of the wall built across Berlin but also a magnificent and brilliantly orchestrated work in its own right. Sallinen has used the string quartet to

---

*He did however, receive a piano diploma from the Sibelius Academy.

†Bergman, Heininen, Kokkonen, and Rautavaara are good examples of composers who have widened their experience by studying serialism and perhaps using it for a period, but whose compositions are no longer tied to this system.

explore the more extraordinary aspects of instrumental technique and executants tend to look for opportunities to play these demanding works—always a challenge—by a composer who continues to explore the exciting new possibilities of a traditional form of music-making. No symphony appeared until 1971—and that was a relatively brief work. Sallinen, a fine constructor of orchestral music, clearly did not, at that time, see himself as a potential symphonist for where other composers might have written Symphony No. 1 Sallinen chose the title Symphony.

Tauno Marttinen (b. 1912) almost qualifies for inclusion among the composers listed in the footnote relating to Bergman and others. His compositional career made a startling change of direction from its neo-romantic beginnings. After the Second World War Marttinen's exposure to serial techniques when studying in Switzerland made an enormous impression upon him and changed the nature of his compositions entirely. More recently a tonal, albeit still astringent, style has become apparent: clearly the composer is not pre-occupied with serialism but neither has he entirely rejected it. With a large output comprising half a dozen symphonies, several concerti and many large-scale choral and orchestral works to his credit, it is intriguing to find the date of the first composition mentioned in the comprehensive listing by the Music Information Centre in Helsinki: *Kokko, ilman lintu* [Eagle of the Air], to be 1956. Did Marttinen not seek to publish his previous works, are they not part of his life's work, is neo-romanticism so unpopular as to be unacceptable to audiences of today that therefore they have mysteriously disappeared? Whatever the reason, it is unthinkable that Marttinen should have waited until the age of forty-four before committing himself to musical creation: is this implied anxiety to break with the past an underlying element of all modern Finnish thought? The number of composers who started composing traditionally, searched unsuccessfully for a time for something more revolutionary only to return to a compromise in which their real self began to appear make it worth pondering over the significance of this recurring pattern.

Usko Meriläinen (b. 1930) has had a career which also falls into this familiar pattern but here all works of whatever style are part of his stated output—including a fairly romantic First Piano Concerto (1955) which, however unrepresentative, succeeded in making sufficient impression to have been made available on a gramophone record. His later works have incorporated electronic techniques.

The youngest Finnish composers of today show an exciting living art with all shades of musical opinion present, yet Einojuhani Rautavaara (b. 1928) seems to represent the most consistently progressive figure. Because of his essentially modern outlook, his large output of compositions and his important appointments indicate that there is no bar to approval by the musical establishment as a result of adventurousness. Rautavaara manages to represent both a father-figure to the youngest modern composers whilst still challenging them by continuing to advance his techniques. His abandonment of serialism is, in one way, significant but it probably served to open many new doors for him. Finnish acquaintances speak of Rautavaara as "one of our modern composers" whereas the rather younger Sallinen, possibly because of his interest in essentially historical Finnish subjects, is thought more as part of the mainstream of music, despite his works sounding anything but traditional.

Even more extraordinary is the placing of so young a composer as Kalevi Aho (b. 1949) in the "traditional" category, but possibly Aho is just as typical of present day Finland as any other deep-thinking composer, for his sense of structure in his relatively few compositions (his output is heavily weighted towards the symphony) is markedly well-controlled. Aho sees music whole and one of his strongest influences has been Rautavaara (he studied with Rautavaara at the Sibelius Academy in Helsinki). His dramatic ideas are, however, very much his own and whilst his methods are largely those of today, the dramatic progress through his works is often related to the timeless techniques of drama, the tautening and relaxing of tensions at critical moments and apotheoses which are either triumphant or despairing according to his programmatic requirements. The waltz in the First Symphony is not too far removed from the world of Mahler. In the Fourth Symphony's huge first movement, Aho builds a final threatening climax by commencing with a labyrinthine melody on the violins which recalls Carl Nielsen's evocation of futureless bleakness in the tragic slow movement of his Sixth Symphony. Aho, one of the very youngest yet also one of the most tonal composers, seems to typify the new generation in Finnish thought, stemming from Sibelius in terms of structure and from Rautavaara in terms of harmonic adventurousness.

Among Aho's latest works is his Sixth Symphony for an orchestra of Richard Straussian dimensions but eschewing the rare colourings found in Aho's Fifth Symphony which includes two saxophones and piano. His Violin Concerto, written in 1981, also exploits a large orchestra colourfully and again has that strange visitor, so beloved of the composer: the baritonehorn.

The most discussed of Aho's recent works is *Avain* [The Key]. The present trends in Finnish music make the exact description of the work vital. That a soloist sings and performs a drama, based on a story by Juhana Mannerkorpi, accompanied by small chamber orchestra, leads to the nomenclature "opera". Certainly the drama has all the elements of opera, being based upon the musings and increasingly irrational actions of Johannes Pontto who sits alone in his apartment awaiting visitors to celebrate his fiftieth birthday. No one arrives.

Such a subject would have appealed to the dry wit of Hindemith and doubtless that composer would have used the term *opera*. Whatever

Leif Segerstam

Jorma Panula

commentators may say about it, the Finnish Music Information Centre Catalogue lists the work as a "scenic monologue for one singer and chamber orchestra". It would be dangerous to assume that this work is part of the rapid Finnish operatic revival, but as an adventurous branch during the progress of an immensely talented young composer it stands as a telling step in his career. To thrust it among its grander operatic contemporaries would be unjust, Aho's delightful diversion remains worthy in its own right. At a later time, this composer may well compose dramatic vocal music of greater import, but for the moment Aho has yet to climb aboard the operatic bandwaggon.

Aho is the antidote to the minor disease of avant-gardisme which troubled the early 1970s in Finnish music. The musicologist Jarmo Sermilä (b. 1939) describes it as an "avantgardist fanaticism". It seems reasonable to give credence to Sermilä's comments since, in the first place, they come from a composer of no little ability himself and one moreover who has also used some avantgardist instrumental combinations such as 26-44 horns (in *Cornologia* 1975), Flugelhorn and Tape (in *Contemplation I*, 1976) and has composed a series of works under the heading Electro-Acoustic music. Sermilä however, has the gift of not taking the latest developments too seriously. His own outlook is catholic (he has recorded as a jazz musician) but he has also trodden a path similar to that taken by his contemporaries Otto Donner, Gottfried Gräsbeck, Antero Honkanen and Usko Meriläinen by working in studios with computerised equipment. No longer is the synthesizer solely concerned with the requirements of popular music and its studio production.

In terms of sheer facility Leif Segerstam (b. 1944) may be said to represent the newest generation of Finnish musicians. If this is true, then currently the climate would seem to be exceptionally healthy. Segerstam's highly successful international career as a conductor in which his sympathies are enormously wide-ranging still leaves him time for composition. This, in addition to his abilities as pianist and violinist, make him one of the most dynamic figures in Finnish music today.

Since 1977 Segerstam has been chief conductor of the Finnish Radio Symphony Orchestra. Despite the inevitable demands of this appointment (to say nothing of those imposed by a similar appointment held simultaneously with the Austrian Radio Symphony Orchestra) Segerstam's output continues unabated.

Refreshingly, many of his compositions are shot through with wry humour, although he is certainly no musical anarchist. That Segerstam's tenth string quartet should be subtitled "Homage to Charles Ives" is no surprise since the two composers take a similarly oblique view of music. One might raise an eyebrow at the title of Segerstam's first wind quintet, *NNNNOOOOOWWW*, and the second work in that form rejoices in the name of *ANOTHER OF MANY NNNNOOOOOWWWS*.

Segerstam has composed twenty-three string quartets at the last count (nos 20-23 all date from 1980) and since he has written string quartets every year since1974, the catalogue may well have grown since 1980.

Segerstam's symphonies are based upon his *Orchestra Diary Sheets*—usually they are in one movement: for example *Orchestra Diary Sheet* no. 22 is the Second Symphony, no. 23 is the Third Symphony. *Orchestra Diary Sheets* nos. 24, 25, and 26 (composed in 1981) have the subtitle "Symphony no. 4 in two or three movements".

The ultimate in Segerstam's inclination towards freedom of performance lies in *Orchestral Diary Sheet* no. 11 (1981). Here, if cello is used as obbligato instrument, the work is Cello Concerto no. 1; if violin it becomes Violin Concerto no. 2; if piano, it is Piano Concerto no. 2 and there are also versions where the solo instrument could become violin and cello; organ; trombone; clarinet in D and even E flat alto saxophone. It would be sad if Segerstam's brilliance in the execution of his musical art should blind posterity to his true ability as a composer. There are certainly some works which were written for the moment but others will retain their impact and continue to be played. Segerstam has yet to write more strongly structured works, including symphonies in more conventional mode, but sufficient has already been composed to mark out this composer as one of exceptional perception.

From the rise of Finnish musical independence—a movement centred upon Sibelius—the twentieth century has shown a parallel, in music, with the Finnish achievement of political independence. It is a romantic notion to suggest that the enormous change from the pseudo-central-European style of early Finnish composers, to the essentially Finnish sound of Sibelius and his successors could have stemmed from the famous meetings between Sibelius, Kajanus, Gallén-Kallela and their companions. These discussions seem to be thought of traditionally as artistic Schubertiades except that music and kindred arts were discussed rather than given performance and where Schubert's soirées included musical instruments as well as food and drink, the latter elements (particularly the last) represented an important centre of attention in Helsinki.*

Nowadays, these meetings are usually spoken of with an air of levity although at the time, eyebrows were raised a little, especially when Gallén-Kallela painted a truthful portrait of one of the more convivial

---

*One delightful legend concerning the lengthy and earnest discussions which, artistically speaking, were designed to put the world to rights during the meetings of Sibelius's circle in Helsinki in the 1890s, has Kajanus able to stay for only a brief drink before going away for three days to conduct in Germany. On his return, his friends were to be found where Kajanus had left them, still happily talking and drinking. On Kajanus's re-entry into the room, Sibelius's only comment is reputed to have been a complaint that Kajanus always left the door open when he went out.

"Ad Astra" (1894) by Akseli Gallen-Kallela a great friend of
both Sibelius and Kajanus — see footnote page 14.
(Photo courtesy Pirkko and Alvi Gallen-Kallela, Helsinki)

occasions which tells something of the outgoing, uninhibited artistic atmosphere. Students and young artists have met since time immemorial and have theorised the nights away in the hope of improving their art, their political aspirations or, as in this case, the artistic individuality of a whole nation.

Miraculously these relatively mature men were able to achieve the aims and principles of which they dreamed in the years of their companionship. If ever fellowship between friends of like mind needed to justify its value here indeed is the proof. In Finnish terms they completed what the vision of Elias Lönnrot has commenced when he published *Kalevala*. Finnish literature, painting, and music had moved forward enormously under this visionary impulse so that the folk tradition had become embedded in the higher art forms.

There is no doubt in Finnish minds as to the significance of this period and, given this understanding, the exciting development of Sibelius's powers alongside an equally powerful sense of nationalism seems entirely logical. The outside world does not necessarily comprehend this significance and Kajanus's importance (except as an interpreter of Sibelius) is not entirely understood, nor is it appreciated that it takes a man of great intellectual stature not only to accept the implied criticism of his own conventional German-derived art—a product of training rather than inspiration—but also to go further by supporting wholeheartedly and with all his considerable influence, an artistic movement in which the revolutionary element was directed against that very tradition of which he was a part.

For all this sense of new musical thought and spectacular change of direction, Finnish music is still seen by the remainder of Europe and America with a certain amount of reserve. Sibelius looms large, but the school of thought which, Sibelius apart, takes little cognisance of Finnish music (with the exception of the Praeludium by Armas Järnefelt) continues to flourish. In English-speaking lands the approach to Finnish language still typifies the suppressed fear of other cultures which so inhibits the linguistic abilities of the British. The splendid old tradition of insularity which led the writer, in a Victorian book on travel, to confine his chapter on Portugal to seven words "very little is known about the Portuguese" remains, in spirit, as late as 1907 when, in the introduction to W.F. Kirby's imaginative translation of *Kalevala* Runo VIII lines 1 to 16 are quoted "as a specimen of the Finnish language". By implication the average Edwardian Englishman had not seen Finnish in print and one must surely be permitted a wry smile when, in praising the beauty of the poetry, the writer avers that many episodes are "by no means inferior to those we find in ballad-literature of better-known countries than Finland".

Such a statement is incredibly patronising: as if Finland were somehow at fault for not being accessible: not in a convenient place in mid-Europe; instead it is thought to lurk inconsiderately upon the outskirts and to remain lesser-known. If such a view can at least be discounted nowadays, there are aspects of *Kalevala* which do remain a little foreign to those of Anglo-Saxon descent. These have mainly to do with the heroes in the legend. Nordic heroes are not necessarily strong, nor are they always powerful. Neither the reckless Lemminkäinen nor the grim Kullervo are the stuff of which great men are made, but in the North, heroes are sometimes weak and indecisive - no better example may be found than Peer Gynt. The British tend to prefer their heroes to be in the Teutonic mould of Siegfried, therefore identification with the heroes of *Kalevala* is less natural. Probably only Ilmarinen measures up to the high standards required of mythological heroes who are appreciated by central Europeans.

In Britain and America Finnish music as represented by Sibelius has always been assured of an appreciative reception. In the United States Koussevitzky, Ormandy, and Stokowski all took pains to perform Sibelius with great frequency (Stokowski was responsible for the American premières of the Fifth, Sixth, and Seventh symphonies) Toscanini showed interest, even performing Sibelius in Milan, whilst Szell and Bernstein retained the tradition in later years. In England Granville Bantock and Henry Wood were champions of Sibelius's cause from the outset whilst, for the greater part of the century, Sir Thomas Beecham, Sir John Barbirolli, and Sir Malcolm Sargent ensured the continued performance of his music. Much has been made of the reaction against the music of Sibelius in England after his death. Since this theory does not speak for the British public but rather for a small coterie of critics, the phenomenon has no real significance. This clique did manage to reduce the number of performances of Sibelius symphonies at the Promenade Concerts (that most accurate gauge of establishment thinking in England) for where in Sibelius's lifetime all the symphonies might be heard in one season, succeeding years found this reduced to merely one or two.

Despite this, the taste for Sibelius never diminished and in the face of the frequently issued recordings of the 1950s and 1960s, including first Collins, then Maazel, Karajan, and Barbirolli conducting all the symphonies, it was a little sad to read critics of established reputation being apologetic about the considerable praise given Sibelius by earlier writers such as Cecil Gray. In the 1960s one distinguished writer—normally thought of in connection with his expertise in French Music—was seen writing a concert report of Sibelius's Fifth Symphony in which the nature of the performance was not discussed at all, but the music was described from first principles as though it had never before been performed in the concert-hall. The writer ended with a somewhat reserved opinion of the music as a whole. It is strange that this small group of "protesters" did not use a more subtle weapon - the achievement of Sibelius's exact contemporary Carl Nielsen whose large-scale works displayed other matters of significance within their compass. It would have been invidious to invoke such an argument, but it might still have been a more powerful weapon than dull disapproval. In the event, those same critics were so concerned to dismiss the enormous significance of Nielsen that this line of attack became automatically unavailable to them.

Perhaps happily, Sibelius's dramatic style no longer fills the minds of composers of film music so thoroughly: at one time almost any air of tension or foreboding in a film was liable to be depicted by a passage of shivering, ostinato-laden quasi-Sibelius. Musicians and music-lovers do take some note of Sibelius's successors but there is still no obvious claimant to actual "popularity" outside Finland. Were Uuno Klami well represented on records, the climate seems right, at least in England, for that composer to rise in estimation. As matters stand, if one name has to be chosen as the most likely to be more fully appreciated in the coming few years in the context of the favourable atmosphere which exists, it could well be that of Joonas Kokkonen.

The appreciation of Finnish music need not be a national matter. The traditional lack of sympathy by the French is no more easily explained than the natural affinity of the British or the Americans. With those who are committed in their appreciation however, there remains the tendency to turn to the roots, both folkloristic and artistic, which are unified in Sibelius. In explaining with succinct brevity the delights of Finland Juha Tanttu explained this feeling of assurance in a few significant words:*

> Every summer, at the music festivals, I think they should play something other than Sibelius; they do, and I say "Good"; and I wait for the Sibelius; then they play Sibelius too; and a shiver runs down my spine.

What We Have Here. Helsinki: Ministry for Foreign Affairs, 1976.

Sweden

The most important era of cultural, and particularly musical, development in Sweden stems from the accession of Gustav Vasa in 1532, the year in which Sweden became independent. By 1526 the Chapel Royal had been founded, with the advantage of a firm tradition of musical activity. The succeeding wars of the sixteenth century hampered cultural progress, but Vasa and his successors encouraged the arts until Gustav Adolphus (Gustav II Adolf), the first essentially musical king, succeeded to the throne. In 1620 he engaged a court band from Germany, largely to assist at the celebrations of his wedding with Princess Maria Eleonora of Brandenburg, but the band remained at court and through this solid basis, Swedish composers began to flourish.

Notable during the reign of Gustav Adolphus were Thomas Boltzius and the various members of the Düben family, whose extraordinary skills have called forth the comparative implication suggested in the phrase "The Swedish Bachs". The king was an accomplished lute player and his personal encouragement did much for music at court. Traditionally the manner of his death has musical connections also, for he was killed at the battle of Lützen on the 6 November 1632 as he was leading his troops into battle to strains of the warrior's hymn "Förfaras ej, du lilla hop".

His daughter Christina succeeded him and carried the musical traditions forward with enthusiasm—indeed her expenditure on the art of music was notoriously extravagant at times. The composers of the day flourished and the standard of performance at court became much higher. The relationship with the English Ambassador Bulstrode Whitelocke was also musically fruitful, for the English entourage proved to be skilled performers and they were asked frequently to entertain the Queen at supper. Towards the end of her reign Queen Christina (who abdicated in 1654,) arranged for exchanges of musicians between the Swedish court and the English Embassy.

In parallel with this healthy musical atmosphere at court, there arose a development of related skills in churches. At this period there are reports of the English Ambassador having received choirs and instrumentalists from Uppsala and from Göteborg. In his memoirs, Whitelocke is amusingly critical of their abilities - especially the musicians of Göteborg whom he spoke of as having sung "in parts, with indifferent good skill and voices". The Anglo-Swedish rapport remained excellent at this period: the Swedish court musicians often eliciting praise from Whitelocke, himself an excellent musician. The Journal of the Swedish Embassy (1772) mentions many of these entertainments but perusal of these reports eventually leads to the assumption that, triumphantly successful though this pleasant interchange of talents must have been, the musical development in the mid-seventeenth century remained firmly locked in court circles. Even so, centred firmly upon the Düben family, music continued to flourish. At this time Anders Düben and his brother Martin (organist at the Storkyrke) were leading figures and must certainly have taken part in this outburst of musical exchange. The Düben family were of German origin and the first to appear in any Swedish documentation is Michael Düben (c. 1535-1600), musician and alderman of Lützen. His son Andreas (1558-1625) became Cantor at St. Thomas's church Leipzig in 1595 and perhaps this appointment triggered the subconscious of those who seek to underline the parallel between the Düben and the Bach families. His son also named Andreas (confusingly known as the Elder) but more commonly referred to as Anders was the leading court musician in the reign of Queen Christina.

Just as today the Bach family is remembered by Johann Sebastian, so the Düben family is famous for producing the founder of Swedish music: Gustaf, 1628-90 the genealogy is shown in the diagram, but Gustaf the Elder must be regarded as the central figure.

Gustaf became Hofkapellmästare [court music director] in 1663. He was firmly grounded in music and could refer to important influences having stayed in both Germany and France. Three sinfonias for viols, written in 1654, show his considerable skill, although his work with the court at that time more often encouraged him to write choral and vocal works. This facility went further when he took on the duties of Hof-kapellmästare. Extended works such as *Surrexit pastor bonus* typify this aspect, but the earlier setting of *Fadar vår* (the Swedish of the Lord's Prayer) first for a small vocal consort with viols and later, in 1654, in a more fully worked polyphonic version, showed, through the declamatory element, this attraction towards the monodic songs of which Gustaf the Elder was such a notable exponent.

Of his successors, his son Gustaf the younger, turned more towards martial music. His association with Prince Karl–later King Karl XII–clearly accounts for this: a warrior prince was obviously liable to demand music of a warlike nature.

The younger Anders Düben found time to compose in a more courtly manner including a notable French-style ballet, but as the eighteenth century began, so the cultured atmosphere of the Stockholm court, with works. This facility went further when he took on the duties of Hofkapell-ence. Anders' tenure as Hofkapellmästare at court lasted for fifteen years, during which time he also received court honours, being elevated to the nobility in 1707, becoming Chamberlain in 1711, Baron in 1719 and Master of the Royal Household in 1721. One of the most helpful tasks performed by the younger Anders in terms of the history of Swedish musical history was to arrange for the large collection of music made by his father, to be transferred to the University Library in 1733. Consisting of 1500 vocal works and 300 instrumental pieces, this has proved one of the richest sources of musicological information, detailing the output of late seventeenth century composers, not all of whom are necessarily Swedish. For example Buxtehude is represented by 105 works whilst two Germans of Bohemian origin: Pfleger and Capricornus (Bockshorn), have 96 and 65 respectively.

In addition to the beneficial influence of the Düben family who had become something of a tradition as directors of court music, this period of established, though by no means fully developed, musical life in the late seventeenth century, brought another important figure to the fore. This was Olof Rudbeck (1630-1702) who was based at Uppsala University, and designed the organ for the cathedral. His work with the choir and orchestra at the cathedral together with his teaching appointment at the University where he became Rector, are reminiscent of Vivaldi's tenure in Venice. His compositions and practical musicianship were in demand by King Karl XI and Karl XII from their respective coronations–where Rudbeck supervised the music–onwards. At a memorable celebration for the victory at Narva in 1700 under King Karl XII, Rudbeck was joined by his university colleagues Walerius and Reftelius.

As the eighteenth century commenced, Swedish music began to

extend beyond the confines of the royal court. The concerts, services, and celebrations may not have been so elaborate, but the cultural expansion was unmistakable. The town musician now began to gain an element of respectability and musicians' guilds developed in the provinces. For regular employment to be available to musicians outside the court circle in Stockholm had been something of a rare event hitherto, but now there came an expansion in provincial towns which paralleled the growing musical awareness of Stockholm which at this time expanded interest in the other arts. In Göteborg there developed a town band which played, not only at public functions, but also at church services and on market days. Wind music would be in demand to a considerable degree and this, in turn, as public interest in music became manifest, began to throw demands upon the repertoire. The average Swedish town musician might play his instrument skilfully and his musical director may have been able to compose the occasional dance, march or even song, but the sudden musical awakening meant a rapid search for more material and Germany was the obvious source.

The movement away from the capital was not entirely coincidental, nor did the influences cease to stem from court. For example, the last year of the seventeenth century saw the appearance of a French acting troupe in Stockholm and they were invited to give performances on the stage in the king's residence. French culture had occupied the court for at least sixty years prior to this and ballets in the French style had been popular. The French actors therefore encountered a sympathetic atmosphere. This appearance, in itself a straightforward enough cultural event, was typical of the several minor examples which engendered broader cultural thinking. The effect in the provinces was more diffused: it could in effect be described as a basic development of taste in pastimes allied to the French outlook with the dances now becoming very popular. The old forms of dance had always been relatively in vogue but the pavane, the galliard, or the courante had probably been thought of as the preserve of the court whereas the newer French dances—including the minuet and the gigue—were now taken up by everyone. This still did not oust the traditional folk-based dances which were shared by peasant and courtier alike, so it would have been possible to have observed in any town of substance, dances of the French style together with those stemming from Swedish folk tradition being performed at the same gathering. Along with the demand for dance music would be a requirement for town musicians to make verse settings for various civic occasions and if the musicians had talent in this direction, he might even employ it at family celebrations.

This mixture of tradition was certainly supra-nationalistic and Queen Christina is known to have attended court gatherings which intermingled French and Swedish dances. The precedent had been set so the broadening of artistic outlook which occurred in the eighteenth century had the advantage of basic appreciation and certainly, regardless of the skills necessary, the town bands had a plentiful supply of instruments, albeit largely those familiar from an earlier period. It is therefore a chastening thought for those whose musicological studies might tempt them to put music into neat pigeon-holes (insisting that it always be performed on the instruments of the period), that an era had arrived in which the minuet was being played and danced, yet the instruments available would often have included the ostensibly archaic shawm, cornett, and sackbut. These splendid, immensely useful instruments might have formed the nucleus of a town band, supplemented perhaps by trumpet and flute whilst viols or lutes might have joined them for indoor performance. The early eighteenth century therefore, showed these splendidly anachronistic occasions when music of the type normally thought of as being the preserve of the classical composers, was played upon instruments with connections stemming back to renaissance or even medieval times.

The changing atmosphere of music in Sweden coincided with the career of Johan Helmich Roman (1694-1758). There is little doubt that Roman provided stabilisation of the development of Swedish music in this time in much the same way as, in England, Handel gave the strong professional basis which collated the Italian and German styles into a logical Baroque-inspired pattern.

Roman's career must bear the use of this parallel, but it is a dangerous comparison, since a direct linking of his art with that of Handel on the grounds of mere similarity of style could be misleading. Where Handel came from Europe and decided to stay in England, there developing a most significant style based on the collation of his musical upbringing, so the slightly younger Roman drew his most important musical influences from England, studying there when in his early twenties under Pepusch. Roman was steeped in music, being the son of a member of the court band in Stockholm, his godfather was Gustaf Düben the Younger. Probably these court connections stood him in good stead in that Ulrika-Eleonora, sister of King Karl XII (a letter from whom praises Roman's musicianship) sent him to London for study. It is known that Roman admired Handel and when in London sought him out, although there is no actual recorded meeting between the two. The pattern of Handel's experience was followed by Roman (albeit over a much shorter period) in that the visit to England brought him into contact with leading exponents of the Italian school of composition including Ariosti, Bononcini and Geminiani. His activities in England were certainly a major influence upon his career and a greater understanding of them would help to put his later style into closer focus. Unfortunately this period of Roman's life (late 1715 or early 1716 to 1721) is ill-documented and few of his activities can be confirmed with any degree of certainty. Whereas his studies with Pepusch are likely to be a matter of fact, his contact with the above-mentioned Italian composers may only have taken the form of exposure to their music. They were in London at the time, therefore he quite probably met them but to say more than that would be conjecture.

A.M. Sahlstedt* states that Roman studied with Handel as well as with Pepusch. This is not impossible, but again there is no documentary evidence and it seems strange that Roman, whilst admitting his admiration for Handel, should never subsequently have been recorded as saying that he had studied with him in London. Sahlstedt also avers that Roman was engaged at the court of the Duke of Newcastle, Sir Thomas Pelham-Holles, but there is a lack of supporting evidence for this, admittedly not unlikely, appointment having been made. There is no doubt that the Handelian element had become evident in Roman's music by the time he returned to Sweden in 1721. It seems reasonable to suppose however, that the reason lay in his having a musical environment similar to that of Handel rather than in any conscious imitation. Roman's wide-ranging artistic outlook was also a characteristic typical of Handel and clearly Ulrika-Eleonora could scarcely have chosen a more propitious time to send him to England, so thriving was the musical life in the second decade of the eighteenth century.

In Roman's absence, Ulrika-Eleonora had succeeded to the throne of Sweden, Karl XII having been killed in battle in 1718. She did however find it expedient to share power with her husband (Frederic of Hesse-Cassel) who became known as King Fredrik I. Immediately upon his return, Roman was commissioned to arrange the music for Fredrik's coronation and at that time the court's musical resources were somewhat modest. The reason was clear enough for despite some demand for martial music, King Karl XII's requirements were summed up in his oft-quoted phrase, "The only music I want to hear would come from whizzing musket balls". Although this somewhat overstates the case, it is hardly surprising that music at court ceased to be the influence on culture that had been the case previously. Indeed provincial expansion in Sweden had gone forward at the expense of development in the capital.

Roman was appointed Vice Kapellmästare in 1721 and took delight in "fertilizing the musical waste-lands" of Swedish music. To a composer who was now worldly, and used to a thriving, organised musical life in London, Sweden must have seemed noticeably to have fallen behind. The measures which Roman took in order to improve this state of affairs included concentration upon the incorporation of the Swedish language as a basis for setting poetic literature. Although to Roman his initial work on Swedish translations of Handel's *Esther* and *Acis and Galatea* together with *Brocke's Passion* to which Roman added chorales in Swedish, may have

---

*in *Äreminne öfwer hofintendenten, Kongl capellmästaren Johan Helmich Roman*.

seemed no more than an expedient way of familiarising Sweden with the works of a notable composer, this gave valuable experience in the use of Swedish in the context of oratorio. Translations of texts for music by some Italian composers (including Carissimi and Lassus) were followed by two important Swedish language works by Roman himself; the *Jubilate* and the *Svenska Massan* [Swedish Mass].

Roman's positive approach towards increasing the influence of Swedish music doubtless met with approval. Apart from the phenomenon of the Düben family, no other Swedish musician had shown such skill or such breadth of outlook. He had come to public attention as early as 1710–largely on account of his virtuosic abilities as a violinist. The important thing was that he was well liked by all who encountered him and surely this was not unconnected with the favour he received in being sent to England for the purpose of study. His first biographer: Sahlstedt, described him as being "of glad and merry disposition in company: a right noble lord to his family, an honourable citizen and friend". This seems a reasonable and helpful indication, even though it stems from the days (1767) of extravagant use of words. That Roman was "of medium stature" and "had eyes of bright lustre" and was "fair of countenance" seems reasonable too, although Sahlstedt does seem to be somewhat subjective when he goes on to say that this "revealed the devoutness and propriety of spirit that his bosom enshrined". Other sources do, however, support Sahlstedt's indication that Roman was of an exceptionally modest disposition and "could not sing the praises of his own person, much less seek the praises of others. He was of constant temper and no stroke of fate could disturb his disposition." Sahlstedt's description of both Roman's physical appearance and his nature is well documented by others and this is how posterity has tended to see him. Unfortunately, posterity is entirely dependent on such descriptions because no authentic portrait of Roman has yet been discovered.

Musically speaking, the important element in Roman's character centres upon his rationality, his objectivity and his thirst for knowledge. This latter trait is suggested by non-musical sources in Kalmar, where a manuscript of his shows deep interest in history through an extensive written collation of information *Något om Rom* [Notes on Rome]. The appointment at court as Vice Kapellmästare was ideal for the creative work upon which Roman embarked. Düben had the court responsibility, Roman could make and invent music whilst grasping the essentials of Düben's task to which, quite obviously, he would succeed one day. The younger Düben, being of good health and in his forties around this time seemed unlikely to be replaced for some time. Roman, nearly twenty years younger, was full of energy and activity and his accomplishments as director and instrumentalist (he being expert on violin and oboe) won him acclaim.

Although today, Roman's career is thought of in terms of the large output of compositions most of which stemmed from the time after his period as Vice Kapellmästare, his practical activities in the 1720s are most important in terms of assisting Swedish music towards recognition as a powerful voice in itself. At the beginning of 1727, Roman was appointed Hofkapellmästare in succession to Düben. From this time, Roman's compositions became more numerous and, no less importantly, he began to improve the standard of the court orchestra which now became his particular responsibility. Concerts in both the Storkyrkan and the Riddarhuset were arranged by Roman and this meant that music-making of court quality was being disseminated and the cultural atmosphere in musical terms, became a little more akin to that of England–the criterion upon which Roman's thoughts seemed to have been based since his return from that country.

The study of Roman's compositions is fraught with complication. Little was published in his lifetime, some has been wrongly attributed to him, other genuine compositions may yet have to be traced.

The Roman collection in the Royal Academy of Music, Stockholm [Musikaliska Akademiens Bibliotek] is uniquely important and at least forms the core of Roman's output. Particularly valuable are the manuscripts obtained from Utile Dulci: a society which flourished a few years after Roman's death. There are several other sources but by far the largest, and in essence the most controversial, is the collection donated by Anders Holmberg (organist at Kalmar Cathedral) on the occasion of the centenary of Roman's death. The controversy arises from the inscription of Roman's name on many of the manuscripts by a hand which cannot be identified. Other collections: notably those at Uppsala and the Roman compositions included in the Alstromer Family's collection (transferred to the Royal Academy in 1948) are much more reliable.

Description of Roman's music is therefore less than easy. Drawing initially from Italian styles (including that of Handel, whose music was noticeably Italianate at the time Roman made his first visit to London) where composers such as Ariosti, Bononcini, Geminiani, the Scarlattis and Veracini - all London-dwellers at one time or another - must have been a strong influence, well documented, early, Italian-sounding music may be attributed with some safety to Roman. Thereafter the style, whilst taking on a firm personality, can mislead a little.

Roman's activities and the development of music went along in happy parallel in the late seventeen twenties and early seventeen thirties. The well-known set of twelve "Sonate a flauto traverso, violone, e cembalo" (the one publication which took place in the composer's lifetime) gives a typically Italianate starting point. It could be argued that despite his enormous reputation in his own country and the tendency for Swedish composers to follow his lead, Roman did not develop any further than those musicians in other countries whose music his own compositions resembled.

Just one distinguishing element began to appear however: a tendency towards the symphonic form in the classical sense. His sinfonias written to precede vocal or choral works (Roman more often used the term *Overture*, but sometimes *Sinfonia*) used the classical mould and he began also to write symphonies in the instrumental sense, further, he tended towards the four-movement pattern, an uncommon predilection at that time.

In the thematic index to Ingmar Bengtsson's comprehensive study *J.H. Roman och hans Instrumentalmusik* (Studia Musicologia Upsaliensia, 1955) the section on symphonies shows eleven three-movement symphonies (one of which has its central movement divided onto two thematically unrelated sections) and six four-movement symphonies which tend to include only one slow movement thereby moving away from the slow-fast-slow-fast pattern of the old concerto grosso.

In 1735 Roman again left Sweden, visiting England once more. In 1736 he travelled, via France, staying for a short while in Paris, to Italy where he stayed in Naples and in Rome over some months; his return journey took him through Austria and Germany. This sequence of visits helped further broaden his outlook and although documentation is once more rather scanty, he certainly met Tartini. Sahlstedt mentions copious correspondence which Roman kept up with other Italian maestri, though again reportage rather than precise authentication is the basis.

During the 1730s Roman's personal life was less than happy despite his success as the chief musician at court and the approval of most of the Swedish musical world, some minor signs of intrigue by rivals began to appear and in later years these saddened Roman. His first wife, Eva Björk, died in 1734 a bare four years after their wedding whilst his second marriage in 1738 ended in his new young wife's death in 1740 at the age of twenty three. This left Roman the responsibilty for five children of his marriages, in addition to which he had to cope with the worry of a gradual increase in deafness - the defect which had persuaded him in 1735 to take the waters at Ischia but, with characteristic enthusiasm, this had become a round tour of Europe. This was a typical temptation for a man of linguistic ability, and Roman had an especial gift in this direction.

Despite personal sadness there can be little doubt that the journey was beneficial to Roman's compositional art and, by implication, to Swedish music in the capital, so influential was his position. It is at this time that stylistic traits became more consistently observable. Above all, Roman's style is unrepetitive and economical. In his symphonies, most of which are relatively brief, there is a great deal of melodic invention with a minimum of notespinning. Modulations are direct and simple and it seems that Roman would rather employ a mere dozen bars in order to incorporate a new linking theme in addition to the formally constructed melodies, than change key by extensive journeys through related tonalities. The use of French dotted (or double-dotted) rhythms is also characteristic of Roman. The general impression, at least in the concerted instrumental music, is one of basic Italian compositional thought of the Baroque period, of an attractively rough-hewn nature, strong on rhythm and never profligate with unrelated sequences of notes. Some of the symphonies of the early 1740s provide the additional interest of having adopted a cyclic form.

In 1744, Crown Prince Adolf Fredrik, married the sister of Frederick the Great. As far as is known, Roman did not travel to Stockholm at all during the first part of that year since 1743 he had moved house to Småland. His rivals may have felt that this was a sign of withdrawal from the influential position in musical life which he held, but he was not idle during that time for the wedding was celebrated to the sound of Roman's most famous composition Drottningholmsmusiken. Here all the elements of his style may be observed: the delicacy of the lighter scored pieces and the grandeur of the brass-laden fanfarish elements. In form and style Handel's *Water Music* is strongly recalled; there are twenty-four movements and one or two of them show fascinating parallels.

Roman's grand and imposing composition has an amazing lack of currency outside Sweden. One would at least have imagined that the English would have taken to it. It is probably true to say that it does not show any notable advance beyond the style of Handel's *Water Music*, of earlier date, however the ceremonial nature of the composition would doubtless account for the ironing out of potential change of style - after all, the *Water Music* was composed in three distinct parts dating from 1715, 1717, and 1736 yet there is no indication to the ear that Handel wished to develop the style as he wrote each section after relatively lengthy intervals.

In 1745 Roman moved to Haraldsmåla, near Kalmar and at this time also was appointed to the respected post of Intendant to the Court. Thereafter he tended to prefer his country home although he did travel to Stockholm to conduct a certain number of concerts, and to be responsible for musical direction at the coronation of both Fredrik I and Adolf Fredrik and Lovisa Ulrika. At some time toward the summer of 1752, Roman left Stockholm and lived at Haraldsmåla until his death in 1758.

Queen Lovisa Ulrika was a great lover of the arts, particularly music and the theatre. She effected the continuance of the French theatrical tradition started in 1699 by engaging another troupe in 1753. In the same year she had a palace theatre built at Ulriksdal and by 1754 the plans for the court theatre at Drottningholm had been put into effect. In 1762 however, the building suffered the fate of so many wood-built court theatres of the eighteenth century and was burnt to the ground. Two years later a similar opera house began to be built on the site and, although the public were free to visit that at Bollhuset (1773) whilst those at Ulriksdal palace and Gripsholm (1782) flourished in the late eighteenth century, musical prestige was best acquired by artists through success at the royal theatre at Drottningholm. It is a strange contradiction that non-Swedish music-lovers tend to associate Roman with Drottningholm. Recordings of his music which frequently depict charming period scenes incorporating the theatre and Drottningholmsmusiken associate the composer by impli- cation, yet Roman had left Stockholm before the first theatre had been built: his association is with the palace but not with the theatre. Had Lovisa Ulrika come to the throne earlier and had her influence therefore encouraged opera at court it would have been intriguing to see if Roman's enormous talent had developed along operatic lines. In the event however, Swedish opera had to start from the very beginning and the first to incorporate a Swedish text did not come into being until 1747. This was "Syrinx eller den uti vass förvandlade vattnymphen". The text was by Lars Lalin but the music was represented by a gallimaufry of compositions, largely dependent on Graun and Handel, but borrowing elsewhere as was thought appropriate. Swedish opera had much to do before it could claim general recognition and whilst Drottningholm theatre began to develop and became the talk of Europe as an extraordinary court opera house, the first successes were largely confined to spoken drama—led by the Queen's French group who performed Voltaire, Collé, Diderot, and Fenouillet de Falbaire. The commencement of opera at Drottningholm depended again on the French influence with music by Duni, Grétry, and Philidor. The King and Queen invited Francesco Uttini to provide operas and he set to work upon texts by Metastasio and produced *Il Re Pastore, L'Eroe cinese, Adriano in Siria,* and *Thetis och Pelée*—the progress towards the Swedish language being obvious from the titling, indeed the last named opera had further Swedish recitatives added in 1773. Uttini became part of Swedish culture, the Italian influence, so strongly supported by the King and Queen, forming a firm basis for the individuality of later characteristically Swedish music.*

In 1771 Adolf Fredrik died and this changed the course of Swedish music in the theatrical sense. Gustav III became king and his tastes inclined less toward the French philosophy. He dismissed the French troupe and even the operatic performances at Drottningholm paused—seemingly awaiting royal directives. Gustav was an artistic king however, he founded the Kungliga Musikaliska Akademien in the first year of his accession. Its charter was to "promote everything which appertains to musical scholarship". He was deeply interested in opera and

---

*Uttini is accepted as part of Swedish musical life and the invaluable publication *Svensk ton på skiva* [Swedish Musik on Records] published by the Swedish Music Information Centre includes the compositions of Uttini.

Gluck was at this time his favourite composer. Uttini was appointed opera director. It was not until 1777 that Gustav actually took over Drottning-holm Palace, but when he did, the beautiful theatre was put to the utmost use.

The theatre, miraculously preserved today, is larger than the original destroyed by a fire in 1762 which broke out during a performance. The original conception of the theatre was as annexe to the palace at Drottning-holm. The rebuilt version was designed and built by the court architect Carl Fredrik Adelcrantz between the years 1764 and 1766.

His brilliant and original conception was directed towards the most up to date mechanical aid for scenic conviction. Two important con-tributors towards this end were Donato Stopani, the Italian expert on stage mechanism and Adrien Masreliez, the French court painter who was entrusted with the decorations.

The stage itself, which is actually greater in area than the auditorium, is designed with the utmost simplicity. Many trap doors are incorporated and the delightfully simple series of rollers to simulate the waves of the sea at the rearmost part of the stage could scarcely be bettered in effect even today. There are no less than three cloud-carriages but above all there is the remarkably efficient series of tabs and sky borders which are changeable within ten seconds. The side tabs are in groups of half a dozen so the changes may be prepared well in advance. The original stage machinery is preserved in its entirety and is part of the magic of the building. The cleverness of the design lies in the concealment of the many devices and the basis of the success of this goes back to Adelcrantz who designed the whole stage and auditorium as one long, deep area so that no seat in the modestly-sized auditorium even when placed at the end of a row allows members of the audience to gaze embarrassingly into the wings at perfor-mers awaiting their entrances since the design ensures that only a frontal viewpoint is provided. There are only about 350 seats in all and originally the most important were specifically allocated to named occupants, with the King and Queen placed centrally in their chairs at the front - doubtless a daunting feature for the actors to whom all the auditorium would appear dark save for the royal couple whose gilded red chairs defined their presence with stark clarity.

It is probably true to say that in the quarter of a century immediately following the completion of the rebuilt theatre, the expansion of its use scarcely ceased. At first, Lovisa Ulrika's beloved French troupe of actors presented the royal family and their court and visiting diplomats with plays by the great French dramatists - Corneille, Racine, Molière. Opera-tic performances were also from French culture including music by Mon-signy and Philidor, whilst the philosophy of Grétry's works was of such similarity that no Swedish onlooker would have been pedantic enough to point out the accident of that French-speaking composer's Belgian birth.

A pause occurred in the fortunes of the theatre when King Adolf Fredrik died and Lovisa Ulrika moved from the palace of Drottningholm. Her son, Gustav III, had at first no use for the theatre and dismissed the French players. This artistically gifted king realised, however, that this building with its unique artistic atmosphere could be exploited for the purpose of a life ambition of his: to make culture at the Swedish court more essentially Swedish. Acquiring the Drottningholm theatre from his mother in 1777 Gustav III set about presenting more substantial artistic fare and, curiously enough, exploited his Swedish nationalistic inclinations through collaboration with a musician of German birth.

Johann Gottlieb Naumann (1741-1801) was subject to immense Swedish influence even though his two stays in Sweden were not long in duration. His operatic talents were even accepted in Italy and his approach to the historical drama *Gustav Vasa*—the libretto of which was drafted by Gustav III and prepared by Johan Kellgren—was based upon the most accomplished Italianate writing and held immense appeal: this Swedish opera by a German composer in the favoured Italian style typifies in many ways the attractively cosmopolitan outlook of Swedish music.

It seems that in 1788 Uttini was replaced as opera director by Joseph Martin Kraus and the implication is that the King found Uttini's services less than satifactory, although no particular evidence of specific dissatisfaction is known. This glorious Drottningholm era ended tragically on 16 March 1792 when Gustav III was assassinated at the theatre. *

Although the performing arts suffered through the decline of performed opera after Gustav's death, the expertise which had made the era possible became an inspiration for later composers. Naumann's superb *Gustav Vasa*, scored adventurously for the resident orchestra, the size of which might have made Haydn, with his band of less than 30 at Eszterháza, feel envious. The orchestra at the time the new opera house was opened in 1782 for public performances, boasted a string strength of 30 (9, 8, 5, 4, 4) 4 flutes, 3 oboes, 2 clarinets, 2 bassoons, 2 trumpets and timpani. The military elements of the opera meant the incorporation of fifes, military drums, and percussion. In 1786 Naumann had enhanced his reputation further through *Orfeus og Erydice*, but this was for the Danish court to a Danish text. Naumann's influence remained however and Vogler, then touring in Sweden, added a Singspiel in similar style whilst Carl Stenborg followed the climate which was moving towards an essentially Swedish influence in his two Singspielen of 1777 and 1778.†

---

*Verdi's *Un ballo in maschera* is based upon this event
†*Gustav Adolfs Jakt* (1777) and *Gustav Vasa in Dalarna* (1778)

These works through the incorporation of folk melodies, became influential despite their modest pretensions. Joseph Martin Kraus (1756-92) also sojourned in Sweden at this time having settled there in 1778. He lived just long enough to compose the magnificent Funeral Cantata for Gustav III. He was basically an operatic composer, and his *Prosperin,* and *Soliman den II* had wide currency in the Gustavian era; posthumous acclaim was afforded *Aeneas i Carthago.* His four symphonies suggest in style the very type of development towards which C.P.E. Bach had been driving in his latest, tautly dramatic symphonies. In particular, Kraus's C minor symphony combines the depth of Mozart of the Fortieth Symphony with the driving force of C.P.E. Bach. The popular term, "The Swedish Mozart", is somewhat misleading—the almost identical birth and death dates bring Mozart to mind, but the music has other elements.

Across this area of Swedish music of the second half of the eighteenth century with its predominance of opera lies the career of Carl Michael Bellman (1740-95). Bellman was an extraordinarily talented poet and his songs to his own texts were created very much in the spirit of the troubadours of earlier times. He would use existing melodies—often courtly dances—quite freely and he had a ready wit. He is famed for his settings of historical events dramatized in his own words but, since his performances were usually given cittern in hand in taverns, a Hogarth-like observation of contemporary life becomes evident in musical and poetic terms. Some of the most famous of his songs have been collected in Fredmans Epistlar (1790) and Fredmans Sånger (1791). They contain acutely drawn portraits of tipplers in Stockholm. The Fredman of the title was a real figure who had fallen from grace as a royal watchmaker, spending the rest of his life between the drink-shop, the gutter and the tavern. Bellman expands this man into a philosopher, often putting into the mouth of the old reprobate deeply considered ideas as in *Ack, du min moder* [Oh, My Mother], *Undan ur vägen* [Make Way] or *Gubben är gammal* [Old Men Honour the Aged] but the Serenades of Schubertian mould such as *Ulla min Ulla* [Ulla My Ulla] or the Mozartian *Haga* show the more delicate and light-hearted side of this remarkable composer.

Gustav III never seems to have held Bellman in any great esteem although he did find some of his brief plays for performance at court acceptable, *Werdhuset* being staged at the Drottningholm theatre in 1787. Bellman was also responsible for the libretto of a Wikmanson opera and in 1773 he tried his hand at an opera of the pastoral genre. No authentic manuscript remains but an operetta entitled *Fiskarena* is performed from time to time at Drottningholm nowadays and this seems to be a reconstruction of Bellman's original. No known performance took place during Bellman's lifetime.

The end of the eighteenth century was a fallow time in Swedish music, the murder of Gustav III in 1792 had severely curtailed opera performances at Drottningholm because Gustav IV Adolph was much less interested in the arts. Since the famous centre of attraction in Swedish musical terms had therefore become less influential, so too the surrounding musical activities lost some of their impetus.

Performances at Drottningholm became less and less frequent and apart from a mere handful of occasions when the building was used a few times in the 1850s, the theatre fell into disuse. Other uses were found for the various rooms, such as supplementary quarters for the palace servants, an officer's mess for the royal guards and a Sunday school for local children together with the use of the auditorium as a mathom house for various paintings and items of furniture from the palace. Even so, care was taken and reasonable respect shown for the building and this meant that the structure stayed in good repair until in 1921 Agne Beijer - an official of the Royal Library in Stockholm realised the magnificence of the neglected building. Everything was in a remarkable state of repair including all the stage machinery. To Beijer's considerable credit he enlisted the financial support of the court and in 1922 the theatre re-opened and has remained the jewel of Swedish opera ever since—probably the most authentically preserved court theatre in the whole of Europe.

The Berwald family had a subtle but undeniable influence on Swedish music and although Sweden's most famous symphonist Franz Adolf Berwald 1796 to 1868 is of surpassing importance in Swedish musical history, the whole family—German in origin—was essentially musical and its establishment in Stockholm goes back to Johann Gottfried Berwald (1737-1814). His music is still performed in Sweden as is that of his nephew Johan Fredrik (1787-1861) Kapellmeister in Stockholm from 1823 to 1849.

Christian Friedrich Georg (1740-1825) had a less obviously remarkable career although like his father and his elder brother, Johann Gottfried, had worked at the Mecklenburg Schwerinska court. In 1772 he gave a highly successful concert as violinist in Stockholm and this was probably a major factor in persuading him to settle there the following year where he became a member of the court orchestra. He married first in 1781 and again in 1789. Franz Berwald was the fourth child of the second marriage and effectively both the last and the most important in the line of musical Berwalds.

In 1805 Christian Friedrich's orchestral appointment was terminated, setting an unhappy seal on the activities of the Berwald family whose abilities seemed at this time to have been frustrated by lack of musical enthusiasm at higher levels. By this time Franz Berwald was showing extraordinary promise, having made his concert debut in the same year at the age of nine as violinist. (At this stage his cousin Johan Fredrik might have been said to have shown even more early talent having presented his first public concert—also as violinist—at the age of six.) That such enormous talent had developed in the family was more than a happy coincidence, for his father's dismissal because of the temporary disbandment of the opera orchestra had made life very difficult. Not until 1807 did circumstances improve a little through the belated award by Gustav IV of a pension to Christian.

Franz Berwald's career is a strange story of progress which could be measured by the success which he achieved in general terms—that is to say his achievements, though mainly musical, were not entirely so. That the last decade of his life brought him respect, initially as manager of a glass works and subsequently as executive of a brick company, must be unique in the annals of musical biography. At this time his musical activities were modestly reduced, but by and large Franz Berwald's career was one of continuing success, building and establishing as it progressed. In this respect, Berwald's business acumen may reasonably be taken as a parallel. For a composer to embrace, in his later years, not only the commercial ventures mentioned above but also a concern for tenants rights, forest preservation, and education, may seem strange, yet the logical and enquiring mind which so obviously lies behind his music is consistent with such an outlook.

In terms of education, Franz Berwald's preparation for life was somewhat skimped. He left school well before completion of his studies following an altercation with his teacher, whereafter his father took responsibility for the completion of his learning.

In 1812, Franz was appointed violinist to the royal orchestra and by 1816 he was giving concerts as soloist. His first extant composition was the Theme and Variations for Violin and Orchestra (1816) but critical acclaim for his early works is usually reserved for his highly original Quartet in G minor (1818) a beautifully turned work with a most skilfully constructed fugue as Finale.

In 1819 Franz and Christian August Berwald toured Finland and Russia with considerable success. Although Franz had wished to earn his living through the monthly *Musical Journal* of which he was editor, by 1820 the demand for this publication fell and he had to rely on his orchestral appointment for his bread and butter. This year saw an increase in his compositional output although the symphony which he wrote at that time, survives only in a partial copy of the first movement. No less important was the C sharp minor Violin Concerto and this, the symphony and his piano and wind quartet of 1819 were performed at a concert during the spring of 1820.

The following years were not especially fruitful for Franz Berwald's output and not until 1827 did he explore larger scale music, composing the Bassoon Concerto and working on the opera *Gustav Vasa*, of which the first act was performed whilst Berwald was still writing the remainder. Whether the public was ready for a nationalistic opera of the same name only forty years after Naumann's very successful essay in that form is another matter. For whatever reason, Berwald never completed *Gustav Vasa* and although in 1829 he worked on, and presumably completed, *Leonida*, the whole manuscript is now lost, as is that of *Der Verräther* composed one year later, whilst during that period also, *Donna Isabella* was started but never completed.

At this time Berwald's creative powers seemed not to progress. The only work of undoubted genius to emerge was the beautiful and melodious Septet - scored for the "Beethoven" combination of clarinet, bassoon, horn, violin, viola, cello, and double bass. Here, as in many of his works of large scale and vision, the slow movement incorporates a Scherzo section. This is a totally characteristic fingerprint of Berwald and it is a highly individual notion which, in formal terms, gives an eloquent symmetry to his music. Most Berwald Scherzi are written with the lightest of touch, usually in the deft Mendelssohnian style and the subtle breaking into a faster tempo, seemingly in mid-slow movement, is always an exciting moment.

The 1830s are not well-documented in respect of Berwald's life. He spent this period between Stockholm and Berlin (*Der Verräther*, as its German title implies was a Berlin-based creation to a text by Moritz Saphir). He did study counterpoint in Berlin and both here and to a lesser extent in Stockholm he also studied medical science and apparently he had some success in treating children suffering from a particular form of spinal defect. As far as can be gathered the composer devoted himself very fully to medicine in the 1830s and his skill in research was much applauded. It was not until 1841 that Berwald disposed of his successful medical practice in Berlin, moved to Vienna and married. At this stage therefore, he may be described as a successful but lapsed composer, successful in all that he essayed despite his lack of basic education. In Vienna, he continued his medical career but now musical interests began to encroach. He worked on his opera *Estrella di Soria*, wrote several tone poems and in 1842, just before his return to Stockholm, a concert of his music was given and the works—including *Elfenlek* [Play of the Elves] and *Minnen från Norska Fjellen* [Memories from the Norwegian Mountains]—were received with considerable acclaim. Only two months later, a concert took place in Stockholm, this time sponsored by Berwald himself. The timing was perfect and the composer's business acumen stood him in magnificent stead on this occasion. A different selection of music was chosen, wisely including excerpts from the as yet incomplete *Estrella di Soria*.

From the moment he returned to Stockholm it became absolutely

Drawings by Timothy Hodgson

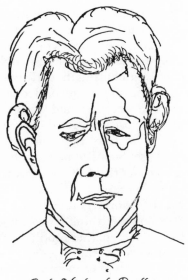

Carl Michael Bellman

Allan Pettersson

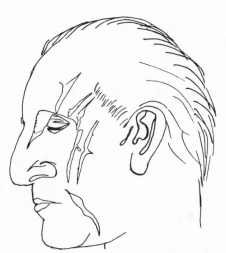

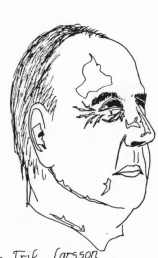

Hilding Rosenberg

Lars-Erik Larsson

clear that Berwald intended to re-establish himself as a composer and he set about this aim with enormous diligence. Already, in Vienna, he had sketched the work which we now know as his First Symphony—The *Sérieuse*—and it was to the symphony that he was to turn as a central feature of his work during the early years of his re-establishment in his homeland.

The numbering of Berwald's symphonies is somewhat confusing, the more so since Berwald was notoriously careless about keeping account of his compositions. As a result it has more or less been left to musicologists to put matters right in this respect. The Swedish musicologist and composer Sten Broman numbers six symphonies, Berwald himself seemed to consider that he wrote only four. It is certainly quite clear that he did not count his early symphony of 1820—nor is the existing fragment of much use to performers today even if it were intended to reinstate it. Broman does however think it worthy of listing as the First and after the *Sérieuse* there arises another problem. Written about the time of Berwald's return to Stockholm from Vienna, the *Symphonie Capricieuse* was completed in a score which gave indications as to the instrumentation required but was not fully written out. It is not certain whether Berwald scored the piece fully at a later date, however one theory has suggested that the rescored version is not the same as the original *Capricieuse* and this, assumedly, is the thinking behind Broman's applying the numbers Third and Fourth respectiveley to the incomplete and the presumably complete (but lost) *Capricieuse*. This leaves the *Singulière* as the Fifth and the E flat symphony as the Sixth. In recent years it has been more common to ignore the symphony of 1820 and to assume the two *Capricieuse* symphonies to be one and the same. One realisation of the incompletely orchestrated score was made by Ernst Ellberg early in the century and another by Sten Broman more recently. Therefore the fully-fledged sketch now properly completed is the only extant performable evidence of a second symphony from 1842. Now since Berwald himself reckoned the E flat symphony to be his Fourth, the most commonly accepted numbering is as follows:

> no. 1 Symphony in G minor-*Sérieuse* (1842)
> no. 2 Symphony in D–*Capricieuse* (1842)
> no. 3 Symphony in C–*Singulière* (1845)
> no. 4 Symphony in E flat—(1845)

This is the numbering used in Great Britain and it probably results from the writings of the leading British authority on the subject, Robert Layton, who makes a strong case for the acceptance of the four symphony theory.

The four symphonies, firmly constructed and invariably showing elements of slow music surrounding scherzo-like features, are regarded as the centre of Berwald's creativity, indeed the early 1840s from which all the symphonies stem represent the most extraordinary outburst of composition. No less than four symphonic poems were composed in 1842 together with an operetta *Jag går i kloster* and a fair amount of subsequent activity between that year and 1845–including the operetta *Modehandlerskan*, the cantatas "King Charles XII's Victory at Narva" and "Gustav Adolf the Great's Victory and Death at Lützen", his second piano trio and the last two symphonies which are usually regarded as his masterpieces of that genre although they were never performed during his lifetime.

In 1846 Berwald toured Europe; in Germany and Austria his music was especially well received. He also spent some time in Paris early in the tour, but details are sketchy and it is generally assumed that this part of his travels turned out to be less than successful.

Even during a musical tour, there was still apparently some time for business ventures and this time, wood was the subject of his trade. In 1848, when in Austria he finally revised *Estrella di Soria* and shortly afterwards turned with renewed enthusiasm to the composition of chamber music - the main pre-occupation of the remainder of his musical career, interrupted only by the piano concerto of 1855 and completed by the operas of the 1860s. The third and fourth string quartets date from 1849, two trios from 1851 and a quintet from 1853. Violin duos were written in the latter part of the 1850s. It will be seen however that on his return to Stockholm in 1849 his compositional activities began to thin out somewhat: financial difficulties were the prime factor and now the glassworks and the sawmill took up a great deal of his energies. It does seem however, that he also built a reputation as a successful music teacher, and of the pianoforte at that, an instrument which he did not pretend to play with anything more than adequacy. He also, as finances improved, aided the careers of pupils and friends alike when he felt that such influence as he could bring to bear–including monetary aid–was merited through outstanding but unrecognised talent.

It was not until 1862 that *Estrella di Soria* was first performed in Stockholm and its success was moderate. It was performed only five times although this may have been sufficient to impress the musically knowledgeable.

The year 1864 saw the completion of another opera, *Drottningen av Golconda* [the Queen of Golconda], and this proved to be his last large-scale composition. For so thorough a musician who intermittently attained considerable success his music is looked upon today with some reserve outside Sweden, yet his music is central to the most skilled of Swedish compositions in the Romantic vein. It might even be true to say that as a symphonist he occupies a central position in the nineteenth century. He was contemporary with Philidor and Albrechtsberger on the one hand, Sibelius and Richard Strauss on the other. His clear-cut thinking and lucid orchestration (the precision of which must have aided those who completed the short score of the *Capricieuse* Symphony) are a model of writing of the period: the shapeliness is similar to Schumann as indeed is a tendency to brevity of thematic material, but the strong point of orchestration is always evident whereas this aspect represented sheer hard work for Schumann. Perhaps Berwald's own comment about the act of compositional creation lets some light into the matter:

> Only from the moment when every note achieves a true value, each harmony a captivating direction, and each grouping of these an elegant and melodic form (and one depends on the other so much that each cannot exist without the other) only then, I say, does one approach the completion of a composition

In Berlioz one finds the explosively sudden contrasts of pianissimo and fortissimo, in Mendelssohn the sense of delicacy in fast movements, in Schumann the logic of overall structure, in Brahms the sense of nobility as climactic moments approach. These features are combined in Berwald and in essence they are typical of symphonic writing: but Berwald's symphonic thoughts spread also into his chamber music: his Quartets in particular and also his Septet. Only in his concerted chamber music with piano - the trios*, the Piano and Wind Quartet of 1819, and the two Piano Quintets from the 1850s—does a romantic expansiveness pervade the music. Otherwise there is a disciplined use of material which never wastes a note. In particular the closing pages of his symphonies are notable for their terse logic - the end of both the *Singulière* and the E flat symphony are positively Sibelian in their economy of utterance. Where the Overtures and tone poems are concerned, Berwald tends to lighten his touch and to write with a less concentrated aspect. Compare for example this theme for *Reminiscences from the Norwegian Mountains* with its homely but somewhat static nature (bars 1, 3 and 5 are identical)

with the urgency of this melody from the finale of the *Symphonie Singulière*

---

*the numbering of the trios sets a problem similar to that of the symphonies: an early trio is lost, the second dating from 1845 is unnumbered, and the remaining four trios of later date are numbered 1 to 4.

This totally different climate of thought which places the symphony in the context of a more serious art form is not necessarily a product of the thinking of Berwald's age. Of contemporaries, Berlioz, Mendelssohn, and Schumann wrote symphonically in their overtures but with Berwald, the overtures and the symphonic poem have an expansiveness which concerns itself less with structure and considered climactic points. In his symphonies however, the form is more closely-knit and impetus is of the essence, insistent rhythms are sometimes a feature but they propel rather than emphasize and are wont to be broken up by syncopation as in the Finale of the E flat symphony.

Berwald's Piano Concerto (1855) was written ten years after his last symphony, there seems to be no advance on the intense cogency of structure evident in 1845. The Piano Concerto remains a skilled, melodious, entertaining work but the symphonies best fit Berwald for the accolade as founder of modern Swedish music because modern Swedish composers still retain respect for symphonic eloquence and tend to treat the symphony as a musical form worthy of deference. Swedish music has taken over this philosophy from central Europe where Germany is now less the spiritual home of the symphony than once was the case.

Berwald died in 1868 leaving work on the harmonisation of the Swedish Choral Book [Koralboken] incomplete. Just as the close of Berwald's life showed a lessening of creative activity (the last major musical effort was the completion of *The Queen of Golconda* in 1864) so the romantic era in Swedish music was contributing less positively to European music than was the case on other countries. Even Berwald's most promising pupils: Joseph Dente (1835-1905) and Jakob Adolf Hägg (1850-1928) have virtually no currency nowadays outside Sweden. Each wrote a worthy symphony and certainly Hägg's *Nordic* Symphony would help clarify in non-Swedish minds something of the nature of music in the period preceding the renascence of Swedish music in the twentieth century. Oscar Byström (1821-1909) seems to have won a firmer, though still tenuous place in Swedish public esteem and once more a single symphony (in the key of D minor as with Dente) is the central feature. Strangely enough Byström's style shows a greater influence from Berwald than does that of Berwald's pupils. Hägg's symphony, though not wildly original manages to avoid falling into such a mould whereas it is difficult to imagine Byström having evolved his style without having been aware of that of Berwald.

The early nineteenth century was not a fruitful period for Swedish composition and Jacob Niclas Ahlström (1805-57), one of the most influential composers of that period, is nowadays somewhat neglected. Born in Visby he started his career as Musical Director of Djurstrom's theatre company and thereafter made a career as a conductor of theatre orchestras largely in Stockholm. As a result his large output consisted mostly of music for theatre productions and hence has lost currency today. His most important works are the opera *Alfred den store* [Alfred the Great], although there is no record of its performance, and another opera *Hassan* remained unfinished. He also wrote a piano concerto and a vocal symphony but despite his enormous musical activity Ahlström cannot be considered an influential figure.

In terms of output at this time, Jacob Edvard Gille (1814-80) merits consideration. Possibly because he was self-taught he seems never to have been regarded as an authoritative figure. He wrote four full-length operas, nine masses, several cantatas, and a *Te Deum* and five symphonies. Instrumental music includes five string quartets.

The remaining figure in the field of early nineteenth century neglect is Ludvig Passy 1789-1870, a fascinatingly skilled musician born in Stockholm of French parents and an outstanding pianist who was a pupil of John Field. He wrote two operas, some chamber music including four string quartets, and a quantity of piano music in a style which concentrates on the exploitation of keyboard technique rather than the advancement of musical style. Unfortunately very little of Passy's music was ever published although manuscripts are kept in Kungliga Musikaliska Akademiens Bibliotek.

The key figure in Swedish music who links the premature end of Swedish romantic composition (personified in Berwald) with the no less premature commencement of twentieth century thought (typified by Wilhelm Stenhammar) is Wilhelm Peterson-Berger (1867-1942). Peterson-Berger had a fecundity of melodic invention which might, at another period, have led to comparison with Schubert. At a time when symphonic structure began to be taken seriously, Peterson-Berger wrote melody after melody of a lyrical, romantic, non-structural nature. This description may sound strange when applied to a composer who actually wrote no less than five symphonies, but the essentially miniaturist nature is everywhere evident. A composer who writes symphonies, four operas, a violin concerto, a good deal of chamber music, and an extensive cantata in addition to having an enviable reputation as a critic and writer yet continues to fall into the area of light music with his songs and melodies frequently arranged into three-minute snippets must surely possess some strange quality which has the facility for encroaching beyond the bounds of serious music.

That another field of music should appreciate Peterson-Berger is not to devalue the composer's achievement, yet the easy flow of tunefulness which he was able to combine so effectively with genuine folk melodies, creating a unique Swedish-Folk-Peterson-Berger style was his personal solution to the ideals of Johan August Söderman (1832-76) who was the keystone of the Swedish romantic movement. A composer mostly for voice, Söderman strove to create a nineteenth-century Swedish tradition—his knowledge of folksong was deep, but his early death prevented his developing it in conjunction with his compositional talents. Peterson-Berger may therefore be considered his legitimate heir. One will hear Peterson-Berger's Violin Sonata or his songs far more often than his symphonies and arrangements of the tunes he wrote - usually from his songs or piano pieces - remain light music fare today, giving a somewhat fogged representation of the composer's true stature.*

Wilhelm Stenhammar (1871-1927), like many Swedish composers had the benefit of a German musical education, but in this instance training was largely confined to the study of piano technique and Stenhammar's compositional talents were refined at the Stockholm Conservatory where one of his tutors was Joseph Dente. He also qualified as an organist and the first public performance of one of his works took place in Stockholm in 1892. Both Stenhammar and Peterson-Berger are representatives of what has come to be called the 1890s style. This is not a reference to a period, rather it reflects a change in the cultural tide - perhaps like the Sturm und Drang movement of the previous century. Colourfulness and contrast of mood typifies this outlook and basically the change was literary, spilling its influence over into music. The movement was something of a reaction against the monochrome intensity of writers such as Strindberg. For musicians it was less a protest, more a way of invoking Swedish character. With Peterson-Berger the colourful imaginativeness came out in his songs, Stenhammar however tended to think in the larger scale, where Peterson-Berger wrote over a hundred piano pieces, Stenhammar's works in that form are concentrated upon two sonatas and three fantasies. Stenhammar's seven string quartets are among the most rewarding of this genre.†

The symphonic nature of Stenhammar's work comes to fruition in his superb Second Symphony in G minor. The subtle colouring, especially in the vivid scherzo, shows a quick-witted response to emotional currents which change direction bewilderingly throughout the work. Where the First Symphony in F (1903) has all the architectural skills, the Second

---

*The treatment of Peterson-Berger can be compared to the extraordinary use of an aria from Rimski-Korsakov's *Sadko* by Tommy Dorsey. Does the average dance-band enthusiast really believe that the rest of the composer's output sounds familiar? So too, the jolly folkish abridged arrangements of Peterson-Berger by Lundquist present a string of graceful tunes, similar in nature and sound of melodic inspiration. These can be heard on a record by Mats Olssons and Egon Kjerrmans.

†Six quartets are numbered, they date from 1894, 1896, 1897-1900, 1904-09, 1910 and, 1916 respectively, the F minor quartet of 1897 has no number.

Symphony takes the imagination into the realms of the half-lit impression-ism which creeps in and out of the solid, formal designs without ever denying the importance of form. With so impressive a work as the First Symphony establishing him as a major force it is surprising that Stenham-mar should have called his second essay in that form Symphony op. 34 for orchestra, as if oblivious of having written a previous composition in that form - one moreover which he was pleased to describe as "Idyllic Bruck-ner". Work on the Second Symphony began at an interesting time how-ever, because in his work as a conductor Stenhammar had concerned himself almost exclusively with contemporary music—including Debussy, Reger, Sibelius, Richard Strauss, and finally Carl Nielsen whose First Symphony made an enormous impression upon Stenhammar and probably this above all led him to begin, in 1911, his magnificent G minor Symphony. As in so many of Stenhammar's works, folk-melodies creep in—a splendid example is to be found in the Scherzo, yet his interest did not lie in folk music and his songs—an important section of his oeuvre—tend to be wholly twentieth century, preferring to use the texts of poets of the recent past or those who were contemporary. In many ways the Serenade in F has elements even more strikingly symphonic and typifies Stenhammar's progress towards the culmination of the 1890s ideals. The Second Sym-phony was composed between 1911 and 1915, the Serenade for large orchestra is from 1911-13 but was revised in 1919. It is not unreasonable to regard it, in its final form, as effectively Stenhammar's Third Symphony for the tensions are certainly symphonic in the seemingly inexplicable appearance of a distant fanfare well into the Scherzo, like a ghost from Debussy's *Fêtes,* is a most dramatically symphonic notion,

so although this Serenade entertains as its name implies, it does so with often gripping feeling.

It is probable that the mere coincidence of the time of the death of Hugo Alfvén (1872-1960) has led commentators to think of this composer as a representative of the twentieth century rather than stemming from the end of the romantic era thus forming the same sort of link as does Stenhammar. For so long the "Grand Old Man of Swedish Music"—a mantle which passed on his death to the twenty-year-younger Hilding Rosenberg—Alfvén was from the outset an essentially Swedish composer, studying at Stockholm Conservatory at the same time as Stenhammar.

Alfvén's composition teacher was Lindegren and he took up a career as a violinist in the Royal Orchestra as early as 1890. His First Symphony (1897) was also his first composition of note and from the fortunate wealth of recordings available, it is possible to study the progress of Alfvén's symphonic thought. Again, as so often in this period, the symphony is central to the composer's output, but Alfvén is clearly the product of late romantic thinking and it seems that whilst his earlier symphonic works (the first three symphonies date from 1897, 1898-99, and 1905) look forward, the Fourth and Fifth (1918 and 1942-52) simply establish the composer's formidable, well-controlled techniques. Most of his tone poems and Rhapsodies tend to be early and his Swedish Rhapsody op. 19 (1904)—the first of three Swedish Rhapsodies—established his fame everywhere in a way in which the Norwegian composer Johan Svendsen's Norwegian Rhapsodies never seemed to manage. Swedish Rhapsody no. 1 has been arranged, (and more often disarranged) for innumerable instrumental combinations and its success is all the more remarkable since its melodies are drawn from authentic Swedish folk tunes. The opportunity to appeal worldwide through local tradition is never to be underestimated and it could well be that this success influenced the composer to allow folk elements into his works from the Third Symphony onwards. The Third Symphony is arguably the most popular. The Straussian element is often discernible in Alfvén's compositions and the subtle colouration evident from his orchestration is entirely appropriate to one who studied painting in his youth. Alfvén is often thought of as a "nature poet" but his landscape, though so close to that which inspired Sibelius, seems often to be observed in the brilliance of the midsummer sun. There are many Swedish forests, but the open aspect of the lakes and clearings which surround them are nearer to Alfvén's pictorial sense than the forests themselves. Although not averse to using pictorial titles* the most obviously programmatic work is the Fourth Symphony which is in four interlinked movements. The essence of Alfvén's delight in Swedish culture and his genius for presenting the nature of nationalism in a manner which attracts the attention of other musical nations, lies in his *Gustav II Adolf Suite*—sometimes referred to as "the festival music Vi" (we) after Nordström. This work is a most skilful combination of pastiche of the music of the Gustavian era and folk elements are ever-present.

Alfvén's compositions incorporate cantatas or choral songs and a number of solo songs. Naturally these travel less well than the folk-based orchestral works, but Hugo Alfvén may properly be regarded as the nationalist composer who achieved remarkable success outside his country

---

*As in the Rhapsodies—*Midsummer Vigil, Uppsala Rhapsody, Dalecarlian Rhapsody*—and the symphonic poem—*The Tale of the Skerries*.

without feeling the need to overstress his nationalistic feelings. These elements grow from Alfvén's music rather than being superimposed upon it and in this lies the essence of his success.

Although not strictly within the mainstream of Swedish music of the early part of the nineteenth century, the course of which was so clearly directed by Stenhammar and Alfvén, the work of Edvin Kallstenius (1881-1967) progresses in parallel. The freedom of form of this composer's melodies is highly individual and although his output contains standard Swedish compositions including *Dalslandrapsodi* (1936) his trend is towards the more recent methods of composition with much harmonic adventurousness. Kallstenius is quoted as once saying "My musical religion is harmonies, everything else is secondary". This does not prevent his use of folk themes although these are set within his own style. His five symphonies, including *Sinfonia su temi 12-tonici* (1960) which, despite the implications of its title, remains tonal, his four sinfoniettas, his Cello Concerto and his Piano Concerto are central to his oeuvre. There are also eight somewhat neglected string quartets and the composer has an especial affection for his Suite for Fourteen Wind Instruments and Drums op. 23 which incorporates a complex fugal Finale.

Ture Rangström (1884-1947) represents the German element of Swedish composition in the first half of the twentieth century. His formal training was sparse although a brief period in Berlin with Hans Pfitzner seems to have been a significant influence. He was a successful critic and also a conductor. His style avoids the conscious incorporation of folk material. His output was considerable and his appeal seems to have captured the attention of German taste.

He composed two operas: *Kronbruden* (1915) and *Medeltida* (1921) whilst a third, *Gilgamesj*, which Rangström started to compose in 1943, was still incomplete at his death from the point of view of orchestration. John Fernström has however created a performing version from his knowledge of Rangström's orchestral style. Rangström has a melodic gift which, at first hearing, seems less than consistent. As one appreciates the nature of the music concerned however, the variety of invention becomes clear and it will often be seen to parallel the intensity of the orchestration at a given moment. Four each of symphonies and symphonic poems are at the centre of Rangström's output with several suites, music for strings and incidental music to plays by Strindberg and Ibsen.

The central composer in the essentially symphonic development of Swedish music is Kurt Atterberg (1887-1974). He composed the symphonist's traditional nine (1912, 1913, 1916, 1919, 1923, 1928, 1943, 1945, and 1957). He has five operas, two major ballets, ten suites, and five concerti to his name these last being for violin, cello, horn, piano, and violin-and-cello. His interest was very largely orchestral, his chamber music is sparse although there are two string quartets, a cello sonata and a piano quintet. Atterberg's official appointments in Stockholm were numerous and may possibly account for a thinning of output in the 1930s. Because his outlook is clearly classical it is not so surprising that his Sixth Symphony op. 31 should have won the International Schubert Competition, held by Columbia Records in 1928 to celebrate the centenary of Schubert's death.

Now that the eccentric uniqueness of the competition is largely forgotten, the symphony can be accepted as part of the Atterberg canon although the reason behind its composition served an excellent purpose in bringing the composer to the attention of the outside world. If the many-talented Franz Berwald may be taken as an example, Atterberg's multifarious activities* seem to be in a good Swedish composer's tradition of skill within more prosaic activities - a circumstance understood also by musicians in Great Britain today. Atterberg's consistent fluency of thought is always highly impressive, his construction is totally professional and he has the ability to hold the interest throughout. His music is firmly tonal and he lightens his touch where suitable: the Fourth Symphony–*Sinfonia Piccola*–is immensely concise and tuneful but the larger-scale works have themes which have a longer-spanning range.

Because Hilding Rosenberg (b. 1892) seems always to have been part of modern Swedish music, he is possibly underestimated outside his own country. In the early part of his career, Rosenberg was given encouraging support by Wilhelm Stenhammar who included the younger man's music in his concerts around the time of the First World War. This was a far-seeing action, for clearly Rosenberg's dissonant, relatively modern style was not at that time the way in which Stenhammar saw orchestral music. It is however, Rosenberg's later music by which he is best known. The First Symphony (1917 revised 1919) is the only major work of Rosenberg's early years to continue to be given occasional performances nowadays. In the 1920s Rosenberg, whose musical education had previously been in Stockholm, furthered his studies in Dresden and this had a radically modernising influence upon his style. The first works of this nature were for small groups of instruments: a trio for flute, violin, and viola, another for oboe, clarinet, and bassoon, and two string quartets. He also wrote a chamber symphony and although the compositional influence of Schoenberg–whom he met in Dresden–does not seem to be direct, the choice of ensembles does very much to match Schoenberg's own ideas at that period.

---

*Founder of the Society of Swedish composers and Chairman 1927-47. Chairman of STIM 1924-49. Secretary to the Royal Academy of Music 1940-53 and in the literary field, critic for *Stockholms-Tidningen* 1919-57, he continued to serve the Swedish Patent office and also among his qualifications numbered that of Civil Engineer.

Rosenberg's talents in music are many-sided, but generally his career shows a switching from one style to another for a sustained period, rather than any intermixing of compositional genres. The mid 1930s to mid 1940s brought a number of church works to the fore and the first *Sinfonia da Chiesa* must be considered a landmark in this area of thought. Perhaps with an especially wide-ranging audience in mind, Rosenberg lightened his style in his very popular cantata *Den Heliga Natten* [The Holy Night] written in 1936 and this continues to be broadcast at Christmastide to the extent that it has become virtually a tradition in Sweden.

Basically however, Rosenberg's strength at that time lay in more earnest music and the *Sinfonia Grave* of 1935 was the first full-scale work to attract the attention of the critics in a serious way. The combination of slow movement and Scherzo in one is an interesting structural feature of this darkly eloquent piece, and one which, since the days of Berwald has seemed to indicate a Swedish structural viewpoint. The Third Symphony (1939) is very much a crossroad of style: not directly dodecaphonic it nevertheless commences with a twelve-tone theme before launching forth into a complex, large-scale forty-minute work - the four movements of which were, through their subtitles, intended to represent the Four Ages of Man. This reference however was subsequently dropped.

Sustained by the popularity of his first opera, *Resa till Amerika* [Journey to America]-the music of which is best known through a suite of music drawn from it—and by the acclaim afforded his Second Symphony, the 1940s found Rosenberg more concerned with teaching than composing and no less distinguished a group of composers than Karl-Birger Blomdahl, Sven-Erik Bäck, and Ingvar Lidholm benefitted from his instruction at this time.

An enormous wealth of music flowed again from Rosenberg after the war. During the war the huge Fourth Symphony had appeared—far more of a cantata than a symphony, based upon the Revelation of Saint John [Johannes Upperbalese]. By 1951 there was a regular flow of works—including string quartets. The two major works of that particular year were the Violin Concerto no. 2 and the Sixth Symphony, both of which are much more sparing in instrumentation than the previous large-scale symphonic works or the ballet *Orfeus i stan* [Orpheus in town] of 1938 where large-scale sweeping orchestration is the order of the day.

That Rosenberg's music is searching, complex and occasionally employs dissonance, should not obscure the remarkable melodic flair nor the sharp wit. In the prewar opera *Marionettes*, first perfomed in 1939, the Overture puts in microcosm Rosenberg's early style: the fast moving element of the Overture and its delightful throw-away ending constrasts with the tongue-in-cheek opening—an irreverent backward glance at the beginning of Beethoven's *Leonore III* Overture.

There is a world of difference between the lighthearted brilliance of the commencement of *Marionettes* and the earnestness of the start of the Third Symphony. Had the analysts not insisted upon drawing listeners' attention to the dodecaphonic aspect of the initial theme of the symphony, the typical combination of growth against contra-rhythmic interruption, which is typical of Rosenberg in more serious mood, would have seemed no more complicated than any other sequence from his larger-scale compositions. Comparison with the sparsely-orchestrated opening of the Sixth Symphony finds a similarity of mood, but Rosenberg has distilled the essence of his thought into lighter yet more distinct contrasts of timbre. Delicate, Nielsen-like percussive touches seem to suggest a subconscious homage to the composer who first entitled a Sixth Symphony *Sinfonia Semplice*.

In the 1960s Rosenberg returned to ballet as a medium having tended in postwar years to pay rather less attention to music for the stage except for the one-act opera *Porträttet* [The Portrait] based on a Gogol story. The ballets comprise *Salome* (1963), *Sönerna* [The Sons, 1964] and *Babelstorn* [The Tower of Babel, 1966]. By 1968 his attention was again turned towards the symphony as an art form and his Seventh appeared in that year. Not long after, the opera *Hus med dubbel ingång* [The House with Two Doors] appeared typifying a constancy of output which, it is virtually impossible to pigeonhole, for Rosenberg's interests have turned briskly from one form of expression to another throughout his long life. Sprinkled amidst his more significant compositions are those of a more individually virtuosic and by implication lighter nature. These include the sunny Second Violin Concerto (dedicated to the violinist Camilla Wicks) and the cheerfully tuneful *Louisville* Concerto. The latter, though basically a "homage to America", includes the tongue-in-cheek introduction of a Lappish theme in the Finale which makes this work (otherwise known as Concerto no. 3 for Orchestra,) a splendid representation of Rosenberg's approachability. Anyone who can write such friendly music must surely be permitted, even by the most conservative of publics, to extend beyond the basis of twelve-tone thought as he does in his searching string quartets of the late 1950s.

The development of Gösta Nystroem (1890-1966) was less rapid than that of Hilding Rosenberg and in terms of influence Nystroem may be regarded as a composer of a slightly later period despite his two-year seniority. Early in life, Nystroem began to assimilate artistic influences slowly, thoroughly, and very often through other related arts. His studies, other than those of a private nature, really only became concentrated in 1923 when he was in his thirties. He made a study of Spanish music in Spain in 1912 prior to going to the conservatoire in Stockholm. After only two years he migrated to Paris where he studied painting. By 1919 he had decided to settle in Paris working as a painter. This brought him into contact with French impressionism in its fullest sense. His paintings reflected this and part of his development as a painter may be linked to the influence of Braque. In his paintings the many-facetted brilliance of the sea was a great influence and his canvases betray a passionate interest in this subject. All this time however, Nystroem was exposed to various aspects of French music with Vincent d'Indy having a particular influence on Parisian musical life at that time. Nystroem was once d'Indy's pupil whilst in turn the influence of Les Six* was never far away from his musical environment. Few musical works from Nystroem's sojourn in Paris remain in existence, but *Ishavet* [Polar Sea] which is dedicated to Amundsen and *Babelstorn* [The Tower of Babel] are depicted in the form of symphonic poems.

Not until he was nearing his fortieth year did Nystroem's long artistic apprenticeship draw to its end. Perhaps his most significant works of this period were the Concerto Grosso for Strings (1929) and the First Symphony–*Sinfonia Breve* (1931). This late flowering may reasonably be regarded as a Nordic equivalent to Brahms's equally steady and inexorable progress, centred upon the symphony as a means of expression. As Nystroem progressed toward recognition he leaned towards the larger instrumental forms in the early 1930s. 1932 saw his return to Sweden and the commencement of his Second Symphony, the work upon which this thorough and gifted composer spent much effort. During this period he came to public attention through a group of works comprising incidental music. Pär Lagerkvist provided the inspiration for the first of these in 1933: *Konungen* [The King] and each year thereafter until 1936 Nystroem completed a similar work. In 1934 he wrote incidental music to Shakespeare's *The Tempest*, in 1935 Pär Lagerkvist's *Bödeln* [The Hangman] was the chosen drama and in 1936 Shakespeare was again taken up in the form of *The Merchant of Venice*.

During much of this time, the Second Symphony–*Sinfonia Espressiva*–was being created. It was eventually completed in 1935 and represents a crystallisation of Nystroem's artistic background at that time. At 45 the strong French influence, the wide appreciation of all the arts and the firm musical grounding represented a coming of age. This firmly-wrought composition is constructed with the utmost cogency and Nystroem's tendency to compose a symphony in one sweep (echoed more recently by Pettersson) is at once obvious. Nystroem even declared the work to be "an intensive musical event". Its tautness and structure supports such a description, but the interesting and revelatory conclusion is that the French and impressionistic influences do no more than aid the subtle orchestral colouring. The actual construction, through carefully building

---

*Auric, Durey, Honegger, Milhaud, Poulenc, and Tailleferre.

Drawings by Timothy Hodgson

Gunnar de Frumerie

Franz Berwald

Gösta Nyströem

Daniel Börtz

groups of instrumental colours, is remarkably nearer to the philosophy of Carl Nielsen or of Hindemith than of a composer of Latin temperament. Clearly there is instrumental experimentation evident in the incidental music with its touches of period charm, although one may argue whether the period aspect is strictly authentic when using harpsichord, guitar, and mandolin with chamber orchestra for *The Merchant of Venice*.

The *Sinfonia Espressiva* typifies Nystroem's method of symphonic unification. Although the other symphonies are not quite so tautly constructed, the melodic and harmonic groups which appear and reappear, usually in varied form, are also featured elsewhere and they are permitted to expand, not only beyond the immediate thematic vicinity, but also across the intervals between movements.

The remaining symphonies of Nystroem's canon are: the Third–*Sinfonia del Mare* (1948); Fourth–*Sinfonia Shakespeariana* (1952); Fifth–*Sinfonia Seria* (1963); and Sixth–*Sinfonia tramontana* (1965). Throughout his life, the sea continued to exert an influence on Nystroem's imagination and it is this element which most often drew the composer towards an impressionistic style that actually strikes the ear rather than merely underlies his thinking. This element is especially strong in *Sånger vid havet* [Songs beside the Sea] which he wrote in 1942 to texts by Ebba Lindquist.

Expansiveness is not a feature of Nystroem's symphonies, but his concerti have a degree of freedom of form. The viola and cello concerti for example, are structurally related to the type of form evolved in the symphonies in terms of building up sound patterns, but the soloistic patterns are allowed to expand across this firm basis. Again in 1948 the sea helped create a non-typical Nystroem invention: five relatively brief songs inspired by sea poems of various authors, set for voice with orchestra. Chamber music features only rarely in Nystroem's output although there are two late string quartets (1956 and 1961) which, like the violin concerto of 1956, show a more dissonant approach to harmony. Opera is represented by the late *Herr Arnes penningar* [Sir Arne's Treasure] and ballet by *Ungersvennen och de sex prinsessorna* [The Swain and the Six Princesses].

Together with Rosenberg and Nystroem a third important figure of this generation also helped urge Swedish music forward from the romantic era into the twentieth century by evolution rather than revolution, this is Moses Pergament (1893-1977) whose stature as critic as well as that of composer had a refining influence upon Swedish musical understanding in the early part of the twentieth century.

Although his early childhood was spent in Helsinki, Pergament settled in Sweden after studying in Paris and Berlin and all of his most important compositional output stems from his years in Sweden apart from the early, highly accomplished, Violin Sonata which dates from his student days. His activities as music critic and writer stretch to over half a century and the reflections upon Swedish taste and its changes throughout the century which can be drawn from his writings are of considerable value. His perceptive championship of Rosenberg's early works indicates a sympathy for the new style although it is probably true to say that Pergament's own style, being strongly lyrical and melodic, is not quite so obviously part of the same progression of thinking as that displayed by Nystroem and Rosenberg. The ballet *Krelentems och Eldeling* (1927) shows Pergament writing very much in the mainstream of Swedish thought at the time, but excursions into music related to his Jewish heritage remain at an intriguing tangent to his main development. One of the most per- formed of his larger-scale works *Den judiska sången* [The Jewish Song] for soprano, tenor, chorus, and orchestra, finds a much talented composer, seemingly preoccupied with the nature of the race from which he descends (a train of thought understandable in the year 1944). Other works include either specifically Jewish ideas or at least subconscious Jewish influence. These include *Rapsodia ebraica* (1935), *Dibbuk* for Violin and Orchestra (1935) and the later operas *Eli* and *Abraham*. Basically Pergament was not drawn towards the symphony as a musical form, although his music progresses in parallel with a movement which has this method of con- struction based firmly at its centre. *Den judiska sången* may however be regarded as a choral symphony, so precise is its structure. The orchestra is exploited imaginatively in his film music whilst in his concerti, the virtuosity is almost as frequently orchestral as soloistic - the main solo instrumental works with orchestra being *Kol nidre* for Cello (1949), the Piano Concerto (1952), the Violin Concerto (1950), the Cello Concerto (1954), the *Canto lirico* for violin (1957), *Fantasia differente* for Cello (1970) and a group of works with flute from the early 1970s. A number of choral settings occupied Pergament in the 1930s and 1940s: *Nedanförmänskliga visor* [Subhuman Songs], *Angest* [Anguish]. Four Chinese Songs and *Fåglar* [Birds]. Later works of this nature include *De sju dödssynderna* (1962) and *Cantata al naharat bavel* (1974).

The Jewish element, although discernible in some works, is not used in a way which attempts to be deliberately coercive of sympathy, as is sometimes the case with the music of Ernest Bloch, nor does Pergament bring in specifically Jewish turns of phrase except in definedly Hebraic works. Pergament may therefore be considered as a composer of the same progressive persuasion as those born just before the turn of the century, whilst working in parallel with, rather than in the mainstream of that school.

It is not unreasonable to suggest that Oskar Lindberg (1887-1955) was a subtle and perhaps unrecognised influence behind the gradual movement away from romanticism. Lindberg, an exact contemporary of Atterberg, is probably overshadowed by the latter's more universal accep- tance, yet Lindberg had a vast knowledge of the traditions of Swedish music and his output of church music together with the substantial work which he did on the 1939 edition of the Church of Sweden Hymn Book, to say nothing of *De sjungade löven* of 1911 a sung drama for schoolchildren which includes hymnic chorales later incorporated in the Church of Sweden Hymn Book. In this way, familiarity with the thoughts of a leading composer was brought to many a layman who may never have listened to Lindberg's better known pieces such as the *Leksand* Suite or the *Little Dalecarlian* Rhapsody. Lindberg was not a leader among those who cajoled Swedish music out of mid-nineteenth-century style, yet his music spoke to many within Sweden.

Sten Broman (b. 1902) well known as a musicologist and an expert on the music of Berwald, has taken a keen interest in contemporary trends, and was Chairman of the Swedish section of the ISCM for almost thirty years up to 1962, as music writer and lecturer he is widely known, but his compositions tend to stem from the latter part of his life, his Second String Quartet (1945-46) having finally brought Broman to public notice as a composer. The nineteen-sixties found Broman concentrating on symphonic composition, the thirteen years between 1961 and 1974 accounting for nine symphonies—the Seventh typifies the direction in which Broman has been moving (and has the advantage of being available on a record for study). It combines orchestra with tape and is concerned with a gradual build up of timbres with unhurried spaciousness.

Hilding Hallnäs (b. 1903) shows interesting development from his years as a teacher, singer, and organist in the 1930s and the 1940s to his very individual style of the 1950s in which small melodic groups and twelve-tone usage are combined. Hallnäs has a large output, biased toward the larger forms, more than half a dozen works of a symphonic nature, and also a sinfonietta and a divertimento. His oboe concerto rejoices in the tongue-in-cheek title of *Momenti Bucolichi*. His vocal work is also extensive including settings of English love poems, poems by Goethe, Lindegren, and as with so many of his compatriots, the poems of Pär Lagerkvist.

Edvard Tubin (1905-82) represents one of the few Swedish composers whose style was influenced by neo-classicism. As a conductor he gave one of the earliest performances of Stravinsky's Symphony of Psalms and was acquainted with both Kodály and Bartók. Within the context of open and clear-cut twentieth century-style Tubin tended towards classical forms and to date has composed ten symphonies, two operas, two ballets, a double bass concerto and several chamber works. Tubin was not strictly in the Swedish line of twentieth-century development but through his Estonian birth and Eastern European influences his music can be said to widen the dimensions of the tonal repertoire of symphonic compositions in Sweden. Composers of this older generation seem to represent a firm basis of melodically inventive music which has stood subsequent composers in good stead.

Dag Wirén (b. 1905), one of the most popular of serious contemporary composers, seems always to have been representative of contemporary Swedish composers noted for their melodic gifts in conjunction with their ability to write on a large scale. Wirén is above all a direct composer, his more romantic earlier compositions have in later years been replaced by a classicism which relates in a distant way to the lucidity of Stravinsky. This is perhaps not entirely surprising since Wirén lived in Paris during the early part of the 1930s after prolonged study at the Stockholm Conservatoire. The mid-1930s found Wirén developing his style. At this time the French influences which perhaps encouraged Wirén's acerbic scoring of basically warm melodies, prompts one to compare the methods of Honegger. The Serenade for Strings of 1937 represents the most popular of all Wirén's work—a beautifully constructed piece, full of melody within which there are echoes of the Sinfonietta of 1934—a work which deserves the use of the diminutive only because it takes less than twenty minutes and employs optimistic melodies, its scale being quite expansive in all other respects. As the 1940s proceeded, so Wirén developed a style more spare and more economical. The melodic flair remains but thematic development tends to spring more from germinal motifs than from full-blooded initial exposition of ideas. Naturally this new development becomes most obvious in the Symphonies. The First and Second were written in 1932 and 1939 respectively, but by the Third Symphony of 1944 methods have begun to change so that in the Fourth Symphony of 1952 a certain severity becomes evident though this is lightened again in the Fifth Symphony of 1964.

The newly acquired seriousness is equally evident in the quartets - the Serenade-like elements of no. 2 (1935) can be contrasted with no. 5 (1970) which is starkly economical in construction. Although not widely known, Wirén's small output of concerti should not be overlooked: the Cello Concerto dates from 1936, the Violin Concerto from 1946, and the Piano Concerto from 1950—three works falling across the period of stylistic change although the progress towards Wirén's later outlook on composition is less evident.

There could scarcely be a greater contrast between the development and style of Dag Wirén and that of his close contemporary Lars-Erik Larsson (b. 1908).*

Larsson's various approaches to composition show only a general pattern, even in recent years, simple, tuneful pieces, often with an element of pastiche in them, have been presented alongside more complex creations—the structure of which may be traced back to the influence of Alban Berg with whom Larsson studied in Vienna in 1929-30. Lars-Erik Larsson first developed his career as critic and then as conductor. Although basically an adjunct to his teaching activities at the Royal College of Music

---

*Notwithstanding their music being coupled on records on more than one occasion.

in Stockholm* the group of works most frequently encountered is his op. 45 (1955-57) which provides a concertino for each orchestral instrument and one for piano. The solo instruments are: no. 1 for flute; no. 2 for oboe; no. 3 for clarinet; no. 4 for bassoon; no. 5 for horn; no. 6 for trumpet; no. 7 for trombone; no. 8 for violin; no. 9 for viola; no. 10 for cello; no. 11 for double bass; and no. 12 for piano. These are far from "difficult" works, but neither are they undemanding. Despite their lack of complication they are sufficiently characteristic to represent the essence of Larsson and it seems strange that hitherto no-one has thought to record this group of ten-minute miniatures as a set.

Larsson, in the 1930s tended towards string writing as in the Sinfonietta (1932) and the *Liten* Serenade (1934) which in nature is almost like a concerted version of the later concertini. Surely his most popular composition is the *Pastoralsvit* op. 19 (1938) in which the swift, pulsing accompaniments underpin the gracefully deft woodwind melodies: though essentially in chamber-orchestra style, it is the chamber-orchestra of Prokofiev's *Classical* Symphony rather than that of the classicists themselves. This is a delightful, tuneful, and infinitely demanding composition in four movements of which the mercurial Finale is the epitome of calm fury—elegant whilst hurtling headlong forward. The lightness of touch is reminiscent of Stenhammar at his most delicate—as in the Scherzo of his Serenade in F.

There had been a certain shift of emphasis by the time Larsson, in 1939, wrote the opera *Prinsessan av Cypern* [The Princess of Cyprus] to a text by Topelius. Here a certain amount of romanticism infiltrated into the music. In the 1940s there was another gradual change of view and a good focal point with which to detail a further shift is the rather sterner, more Germanically-scored Music for Orchestra of 1949. The Violin Concerto of 1952 carries this tendency further still and even the *Missa Brevis* of 1954 does not yet revert to the earlier lightness of touch - in fact the Kyrie of this work suggests dodecaphonic thinking.

The Three Pieces for Orchestra of 1960 and the Orchestral Variations of 1963 are certainly atonal and have a close affinity with serial style. Why Larsson chose to launch into this particular backwater during the 1960s is difficult to comprehend. True, Stravinsky also toyed with such ideas, but one might have assumed that if the teaching of Berg thirty years before were to have been influential in this direction, then Larsson might have been expected to have adopted such techniques at an earlier stage. By the time *Due Auguri* was composed in 1971 there were indications that Larsson had moved away from his austere outlook of the 1960s and although the tonal palette avoids homely harmonies, the underlying wit is always there.

---

*This is the Conservatoire in Stockholm the terminology having been changed to "College" in 1940.

It bursts forth even more fully in *Pastisch och Pastoral* - a suite based on every style except his own with excrutiatingly tantalising snippets of the great masters flitting in and out of this splendidly alarming pastiche, the amalgam of elements within it coming out as pure Larsson in the last analysis.

With works such as the *Pastoralsvit* and the very popular *Förklädd Gud* [The Disguised God, 1940] a clear-cut and natural cantata with all the pastoral freshness of Carl Nielsen's *Fynsk Foraar* (to name yet another choral Scandinavian work of genius which is all the more convincing through its gracious subtleness) Larsson may well remain at the centre of the contemporary scene in Swedish music with the notable added advantage that the public is unable to pigeonhole his style. This means that the nature of any composition which he may currently prepare, is unlikely to be foreseen before its appearance in the concert hall and this is surely an excellent key to continued success.

Gunnar de Frumerie (b. 1908) breaks the pattern set by other composers of his era in that he was far from late in developing. The classic case of brilliant late development is perhaps Nystroem, but de Frumerie, with a background which shows some similarity was composing copiously even during his student days. He was a pupil at the Stockholm Conservatoire at the age of only fifteen. Lundberg and Ellberg were his tutors and at twenty, after winning no less than three prizes in a composition contest, de Frumerie went to study music in Vienna—including piano tutelage under Emil von Sauer—and in Paris with Afred Cortot (piano) and Sabanejev (composition)—the latter also being Nystroem's tutor. De Frumerie's professional career began as that of concert pianist and despite his substantial early output, public notice does not seem to have been taken of his work until the time when his intense performing career mellowed into a combination of performer and composer. The *Chaconne* of 1932 caught the public attention, but it was very much the conception of an active concert pianist. His piano suites (1930, 1936, and 1948) are based on cogent, clearly defined, classical structures, beautifully written. Possibly because of de Frumerie's confident control of his medium, there is no real indication of development between the suites: not because the composer did not progress but more likely because so successful a technique was in no need of change.

In the orchestral field, de Frumerie again shows a parallel with Nystroem (although sonically, judged composition against composition, the theory would be a little difficult to support in terms more positive than passing similarity). The common ground seems to lie in the first place with the French impressionist background (he had a great admiration for Debussy when in Paris) and in the second place with a development of personal style which, whilst using some of the impressionist techniques of colouration, became more firmly wrought and symphonically inclined than the contemporary French music. Nystroem travelled along a similar path and was firmly drawn towards composing symphonies, Gunnar de Frumerie on the other hand used divers forms whilst exploiting his early influences.

Not unexpectedly, the piano has remained quite central to de Frumerie's output. The five piano concerti are classically structured and romantically scored whilst still belonging to the twentieth century, there is also a powerful double piano concerto, and an early (1932) Variations and Fugue for Piano and Orchestra. There are two piano quartets and two piano trios. De Frumerie has turned to opera only once - *Singoalla* receiving its first performance in 1940. There is also a ballet on a typically Swedish subject: *Johannesnatten* (Johannesnatten falls on Midsummer's eve), a violin concerto was written in 1936, and there are several concerti for wind instruments including clarinet (1958) trumpet (1959) oboe (1961) and flute (1969).

Erland von Koch (b. 1910) works from a deep-rooted basis of folk-music which influences the nature of many of his compositions. Although his musical education did not differ radically from that of several of his contemporaries (Stockholm Conservatoire, France, Germany) the influences seem to have made an impression which is somewhat individual. The preoccupation with sonorities perhaps stems from his study of the organ, his ability to manipulate the orchestra in order to express these ideas in sound is surely not unconnected with his studies of conducting with Clemens Krauss and through all this, there runs the thread of Swedish folk music based on the area of Dalecarlia. This is not so much a promotion of Swedish folk music, more an infiltration of its tones and rhythms into larger scale compositions. Von Koch was at his most prolific in the 1950s but the large-scale element commenced with the symphonies at an earlier time: the First Symphony dates from 1938, the unashamedly folkish Second Symphony *Sinfonia Dalecarlia* from 1944 and the Third Symphony from 1948. A sinfonietta dates from a year later with the Fourth Symphony (*Sinfonia Seria*) being composed in 1953. There are several full-scale orchestral works of the 1950s, the most popular of which being the *Oxbergvariationer* (1956). The chamber output includes six string quartets spread over thirty years from 1934 onwards although the most sheerly popular group from this field remains the five dances for violin and piano. There are no less than ten concerti two of which are for saxophone.

In a work such as the Third Piano Concerto, the wind and percussion orchestration reflects the nature of Hindemith - a known and admitted influence but the use of syncopation is anything but Germanic, Aaron Copland is much more easily brought to mind. This work of 1970 shows a keen interest in advance and experiment with timbres but the harmonic structure would not shock those who appreciate Bartók on the one hand and enjoy the racy rhythms of the more outspoken French composers of the

1920s and 1930s on the other. The wide range of Koch's style makes his concerto a splendid contrast with the lyrical solo piano works accompanied by other instruments written a decade or more earlier. Even the piano quartets are written in an orchestral style. Piano-with-accompaniment seems not to be part of the composer's conception.

An effective way by which to confuse hearers concerning the significance of one of Sweden's most individual contemporary composers is to lay stress upon the importance of the *Barfotasånger* [Barefoot Songs] by Allan Pettersson (1911-80). These were written during the war years and imply his concern for his fellow human beings—it causes no surprise when one learns that the composer comes from very humble circumstances. The sudden renewed interest in these early works seems much influenced by the fact that Pettersson's enormous compositional skill has been appreciated only relatively recently: the focal point most often quoted by commentators is the success attendant upon the presentation of the Seventh Symphony written in 1967 and dedicated to Antal Doráti.

Of the many Swedish composers born early this century who have been attracted to symphonic form Pettersson seems one of the most innately symphonic. One tends to think of a Pettersson symphony as being a one-movement arching whole. This is true of a central block of symphonies (the Fifth, Sixth, Seventh, and Ninth) but even the Twelfth (of his fifteen symphonies), though it incorporates settings of nine poems, is still in the same tautly constructed frame. With Pettersson, symphony has a structural significance although one cannot pretend that the logical system of growth which typifies his structural methods is in any sense classical but the sense of living development, reminiscent in spirit, though not in sound, of Carl Nielsen, has a consistent sense of burgeoning life forces.

As with many of his contemporaries, Pettersson had some French musical education (with Honegger, Leibowitz, and Milhaud in Paris) although there always remains a self-made element in his music. His Concerto no. 1 for String Orchestra has an intriguingly academic nature—most demanding, very lucid—rather like Svend Schultz with darkly angry syncopations added. The interesting aspect of this full-scale and thorough piece of modern string writing is that it was composed before Pettersson set about the major part of his compositional studies in Paris.

Whilst the events of a composer's life cannot be taken as representing an overwhelming influence upon the music which he composes his environment is bound to affect his thought. Pettersson has described his life as *"det välsignade det förbannade"* [blessed and damned] his poverty-stricken childhood having been overcome, his studies taken up, a steady career as orchestral violinist (1939-51) pursued, and some success as composer achieved, the heavy blow of rheumatoid arthritis struck him. That one of the most cogent of all his symphonies—the Fifth—should have been generated at this unhappy time (1963-66) is a tribute to Pettersson's single-mindedness. But it is typical of a man who is quoted as saying, *"Hur tror dom att man kan skriva musik när man sitter inkrökt i sig själv? När man skapar måste man stå ovanför och utanför sånt"* [How can anybody write music if one is all wrapped up in oneself? When you create, you have to stand outside and above such things]. The outgoing nature of his music (outgoing even when tragic) suggests that this was also a characteristic of the man himself.

Perhaps part of the still limited awareness of Pettersson's importance, as far as countries outside Sweden are concerned, has to do with the absence of real written appreciation of the composer's work, because too much concentration is placed upon his personality and views. One may write of his Twelfth Symphony in appreciation of the superb welding of poetry and musical organisation - but foreign readers may be forgiven for permitting themselves a wry smile when reading pseudo-political accretions about "fascists seizing power in Chile" or, if one looks at it from a different viewpoint one might alternatively say, "defeat of the repressive communist regime in Chile". It is all amusingly irrelevant because this symphony was more or less completed (based on Chilean poems inspired by events in 1946) before the latest Chilean revolution took place. Fortunately, art is above politics and although the words of the political interferers who wish to harness Pettersson's circumstances and inherent humanity to their own hobby-horses may stick in the mind more easily than Pettersson's counter-comments, *"Mitt engagemang i detta work är inte politiskt"* (My commitment in this work is not political), the real justification lies in the directness of the music itself.

Apart from the symphonies, Petterson's output includes two further concerti for string orchestra, the seven sonatas for two violins, and the concerto for violin and string quartet. The belated interest taken in his *Barfotasånger* is typified by the appealing choral setting of six of them for mixed choir by Eskil Hemberg.

It is an interesting anomaly that at one time Pettersson studied with Karl-Birger Blomdahl (1916-68) and an intriguing thought that Pettersson should have sought the younger man's guidance especially when the nature of the composition of the two differs so vastly: Blomdahl was a pupil of Rosenberg and not surprisingly the war years found him among that group of composers whose development was based on the basic methods of Rosenberg and Hindemith (the so-called Monday Club of like-minded Rosenberg pupils).

The 1950s found Blomdahl regarded as very much a leader of the avant-garde of the day. Certainly he had a forward-looking attitude although his most immediately striking work was the Chamber Concerto for Piano, Woodwind, and Percussion which seems to betray a more Slavic attitude to neo-classicism. Symphonic thought was not central to Blomdahl's compositions at this time and his first two symphonies seem to be entirely neglected, however the Third, *Facetter* is important because its incorporation of serial techniques was virtually unique in that it became the first such composition from a Swedish composer to win general acclaim in other countries. Valuable though it may have been in setting Blomdahl upon a successful career, serialism seems not to have retained a particularly important place in his repertoire. Blomdahl's real fame tends to spread outward from the extraordinarily original opera *Aniara*. This is the first notable "space opera" and is set in a spacecraft which is off course and doomed to speed across the galaxies eternally. The opportunity for exploration of the emotions of the characters through Harry Martinson's poem, which forms the basis of the libretto is very exciting, further, Blomdahl can very reasonably justify the use of electronic sounds, especially as the spaceship's computer becomes very much a central feature of the plot. From the time of this opera, the lure of scientific advance gripped Blomdahl. His second opera did not quite follow the same path - this was *Herr von Hancken* (1965)–although the unreal atmosphere of *Aniara* is often evident, but his third opera *Sagan om den stora datan* [The Story of the Big Computer], like *Aniara* a stern warning of the overwhelming power of science, again incorporates electronic principles and betrays the composer's scientific pre-occupations. Unfortunately Blomdahl died before completing the work.

The furthest musical extremity to which Blomdahl's scientific interests led him was *Altisonans* (1966). Whilst electronic music is now acceptable as a valid art form, it is still a little difficult to know whether this montage of signals from satellites in orbit together with sonic impulses caused by sunspots may reasonably be described as a composition. It lasts for a long time and one wonders if there might be value in beaming it into space. For all one's reservations however, it is quite obvious that Blomdahl's searching mind continued to explore every possibility right up to his premature death. The contrasting aspect of his works lies in the dance—both in his dance suites and in his ballets wherein he collaborated with the choreographer Birgit Åkesson in three important ballets: *Sisyphos* (1954) *Minotauros* (1957) and *Spel for åtta* (1962).

A colleague of Blomdahl's in the Monday Club was Sven-Erik Bäck (b. 1919) whose musical upbringing followed a similar pattern and the early influence of Rosenberg was clearly in evidence. Bäck's inspiration lay in diverse areas. His musical education came from around the war years, his knowledge of Gregorian Chant emerged in practical terms, his chosen instrument was the violin. Despite his swift development along modernist lines, Bäck has retained a considerable following and the success of his operas - commencing with *Tranfjadrarna* [The Crane's Plumage] for radio in 1956, followed by *Gastabudet* [The Banquet] (1958) and *Fågeln* [The Birds] in 1961 (written economically for chamber orchestra)–proved an excellent channel towards recognition. Vocal music provides an important part of his output in addition to those mentioned, there is an opera for children: *Kattresan* [The Cat's Journey, 1951] an extensive play for children with music and several choral cantatas. The older styles manifest themselves in Bäck's earlier music—there are eighteenth-century characteristics in his *Sinfonia per Archi* of 1951 although the *Sinfonia da camera* of 1955 shows a markedly more modern style.

Ingvar Lidholm (b. 1921) was yet another Rosenberg pupil but his profession took a route rather different from that of Bäck. Fortner and Seiber were also his tutors and in addition he had practical experience as a concert violinist with the Royal Court Orchestra and as leader of the Örebro Orchestra (this was between 1947 and 1956). It is not perhaps surprising that the neo-classical style inhabits his earliest compositions—of which *Toccata e canto* (1944) is notable. By 1955 the unconventional modernism of *Ritornell* had attracted attention. The mid-fifties seems to have been a time for acceptance of more advanced styles. Whilst the striking cross-rhythms and wide dynamic contrasts prepare the listener for its use in later choral works, *Ritornell* seems more a firm point of progress towards more daring textures than an entirely revolutionary concept. Regard for this work remains high certainly, although appreciative comments which describe the elements of contrast in colourful terms such as "lyrical sections are contrasted to ecstatic paroxysms" probably overstate the case in terms of where Lidholm should be placed in relation to other modern Swedish music, graphic though that description may be. Lidholm probably stands or falls by *Riter* [Rites] dating from 1959 and incorporating taped electronic music, whilst still full of dance rhythms and also *Nausikaa ensam* [Nausicaa Alone] of 1963—a "lyrical scene for soprano, chorus and orchestra". Ancient legend and the potential of modern methods in creating evocative scenes—particularly the seascape and the pastoral elements—give rein to Lidholm's especial gifts in this direction.

Within Lidholm's development there is a subdued element of dodecaphonic writing but this seems to have been more a convenient method of protest when first embarking upon his career than a considered compositional philosophy.

Laci Boldemann (1921-69) may reasonably be regarded as a Swedish composer despite his Finnish birth. His childhood was in Germany, where he had to return after commencing studies with Gunnar de Frumerie because of his liability for military service. His compositional career therefore commenced late and initially made more impact in Germany than in Sweden. The collection of songs: *Möss i månsken* [Mice in the moonlight] and the opera *Svart är vitt* [Black is white] brought Boldemann's name to the fore in the 1960s when Sweden suddenly realised that here was a composer able to combine a respect for traditional fully tonal composition with his own brand of originality. Even the earlier works such as the Sinfonietta (1953) and the Piano Concerto (1956) avoided the reliable elements of neo-classicism with which many young composers cut their teeth. Larger scale works include a symphony (1962), violin concerto (1959), and trumpet concerto (1968) whilst the extensive Oratorio *John Bauer* (1967), and the stage setting of *Dårskappens timme* [Hour of Madness] (1966)—which falls halfway between the art of opera and that of the musical—were composed as Boldemann seemed to be reaching the height of his career. Had it not been cut short by his premature death, Boldemann's output could have proved a focal point for Swedish music, knitting the progressive and the traditional with supreme skill and capturing the public imagination during the 1960s.

It seems that whilst in the 1950s, Sweden accepted warmly all the advances that the most progressive composers could invent, the succeeding decade was a period in which to re-establish more traditional values. Part of the reason for the willing acceptance of experiment and avant-garde thinking of the 1950s probably stems from the excellent grounding of the protagonists—frequently pupils of Rosenberg and often in sympathy with Monday Group thinking. It is part of the innate stability of Swedish progress that amidst developments and modifications of those very twentieth-century trends started by Rosenberg, it is still this venerable master who has continued firm progress, refining and developing his own style—the very musical thinking which has engendered tangents to the central compositional truths. Often Rosenberg's own pupils have explored these tangents. In the 1960s some composers rejoined the special brand of Nordic progress found in Sweden with its mild German influences. To that extent Torbjörn Iwan Lundquist (b. 1920) appearing from a very different background as conductor of music at Drottningholm, director of a chamber orchestra and successful composer of film music to be one of several composers who have helped re-establish the Swedish mainstream. Lundquist is again a symphonist. Pastoral and natural scenes lie behind his non-programmatic works of which the Third Symphony (*Sinfonia Dolorosa*) completed in 1975 is the best known. Lundquist's entirely individual yet still fully tonal style comes to the fore at an appropriate time in the twentieth century and the different sources and roots of the composers of the 1960s and 1970s seem to come together in agreement over a pattern of lyricism and drama which is immensely appropriate. Petterson's music—though less melodically yielding—and the tunefulness of Lundquist are very closely related. It is not surprising therefore that younger composers (such as Daniel Börtz) have also adopted styles which incorporate the secret of forward impetus. Whatever one may think about Lundquist's incorporation of pseudo-American syncopation towards the latter part of his Third Symphony, it cannot be denied that his sense of forward movement is immaculate. The symphonic period of Lundquist's writing is relatively recent for, film music apart, the 1950s and early 1960s found Lundquist concentrating on vocal composition: *Elegie från Bergen* (1958),

Anrop [Call] of 1963 being the most substantial.

Maurice Karkoff (b. 1927) is one of those who managed to impress the public with lyrical tonality when his first compositions were published in the 1950s. His Serenade for String Orchestra of 1953 displayed his basically romantic inclinations and these remain despite the exploratory nature of later works. Karkoff's development has not entirely stabilised. It may perhaps be argued that the scattering of works which include the intention of sympathising with the persecution of the Jews is a line with romantic predilection. The Fourth Symphony (1963) and *Epitafium för nonett* (1968) concern themselves with the aspect and the conflict betwixt Israel and Egypt is reflected in *Das ist sein Erlauten* (1965). To this extent, Karkoff has elements in his nature which result in an inward view, but respect for Hebrew ancestry is not all-embracing and an interesting offshoot of Karkoff's imagination is to be found in his balalaika concerto. Other concerti include those for piano, cello, clarinet, violin and trombone whilst his chamber music includes quartets both for strings and trombone.

The same subjectivism although based on entirely different principles creeps through also in the music of Jan Carlstedt (b. 1926). The slight Russian flavour - noticeable in his earlier works such as the First Symphony, written when he was 26 seems to be very much a personal trait since by no means every pupil of Lars-Erik Larsson takes such a view.

His valuable studies of folk music in Dalarna have influenced his music and the chamber music which incorporates violin or violins shows a familiarity with the techniques of folk fiddlers. To have composed the *Brotherhood* Symphony (1967) in memory of Martin Luther King is another matter altogether—to what extent is it worth a composer's prospects to invest in so important a form as a symphony (in this case the Second Symphony) only to base it on an occasional subject, admirable and emotive though it may be at the time and welcome though it may prove to an audience sympathetic to the subject? Carlstedt's music has an attractive bitter edge however—the reflection of the early influence of modern Russian composers perhaps. The nature of the music of this particular generation (i.e. those born around fifty or more years ago) is more concerned with euphony than that of the composers born around 1920 or earlier but Bengt Hambraeus (b. 1928) falls interestingly between the two stools and he enjoys the appreciation of the scholarly element in Sweden: how could it be otherwise for a composer who studied in Darmstadt?

A noted organist, a musicologist and an expert in ancient choral music, Hambraeus achieves sonority within the confines of modern (including dodecaphonic) methods. Shortly before his emigration to Canada in 1972 Hambraeus, in his *Rencontres pour orchestre* makes a strange, immobile collage of elements from other composers—largely those of the High Romantic era—and presents a study in timbre. It seems significant that a composer, so well versed in Swedish tradition should not only embark upon a direction in which the new impulse-loving symphonists and orchestral writers are tending to avoid, but that he should also decide at that time that his work should be continued in another country.

More central to the new school of lyrical composers whose work came to be taken more seriously in the 1960' in Bo Linde (1933-70) who was even shorter-lived than Boldemann to whose lyrical form of expression Linde's music bears a passing resemblance. A pupil of Lars-Erik Larsson, there is often more than a hint of his tutor's wry humour–typically so in *Slotts-skoj* [Fun in the Castle] which he wrote in 1969. He wrote a violin concerto in 1957 and two piano concerti which avoid the earnestness and grand gestures of similar works of the period. Other concerti include one for cello, another for bass clarinet with strings and a concertante for wind quintet with strings. Again it seems that the flowing tonalism which was being used and capturing public attention in the 1960s alongside the more radical compositions, was cruelly robbed of a brilliant protagonist through Linde's early death.

The Swedish composers who were born in the 1930s have lived through an age of protest and often studied with, or at least come into contact with composers who were protesting. Whilst Swedish music still seeks new effects and new means, there is a face of humanity in the latest creations. They continue the new traditions and they search further, yet there comes a time when, since protest is accepted as representing success- ful and influential opinion, it is difficult to protest further. A composer not afraid to experiment is Arne Mellnäs (b. 1933), yet in his music there lies so much tongue-in-cheek humour that it really will not do to suggest that he belongs to any school nor does it seem he is intent on influencing the course of Swedish music. Mellnäs seems happily to remain himself and if he succeeded in shocking the International Society for Contemporary Music in Prague in 1967 with his unconventional work *Aura*—written three years previously–by having a multiplicity of balloons bursting at the close of the work it seems on reflection, reasonably typical of a modernist who refuses to be too earnest. More experimental yet is *Capricorn Flakes* based on note groups representing the Constellation of Capricorn and incorporating also astrological significances. Mellnäs's output includes also several choral works, including *Dream*, commissioned by Rikskonserter.

Rikskonserter (Foundation for Nationwide Concerts) is a very influential Swedish body–governement-based and with the facility to instigate recordings using the Caprice label. Although contemporary composers are of special interest, the Foundation is concerned with the dissemination of Swedish music everywhere, concerts, tours by Swedish musicians, and foreign exchange. There is the facility also to commission works; usually, but not exclusively, from Swedish composers. A leading figure in the development of Rikskonserter is Eskil Hemberg (b. 1938), one of three closely contemporary conductor-composers, the others being

Lennart Hedwall (b. 1932) and Ulf Björlin (b. 1933). Hemberg, conductor of the Academic Choir of Stockholm University has himself concentrated on choral compositions including a highly original choral opera for unaccompanied choir and actors. Hemberg is well known for his mixed choir settings of some of Pettersson's *Barefoot* Songs. His appointment to Rikskonserter was in 1970 and a year later he became Chairman of the Association of Swedish composers.

Three composers of this period stand apart from the others in their exploration of modern techniques including subtleties such as "tone gestures". The composers concerned are Bo Nilsson (b. 1937), Björn Wilho Hallberg (b. 1938) and Jan Morthenson (b. 1940).

Nilsson has sometimes incorporated tape effects with conventional writing for the symphony orchestra—his works tend not to be extensive but this does not prevent his use of sizeable forces as in *Entrée* (1963) for large orchestra and loudspeakers, *Taqsm* (Caprice), *Maqam* (1973) for piano, orchestra and tape, or *Vier prologen* (1968) for orchestra. The "tone gestures" (a phrase used in description of Nilsson's music by his publishers) are probably an indication that Nilsson's thematic material includes among his most modern of techniques, melodies redolent of the romantic era.

Hallberg's brand of originality may have been influenced by his central European encounters especially those with Boulez and Nono before studying with Blomdahl. The year 1967 saw the completion of Hallberg's mass based on poems of Dag Hammarskjöld. *Aspirations* (1971) is perhaps his best known orchestral work and although Hallberg has suffered being paid the damning compliment of being deeply involved personally in current questions on account of his opera *Evakveringen* being about the destruction of the environment, his genuine originality should prove to be sufficient to overcome such criticism.

Morthenson has developed a system of chordal sequences which has grown into a most individual approach to sonority. Although microtones are incorporated the sonorous textures provide sufficient stability to hold the attention of the listener. There are certain examples of aleatoric techniques within Morthenson's music and his development through his series of coloratura works suggests that however experimental his style, his intense originality may well assure Morthenson of popular attention as the twentieth century proceeds.

The music of Daniel Börtz (b. 1942) typifies the new and very gradual structural revolution which is driving Nordic music forward into a contemporary view which transforms yet also respects traditional structures and harmonies. It is not surprising that Börtz, one of the youngest yet most responsible of the new generation of Swedish composers, should be attracted to the symphony as a mode of expression. Every time that a new look is taken at the current trends of music in Sweden it would appear that a symphonist stands there pointing the way. Börtz is just such a composer. The parallel (though not comparison) with Kalevi Aho, one of Finland's most remarkable young composers, is probably valid because the closely knit structures of both have something significant to say. The sheer euphony of the radiant opening chord of Börtz's First Symphony grasps the attention from the outset. Again like Aho, Börtz's output is not extensive, but it is immensely significant. A pupil of Rosenberg (to whom he is related) continuing later studies with Blomdahl and Lidholm, Börtz has achieved his individual style from a basically Swedish environment and his interest in contemporary trends led him to the position of Secretary to the Society of Swedish Composers.

His interest in literature has influenced his choice of musical subject matter—notably the *Kafka Trilogy* (1966-69). Speaker, soloists, chorus and orchestra are employed and one of the three, Josef K, to Kafka's own text from *The Trial* stands alongside Börtz's symphonies as among his most widely known works. The remaining two Kafka works, *Voces* and *In memoria di* ...., represent a Kafka-esque development where Börtz's imagination, as influenced by Kafka, is allowed to flower. Kafka being important to him it is not perhaps surprising to note that Börtz has suggested that his view of life is not entirely optimistic, "I sway betwixt two poles: love of beauty and awareness of insignificance and mortality". *Voces* incorporates three voices, tape, and orchestra but this is something of an exception since this composer's experiments with timbre are more often confined to conventional instruments.

The first three symphonies are closely related, the composer having declared that Sinfonia I is "the first stage in a three-stage rocket". He declared the First Symphony to represent pure form—as such it is an independent entity—and is usually performed separately. The other aspects explored in this trilogy are the contradistinction of major and minor and the use of melody. It would perhaps be misleading to suggest that the First concentrates upon form rather than melody (after all the former would make but minimal impact without the latter) but disruptive influences against the calm coolness of major-keyed, consonant chords raise an edifice which it is extraordinarily easy to follow. Börtz has written a number of chamber works including several *Monologhi* for various solo instruments and his string quartets (the second of which, dating from 1971, the composer considers to be of especial importance in his output) are often exploratory in nature. His opera *Landscape with River* (1972) inspired by Hesse's *Siddhartha*, turns again to less revolutionary structuring and clarifies the text with notable skill. Where the *Monologhi* are sometimes highly experimental (no. 5 for example elicits timbres rather than words from the solo soprano), the works comprising more complex scoring tend towards a more firmly tonal conception and the symphonies have a fine logic which stands Börtz firmly among the leaders of those who are currently carrying forward Swedish traditions.

In recent years Swedish music has tended more towards experimentation and is currently beginning to divide. There are tonal modernists such as Börtz and Stig-Gustav Schönberg (b. 1933), who do not dispense with the infant of tradition although they are prepared to do without the bath-water of habit. There are also progressive modernists such as the self-taught Johnny Grandert (1939) whose skilled use of orchestral methods justifies his art in conventional eyes (or ears) but this is intermixed with works for extremely unconventional instrumentation (machine gun; twenty flutes, etc.). In this genre also is Per-Gunnar Alldahl (b. 1943) whose *Light Music* for five flutes, vibraphone, and electric organ of 1968 attracted some attention: the contrast is not really between these two groups however for basically they remain on the same side of the aural fence: but the other tributory (or the cynical would say backwater) of the mainstream of modern Swedish music is represented by a thriving school of electronic composers.

This division is an interesting phenomenon because overlap between composers devoted to electronic music and using conventional instrumentation is becoming less frequent. In Sweden, electronic works were first explored by Rune Lindblad in 1954. *Musique concrète* and taped electronic music became viable as audio science in the 1950s increased the possibilities of exploiting the recorded tape. A great deal of hard work was put in by the protagonists of this medium, printed information and lectures sought to spread this new gospel. The most notable early works came from composers interested but by no means exclusively concerned with the new medium were *Doppelrohr II* by Bengt Hambreaus (1955) and *Audiogramme* (1957) by Bo Nilsson—even then the realisation of these compositions did not take place in Sweden but in Cologne. Not until the mid 1960s was real progress made in Sweden but then electronic composition received considerable encouragement. This came about through the creation of the Electronic Music Studio in 1964, largely through the influence of Karl-Birger Blomdahl. Where Blomdahl clearly saw electronics as an ideal aid to his outlook on conventional scoring he still did not espouse the medium entirely. The chief pioneer in that field was Ralph Lundsten (b. 1936), who together with Leo Nilson (b. 1939) established the Andromeda studio. Lundsten being a film-maker, was able to develop what we know nowadays as mixed-media presentations. Lundsten's output is enormous and the informative English-language booklet *Electronic Music in Sweden* (Stockholm: Swedish Music Information Centre, 1972) lists no less than 31 electronic compositions by Lundsten and a further 13 in combination with Nilson. * Having been surprised by the sheer quantity of works by

---

*The listing of the same works twice, firstly under Lundsten + Nilson then again under Nilson + Lundsten does seem to be a little confusing despite the admirable intentions of equality.

Lundsten and Nilson against which should be mentioned the considerable output of Lindblad (70) it should be added that the date of this survey was as long ago as 1972, but even so the Lindblad/Lundsten/Nilson contribution is of the order of forty percent of all Swedish electronic music at that time.

Since currently the technology which enables recorded sounds to be made using digital techniques is very much a talking point for those interested in the electrical reproduction of music, it is an intriguing thought that Knut Wiggen of the Electronic Music Studio (EMS) was able to write in 1972:

> The studio does in fact allow analogue control. It is true that most of us at EMS probably consider the analogue control as a step backwards from a technological point of view but the availability of an analogue controlled apparatus must be seen as a service for composers who prefer this type of control system.*

So in 1972, analogue control was thought to be outdated—therefore any conventional commercial recording must be taking the electronic pioneers back in time.

Two composers of electronic music who seem in recent times to be creating the type of sounds which grip the listener are Lars Gunnar Bodin (b. 1935) and Bengt-Emil Johnson (b. 1936). Amid the small forest of electronic composers, current Swedish opinion sees these two musicians as having something to say within their own medium, even by those who feel the nature of these composers' art to be somewhat eclectic. It seems likely however, as the electronic revolution rationalises itself, that some compositions of the moment in the 1970s by artists such as Åke Hodell and Sten Hansson which incorporate irrelevancies such as Black Panthers, Che Guevera and American Military Deserters, will die (or may already have died) just as quickly as the popular press has tired of the subjects portrayed. Hansson was sufficiently regarded however to succeed Bodin as Chairman of the avant-garde Fylkingen Association.

Sten Broman's interest in electronic music is so relatively recent that *Electronic Music in Sweden* fails to list him and does not even include his large-scale Seventh Symphony, the electronic tape of which he completed as long ago as 16 April 1971 and which was put on to disc in combination with the collaboration of the Swedish Radio Symphony Orchestra the following year. Broman's highly imaginative juxtaposition of tape and symphony orchestra represents an exciting aspect of electronic music and may well be the key to turning the electronic backwater into a rivulet parallel to and flowing in the same direction as the mainstream of Swedish music after all.

---

*Electronic Music in Sweden, p. 49.

The proliferation of young composers following avant-garde trends in Sweden is sometimes thought to represent a mere taking advantage of the generally liberal attitude to modernism shown by the Swedish public. There is music which says and relies on current trends and it may not be unconnected with the benevolent atmosphere which led the Swedish Council of Cultural Affairs to draw up a new cultural policy and present it as a bill in Parliament in 1974. In Great Britain, where the notion of having a minister responsible for the arts is novel and discussions on the possible creation of a Ministry of Arts fairly controversial, the Swedish approach may seem a little indulgent. When Swedish writers explain about the thriving contingents of avant-garde composers there is a tendency to wonder if the mesh of the net is too fine, for in attempting to capture as much musical talent as possible, there is a risk of promoting mediocrity along with the talent. Certainly some Swedish commentators conversant with the subject are not entirely uncritical. Claes Cnattingius (best known as music critic for *Dagens Nyheter*) has frequently written at length introducing new and often revolutionary composers to his readers, but neither he nor other writers in English on the subject such as Göran Bergendal or Lennart Reimers show unreserved acceptance of any and every composer who chooses to nail his colours to the avant-garde mast. Currently Swedish music thrives with such extraordinary success that it is easy to overlook its tradition. Contemporary composers are numerous, more encouraging still, they are, on the whole, possessed of enormous talent. It should be remembered however that Government-subsidized organisation of music in Sweden supports not only the youngest composers who show talent in creating electronic music but also the artistic achievement of the past, as for example the historic Drottningholm theatre and all it stands for, making viable productions which, if dependent upon box office takings would be financially disastrous despite full houses.

The musical roots are less strongly traditional in Sweden than in some neighbouring countries. Folk rhythms run through music in a natural, almost subconscious manner and Carl Michael Bellman is so much a part of musical thought that Swedes seem scarcely to mention that his songs have probably run through their minds for as long as they can remember.

Swedish music tends to involve the listener, and it seems an essentially Swedish way of drawing Blomdahl's *Aniara* to a revelatory conclusion by closing down all light on the stage, thereby representing the terrible finality of death as the blackness descends upon the lifeless occupants of the spaceship. The first production—and as far as I know, the remainder too—also blacked out the auditorium so the audience became one with those on the stage. Involvement is natural, and occurs at Drottningholm where today's music-lovers may sit in the same seats as the royal court of old, viewing operas of the eighteenth century which are presented in a way not too far removed from that experienced by King Gustav III (no one but a pedant would complain about the bewigged orchestra wearing wrist-watches or modern spectacles). The attractive aspect of Swedish music is that the outsider may also experience such aspects on visiting Sweden. The festive atmosphere of midsummer night can be assimilated too, in fact only the relative rareness of recordings of Swedish music outside their country of origin puts difficulties in the way of understanding its nature. The fetish of the big name, the admiration of the well-known and extremely popular composer dies hard. This works to the disadvantage of the Swedish, but because of this demand, there is a marvellously low incidence of second-rate music, there may not be a Beethoven or a Bach of Swedish music and a few modernists may stray off at an introverted tangent, but the quality of the best over the years incorporates many composers of great talent.

An ideal starting point might still be with the enormously popular - perhaps Alfvén's *Midsummer Vigil*, preferably supplementing the sound of the music with the composer's own delightful description of it. Thereafter work outwards, always remembering that some of the most remarkable discoveries are to be found in earlier years. The Swedish kingdom has a long history and its cultural progress with its art forms expanding from the royal centres to reach the people shows a gradually increasing artistic sensitivity which totally transcends political considerations. Whether the spread of fine music results from the efforts of a king or queen encouraging artistic endeavours to be heard outside court in the people's theatres—events which occurred more frequently as the eighteenth century drew to its close—or whether the modern conception of twentieth-century government replacing royal patronage is the source, the result has always been a widening of artistic spectrum and a disinclination to allow artistic laurels to be rested upon.

Tables

Musical representatives of the Düben Family

Michael *c.* 1535-1600
musician of Lützen

Andreas 1558-1625
Cantor at St. Thomas's
Church, Leipzig

Andreas (Anders)
the Elder
c. 1597-1662
Born in Leipzig but
settled in Stockholm
1620. Pupil of
Sweelinck 1614-1620
appointed Hofkapell-
mästare in 1640

Martin *c.* 1600-50
Organist of the Storkyrke
in Stockholm from 1625

Gustaf, the Elder
c. 1628-90. Member
of the Hofkapell from
1647, appointed Hofkapellmästare in 1663 after
the death of his father.
Retired in 1687.

Gustaf, the Younger
1660-1726
appointed Hofkapell-
mästare 1691;
ennobled 1698

Andreas (Anders),
the Younger
1673-1738.
Hofkapellmästare
1698-1713;
ennobled 1707

Joachim
1676-1730

Carl Gustaf
1700-58
director of
the Court
Orchestra
1741-58

Carl Vilhelm 1724-90
succeeded his cousin Carl
Gustaf as director of the
Court Orchestra 1758-64.
Became President of the Royal
Academy of Music

Musical representatives of the Berwald Family

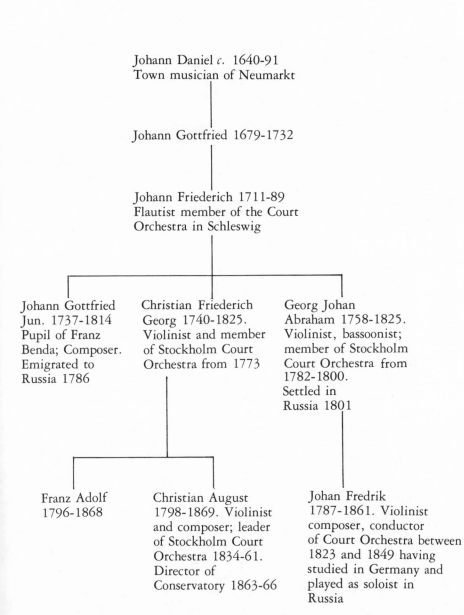

Johann Daniel *c.* 1640-91
Town musician of Neumarkt

Johann Gottfried 1679-1732

Johann Friederich 1711-89
Flautist member of the Court
Orchestra in Schleswig

Johann Gottfried
Jun. 1737-1814
Pupil of Franz
Benda; Composer.
Emigrated to
Russia 1786

Christian Friederich
Georg 1740-1825.
Violinist and member
of Stockholm Court
Orchestra from 1773

Georg Johan
Abraham 1758-1825.
Violinist, bassoonist;
member of Stockholm
Court Orchestra from
1782-1800.
Settled in
Russia 1801

Franz Adolf
1796-1868

Christian August
1798-1869. Violinist
and composer; leader
of Stockholm Court
Orchestra 1834-61.
Director of
Conservatory 1863-66

Johan Fredrik
1787-1861. Violinist
composer, conductor
of Court Orchestra between
1823 and 1849 having
studied in Germany and
played as soloist in
Russia

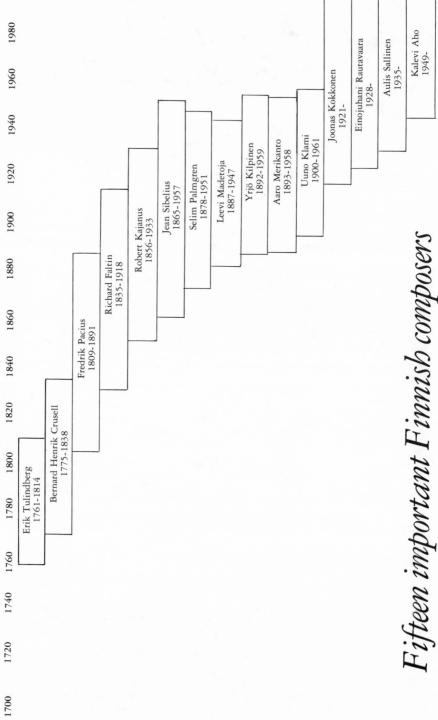

Fifteen important Finnish composers

Erik Tulindberg
1761-1814

Bernard Henrik Crusell
1775-1838

Fredrik Pacius
1809-1891

Richard Faltin
1835-1918

Robert Kajanus
1856-1933

Jean Sibelius
1865-1957

Selim Palmgren
1878-1951

Leevi Madetoja
1887-1947

Yrjö Kilpinen
1892-1959

Aaro Merikanto
1893-1958

Uuno Klami
1900-1961

Joonas Kokkonen
1921-

Einojuhani Rautavaara
1928-

Aulis Sallinen
1935-

Kalevi Aho
1949-

1700   1720   1740   1760   1780   1800   1820   1840   1860   1880   1900   1920   1940   1960   1980

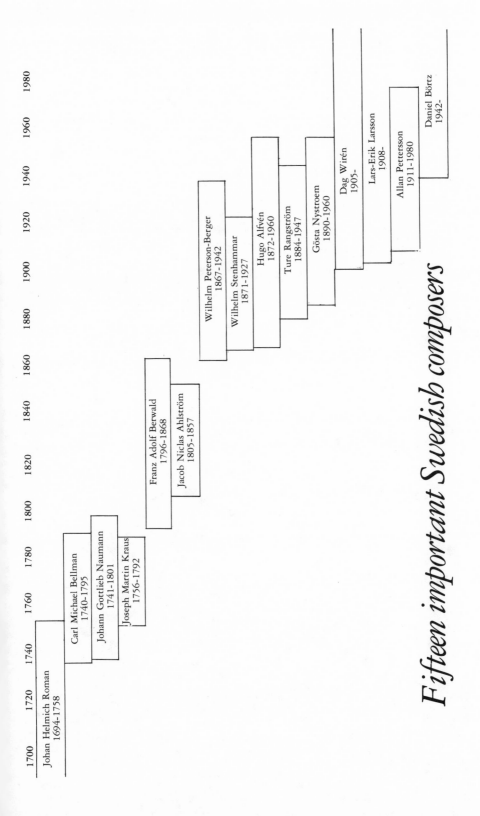

Fifteen important Swedish composers

Part 2

Discography

These selective discographies of Finnish and Swedish music are intended to show the recorded material available featuring music mentioned in the main sections of the book. Comments on individual performances and recordings are to be found in the form of footnotes to the text.

If a recording is known to be recommendable, age or unavailability has not prevented its being listed, it does seem however that in Finland and Sweden, records remain on the market far longer than is the case in central Europe, United Kingdom, or United States. Many recordings, though far from new, retain their attractiveness: for example, those of the Alfvén Symphonies have been in the Swedish Society catalogue for many years but they remain attractive to the collector.

The quality of pressings on Finnish and Swedish "domestic" labels was found to be exceptionally high and without question far more consistently satisfactory than the standard found in Britain or America. Another welcome factor in locally recorded presentations is the considerable success achieved in reproducing public performances with the minimum of audience distraction and here too, balancing by the engineers is frequently as convincing as in many a studio production.

The Finnish recording company Finnlevy used the company name on its discs until 1979 when it changed to Finlandia as records were re-pressed and a greater proportion exported than hitherto. It is therefore possible to encounter identical recordings where some have the legend Finnlevy on the sleeve and others Finlandia with a new numbering system. In the listings, the latest number and description available has been used.

The following points should be noted:—

Couplings are shown in brackets before the record number: Works by the same composer are in *italics* and other couplings are referred to by composer's name only.

All discs are 12" stereo 33 $^1/_3$ rpm unless otherwise stated; (M) = mono. Availability of many discs is limited in Britain and America and may require the help of specialist dealers. Where a record number differs on the American market the number is identified by the prefix "US".

Recital discs containing music by several composers are listed at the end of each discography and are given arbitrary list numbers ("F" for Finnish and "s" doe Swedish) so that cross-reference may be made in the main body of the discography under the individual composers' name.

Selective Discography
of Finnish Music

AHO, Kalevi (1949-   )

Lasimaalaus [Stained Glass]
Andersen–Cantemus Chamber Choir of the Sibelius Academy
    (Englund, Rautavaara) Finnlevy SFX 52

Oboe Quintet
Jouko Teikari, Olavi Palli and Hannele Segerstam, Pentti Kikkonen,
Risto Poutanen
    (Crusell, Mozart) Finlandia FA320

Quintetto per oboe e quartetto per archi
Teikari, Palli, Segerstam, Kikkonen, Poutanen
    (Crusell, Mozart) Finlandia FA 320

Symphony no. 4
Rautio–Tampere Philharmonic Orchestra
    Finnlevy SFX 44

BASHMAKOV, Leonid (1927-   )

See Recitals: F3

CRUSELL, Bernhard (1800-50)

Clarinet Concerto no. 2 in F minor, op. 5
Peyer. Jacob—London Mozart Players
    (Copland) Unicorn RHS 314; US: Unicorn 75002

Clarinet Concerto no. 2 in F minor, op. 5
The Music Party
    (Hummel) UK and US: L'Oiseau-Lyre DSLO 501

Divertimento per oboe e quartetto
Teikari, Palli, Segerstam, Mikkonen, Bister
    (Aho, Mozart) Finlandia FA 320

DONNER, Henrik Otto (1939-   )

XC, for soprano, chorus and chamber orchestra
Andersén—Finnish Radio Chamber orchestra and chorus
    (Heininen) Fennica Nova Feno 1

BERGMAN, Erik (1911-   )

Aubade
Panula—Helsinki Philharmonic Orchestra
    (Sibelius) Finlandia FA 314

Aspekter
Pohjola
    (*Exsultate*) HMV5EO63-34484

Exsultate
Forsblom
    (*Aspekter*) HMV5EO63-34484

Concertine da Camera
Travis–Miksi ei Ensemble
 (Merikanto; Webern) LRLP 228

Colori Ed Improvvisazoni
Segerstam - Finnish Radio Symphony Orchestra
 (Noa) Finlandia FA 330

Noa
Lehtinen. Segerstam–Finnish Radio Chamber Choir & Symphony
Orchestra
 (Colori Ed Improvvisazioni) Finlandia FA330

See also Recitals: F.1.

ENGLUND, Einar (1916-)

Epinikia
Berglund–Helsinki Philharmonic Orchestra
 (Symphony no. 2) Finnlevy SFX 34

Hymnus sepulcralis
Cantemus Choir
 (Aho; Rautavaara) Finnlevy SFX 52

Piano Concerto no. 1
Izumi Tateno. Panula–Helsinki Philharmonic Orchestra
 European EMI 5E 063 34471; U.S.: Angel AA 8874

Sokerileipuri [The Sugar Baker]
Nikkonen. Raiskinen–Finnish National Opera Instrumental Ensemble
 European EMI 5E 062 34960

Symphony no. 1
Pekkanen–Turku Philharmonic Orchestra
 Finlandia FA 304

Symphony no. 2, *Blackbird*
Pekkanen–Helsinki Philharmonic Orchestra
 (Epinikia) Finnlevy SFX 34

Symphony no. 4
Pohjola–Espoo Chamber Orchestra
   (Kokkonen) Finlandia FA 329

HANNIKAINEN, Ilmari (1892-1955)

See Recitals: F 6

HEININEN, Paavo (1938-   )

Arioso
Lukácsy–Heidelberg Chamber Orchestra
   Da Camera Magna SM 91022

The Autumns, op. 22
Andersén–Finnish Radio Chamber Choir
   (Donner) Fennica Nova Feno 1

Concerto per Orchestra in forma di variazioni: Adagio
Gillespie. Susskind–Royal Philharmonic Orchestra
   (Meriläinen) Philips 802 854 LY

Sonatina della primavera, op. 28a
Pohjola
   Konserttikeskus KKLP 174

Sonatine, op. 2
Tateno
   (Kokkonen, Meriläinen, Rautavaara) Toshiba TA 60001/4

JÄRNEFELT, Armas (1869-1958)

Praeludium
Berglund–Bournemouth Symphony Orchestra
   (Alfvén; Grieg) HMV ASD 2952

JOHANSSON, Bengt (1914-   )

Vesper
Andersén–Klemetti-Opiston Institute Choir
    HMV 5E063-34517

See also Recitals: F 1; F 4

KILPINEN, Yrjö (1892-1959)

6 Fjeldlieder; 5 Lieder der Liebe I, op. 61
Niemela, Koskimies
    (Sibelius; Grieg) US: WCFM 5(m)
(The Kilpinen Song Society issued a set of five 78rpm discs in England
containing a selection of 19 songs on HMV DB 2594-8)

See also Recitals: F 6

KLAMI, Uuno (1900-61)

Kalevala Suite, op. 23
Panula–Helsinki Philharmonic Orchestra
    (Cheremissian Fantasy) Finlandia FA 302

Cheremissian Fantasy, op. 19
Noras. Panula–Helsinki Philharmonic Orchestra
    (Kalevala Suite) Finlandia FA 302

KOKKONEN, Joonas (1921-   )

Bagatelles (5) for piano
Tateno
    (Heininen; Meriläinen; Rautavaara) Toshiba TA 60001-4

Cello Concerto
Noras. Kamu–Helsinki Philharmonic Orchestra
    (Haydn) Finlandia FA 310

Music for string orchestra
Berglund–Heidelberg Chamber Orchestra
   (*Sinfonia da camera;* Heininen) Da Camera Magna SM 91022
Pohjola–Espoo Chamber Ōrchestra
   (Englund)

Piano Quintet
Gothóni. Finlandia Quartet
   EMI 5E063 34330

Piano Trio
Tateno, Arai, Kimanen
   Love LRLP 203

Sinfonia da Camera
Lukácsy–Heidelberg Chamber Orchestra
   (*Music for string orchestra;* Heininen) Da Camera Magna SM 91022
Baumgartner–Helsinki Chamber Orchestra
   (*"Durch einen Spiegel ..."*) Finlandia FA 323
Durch einen Spiegel ...
Hamalainen. Baumgartner–Helsinki Chamber Orchestra
   (*Sinfonia da Camera*) Finlandia FA 323

String Quartet no. 1
Finlandia Quartet
   (Rautavaara) HMV 5E063-34444

Symphony no. 2
Segerstam–Finnish Radio Symphony Orchestra
   (*Symphony no. 4*) BIS LP 189

Symphony no. 3
Berglund–Finnish Radio Symphony Orchestra
   (Sibelius) Finlandia FA 311; Decca SXL 6432

Symphony no. 4
Kamu–Finnish Radio Symphony Orchestra
   (*Symphony no. 2*) BIS LP 189

Viimeiset Kiusaukset [The Last Temptations] (Opera)
Talvela, Auvinen, Rouhonen, Lehtinen. Söderblom–Savonlinna Festival
Chorus and Orchestra
   DG 2740 190 (3, nas)

See also Recitals: F 1; F 3; F 5

KUULA, Toivo (1883-1918)

Piano Trio in A, op. 7
Pohjola Trio
    BIS LP 56

(14) Songs
Hynninen, Gothóni
    Finnlevy SFX 46

Songs
Valjakka, Gothóni
    (Sibelius; Sallinen) Finnlevy SFX 11

Works for mixed choir
Andersén–Klemetti Institute Chamber Choir
    Finlandia FA 306

See also Recitals: F 6

KUUSISTO, Ilkka (1933-   )

See Recitals: F 4; F 5

MADETOJA, Leevi (1887-1947)

Comedy Overture
Panula–Helsinki Philharmonic Orchestra
    (*Symphony no. 3*) Finnlevy SFX 20

Pohjalaisia [The Bothnians] (opera)
Lokka, Karpo, Hynninen, Erkkilä. Panula–Finnish National Opera Choir
and Orchestra
    Finnlevy SFX 22/4 (3)

Symphony no. 3 in A, op. 55
Panula–Helsinki Philharmonic Orchestra
  (Comedy Overture) Finnlevy SFX 20; Finlandia FA 307
  (Symphony nos. 1 and 2, Okon Fuoko, Kullervo, Comedy Overture) Finlandia FA 202 (3 nas)

See also Recitals: F 5

Symphony no. 1
Kamu–Finnish Radio Symphony Orchestra
  (Symphony nos. 2 and 3, Okon Fuoko, Kullervo, Comedy Overture) Finlandia FA 202 (3 nas)

Symphony no. 2
Segerstam–Finnish Radio Symphony Orchestra
  (Symphony nos. 1 and 3, Okon Fuoko, Kullervo, Comedy Overture) Finlandia FA 202 (3 nas)

MARTTINEN, Tauno (1912-   )

Delta, op. 9, for clarinet and piano
Munter, Koskimies
  Ponsi PEALP 10

Rembrandt, op. 11, for cello and piano
Laamanen, Mikkilä
  Finnlevy SFX 37

Septemalia, op. 97, for seven double basses
Helsinki Philharmonic Orchestra
  Tactus TA 8002

MELARTIN, Erkki Gustav (1875-1937)

The Sleeping Beauty Suite
Jalas–Finlandia Orchestra
  Fennica SS 2

Der Traurige Garten, op. 52
Gothóni. (Palmgren)
    Finnlevy SFX 6

See also Recitals: F 6

MERIKANTO, Aare (1893-1958)

Concert Piece for cello
Hölä. Söderblom–Finnish National Opera Orchestra
    (Piano Concerto no. 2; Partita) HMV 9C 063-36024

Intrada
Fougstedt–Finnish Radio Orchestra
    Fennica SS 7

Juha (opera)
Lehtinen, Kostia, Krumm, Valjakka. Söderblom–Finnish National Opera
Chorus and Orchestra
    Finnlevy SFX 1-3 (3, nas)

Lemminkäinen
Similä–Finlandia Orchestra
    Fennica SS 4

Partita for Orchestra
Söderblom–Finnish National Opera Orchestra
    (Piano Concerto no. 2; Concert piece for cello) HMV 9C 063-36024

Piano Concerto no. 2
Heinonen. Söderblom–Finnish National Opera Orchestra
    (Concert piece for cello; Partita) HMV 9C 063-36024

Piano Concerto no. 3
Valsta. Hannikainen–Helsinki City Symphony Orchestra
    Fennica SS 11

Songs
Borg, Kostia, Urrila, Viitanen, Kuusisto
    Rytmi RTLP 7522

Valse lente (arr. for string quartet)
Finlandia Quartet
    HMV 5E063-36007

Violin Concerto no. 2, *The Echo*
Hastbacka. Berglund–Finnish Radio Symphony Orchestra
    (Raitio) Fennica Nova FENO 2

See also Recitals: F 2; F 6

MERILÄINEN, Usko (1930-   )

Notturni (3)
Tateno
    (Heininen; Kokkonen; Rautavaara) Toshiba TA 60001/4

Notturni (3)
Pohjola
    (Piano Sonatas nos. 3 and 4) EMI 5E 063 35064

Piano Concerto no. 1
Gillespie. Susskind–Royal Philharmonic Orchestra
    Philips 802854 LY

Piano Concerto no. 2
Gillespie. Bělohlávek–Helsinki Philharmonic Orchestra
    (Symphony No 3) Finlandia FA 305

Piano Sonata no. 2
Solomon
    (Rautavaara) Philips 802855

Piano Sonatas nos. 3 and 4
Pohjola
    (Notturni) EMI 5E 063 35064

Symphony no. 3
Söderblom–Finnish Radio Symphony Orchestra
    (Piano Concerto no. 2) Finlandia FA 305

See also Recitals: F 2

NUMMI

See Recitals: F 4

PACIUS, Fredrik (1809-91)

King Charles's Hunt (Ballad)
Kuusoja, Oja
    Rytmi RTLP 7502
(See Recital F 6)

PALMGREN, Selim (1878-1951)

Cinderella (Incidental Music)
Järnefelt–Symphony Orchestra
    (Askungen; Tuhkimo) 10" Odeon PLD 18(M)

Piano Concerto no. 2
Tateno. Panula–Helsinki Philharmonic Orchestra
    Toshiba EMI 0643-34471

Piano Works
Gothóni
    Finnlevy SFX 6
Palmgren
    10" Odeon PLD 8(M)

PANULA, Jorma (1930-   )

Jaakko Ilkka (Excerpts from the opera)
Häkkilä, Auvinen, Kuoppa, Hynninen, Koskinen. Panula–Ilmajoen
Opera Chorus and Opera Orchestra
    Gold Disc GDL 2014

PYLKKÄNEN, Tauno (1918-1980)

See Recitals: F 5

RAITIO, Vaino (1891-1945)

Joutsenet [The Swans]
Jalas–Finlandia Orchestra
Fennica SS 2
Kamu–Finnish Radio Symphony Orchestra
  (*Kuutamo Jupiterissa*; Merikanto) Fennica Nova FENO 2

Kuutamo Jupiterissa
Urrila, Valjakka. Kamu–Finnish Radio Symphony Orchestra
(*Joutsenet*; Merikanto) Fennica Nova FENO 2

Scherzo *(felis domestica)*
Fougstedt–Finnish Radio Orchestra
Fennica SS 8

RAUTAVAARA, Einojuhani (1928-   )

A Book of Life [Eldman kirja], op. 66
  Finnlevy SFX 58

Divertimento
Panula–Sibelius Academy Chamber Orchestra
  (*Lorca Suite;* Grieg) Finnlevy SFX 52

Piano Sonata no. 1
Tateno
  (Heininen; Kokkonen; Meriläinen) Toshiba TA 60001-4

Lorca Suite
Andersén–Cantemus Chorus
  (*Divertimenti*; Aho, Englund) Finnlevy SFX 52

Piano Sonata no. 2
Karhilo
  Finnlevy SFX 45; U.S. Musical Heritage 3401

Pelimannit, op. 1
Segerstam–Helsinki Chamber Orchestra
  (Sibelius; Segerstam) BIS LP 19

Requiem in our Time, op. 3
Panula–Helsinki Philharmonic Orchestra
    (Sibelius: Symphony No. 5) Finlandia FA 313; UK: Decca SXL 6433

String Quartet no. 1
Finlandia Quartet (Kokkonen)
    HMV 5E063-34444

String Quartet no. 3
Delme Quartet
    (Meriläinen) Philips 802855

String Quartet no. 4, op. 87
Voces Intimae Quartet (Shostakovich)
    BIS LP 66

See also Recitals: F 1

RECHBERGER, Herman (1947-   )

Missä päiväne? [Where is the Day?]
Ketonen, Choir of the Vantaa Co-educational School. Korhonen–Instrumental Ensemble
    Finnlevy FL 7005 045

Vanha Linna [The Old Castle]
Tirilä–Oulainen Youth Choir
    ONKLP 2

SALLINEN, Aulis (1935-   )

Chamber Music no. 1, op. 38
Stockholm Chamber Ensemble
    (Larsson; Roman; Telemann) BIS LP 46; US: HNH 4011

Chamber Music no. 2
Bahr. Kamu–Stockholm Chamber Ensemble
    (*Elegy; Quattro; String Quartet no. 3*) BIS LP 64

Chamber Works
Cadenze per violino solo; Cello Sonata; Elegy for Sebastian Knight, for
cello; String Quartet No. 4
Ignatius, Rautio, Suhonen Quartet
Scandia SLP 575

Chorali
Berglund–Helsinki Philharmonic Orchestra
(*Symphonies nos. 1 and 3*) BIS LP 41; US: HNH 4002

Elegy for Sebastian Knight
Helmerson
(*Chamber Music no. 2; Quattro; String Quartet no. 3*) BIS LP 64

Mauermusik
Berglund–Finnish Radio Symphony Orchestra
(Sibelius: Symphony no. 4) Finlandia FA 312; UK: Decca SXL 6431

Punainen Viiva [The Red Line]
Valjakka, Hynninen, Viitanen, Hietikko. Kamu–Finnish National Opera
Chorus and Orchestra
Finlandia FA 102 (3, nas)

Quattro per quattro
Bahr, Angervo, Höylä, Nordwall.
(*Chamber Music no. 2; Elegy; String Quartet no. 3*) BIS LP 64

Ratsumies [The Horseman] (opera)
Salminen, Valjakka, Erkkilä, Välkki, Wallén, Nieminen, Viitanen,
Toivanen. Söderblom–Savonlinna Opera Festival Chorus and Orchestra
Finlandia FA 101 (3, nas) UK: Finnlevy SFX 41-3 (3, nas)

Songs
Valjakka, Gothóni
(Kuula; Sibelius) Finnlevy SFX 11

String Quartet no. 3
Voces Intimae Quartet
(*Chamber Music no. 2; Elegy; Quattro*) BIS LP 64

Grammaticale Suite
Sallinen–Tapiola Chorus, Chamber Orchestra
Columbia 5E062 34670

Symphony no. 1
Kamu-Finnish Radio Symphony Orchestra
(*Symphony no. 3; Chorali*) BIS LP 41; US: HNH 4002

Symphony no. 2
Kuisma. Okko Kamu–Norrköping Symphony Orchestra
(Nilsson, Milhaud, Kuisma) Caprice CAP 1073

Symphony no. 3
Kamu–Finnish Radio Symphony Orchestra
(*Symphony no. 1; Chorali*) BIS LP 41; US: HNH 4002

See also Recitals: F 2; F 5

SALMENHAARA, Erkki (1941-   )

Wind Quintet
Göteborg Wind Quintet
(Mortensen; Holmboe; Carlstedt) BIS LP 24

Piano Sonata no. 1 in E flat
Liisa Pohjola
(*Piano Sonata no. 2*) HMV 5E 063 35065

Piano Sonata no. 2
Liisa Pohjola
(*Piano Sonata no. 1*) HMV 5E 063 35065

See also Recitals: F 1

SEGERSTAM, Leif (1944-   )

Concerto Serioso for violin and orchestra
H. Segerstam (violin). L. Segerstam–Austrian Radio Symphony Orchestra
(*Patria; Skizzen*) BIS LP 84

Divertimento
Segerstam–Helsinki Chamber Orchestra
(Sibelius; Rautavaara) BIS LP 19

Moments Kept Remaining
Hannak, Kovatcher, Gobel
   DGG 0666937

Patria
Segerstam–Austrian Radio Symphony Orchestra
   (Concerto; Skizzen) BIS LP 84

Rituals in La (with Lasse Werner)
Segerstam, Werner
   (String Quartet No. 6) BIS LP 20

Skizzen aus Pandora
Segerstam–Austrian Radio Symphony Orchestra
   (Concerto; Patria) BIS LP 84

String Quartet no. 4
Segerstam Quartet
   (5 *"Lemmelkvartetten"*) Swedish Society SLT 33222

String Quartet no. 5 *"360°"; Lemming*
Segerstam Quartet
   (String Quartet no. 4) Swedish Society SLT 33222

String Quartet no. 6
Segerstam Quartet
   (Rituals) BIS LP 20

String Quartet no. 7
Segerstam Quartet
   (Three Moments) BIS LP 39

String Quartet no. 8
Segerstam Quartet
   Finnlevy SFX 54

String Quartet no. 10 *Homage to Charles Ives;*
String Quartet no. 12
Segerstam Quartet
   (Trio) Phonodisc 0120219

Three Moments of Parting
H. Segerstam, Gothóni
   (String Quartet no. 7) BIS LP 39

Trio in One Movement of Thoughts
Suth, Bachtiar, Segerstam
　　(*String Quartets nos. 10; 12*) Phonodisc 0·120219

See also Recitals: F 2; F 3

Concert
Nocturne; plays for 2 celli, percussion and little orchestra; Concertino–
Fantasia
Wallisch, Bachtiar, H. Segerstam, Kenschnig. L. Segerstam–Finnish Radio
Symphony Orchestra
　　Phonodisc 0120279

SERMILÄ, Järmo (1939-　　　　)

Monody for mellophone or horn and percussion
Sermilä, Verala
　　Love LRLP 57

SIBELIUS, Jean (1865-1957)

In the case of Sibelius there exists a large number of discs, and in some cases
multi-disc sets, containing more than three works. These "Concerts" are
numbered arbitrarily for our discography and listed at the end of Sibelius
entries. Recommended items among the contents are also listed under
their separate headings, where couplings may be found by reference to the
"Concert" number.

Andante Festivo for strings
Groves–Royal Liverpool Philharmonic Orchestra
　　HMV ASD 3287 (Concert no. 2)
Jalas–Hungarian Stat Symphony Orchestra
　　(*King Christian; Swanwhite*) Decca Ace of Diamonds SDD 506; US:
London 7005
Sibelius–Finnish Radio Orchestra
　　(*En Saga; Violin Concerto*) World Records SH 207(M)

The Bard (Tone Poem) op. 64
Beecham–London Philharmonic Orchestra
　　(*In Memoriam; Legend No. 4; Symphony No. 4*) World Records SH
113(M)

Boult–London Philharmonic Orchestra
    Pye GGCD 305(2)(M) (Concert no. 6)
Gibson–Scottish National Orchestra
    CFP CFP 40273 (Concert no. 5)
Gibson–Scottish National Orchestra
    RCA RL 25136(2) (Concert no. 7)
Kamu–Finnish Radio Orchestra
    DG 2736 003(6) (Concert no. 10)

Belshazzar's Feast (Incidental Music), op. 51
Kajanus–London Symphony Orchestra
    World Records SH 191/2(2)(M) (Concert no. 9)

Canzonetta for strings
Groves–Royal Liverpool Philharmonic Orchestra
    HMV ASD 3287 (Concert no. 2)
Segerstam–Helsinki Chamber Orchestra
    (Suite Mignonette; Rakastava; Rautavaara) BIS LP 19
Chamber Works
Romance in F, op. 78 no. 2. Telmanyí, Moore
Dance Champêtre no. 1, op. 106, no. 1 Telmanyí, Vasarlehy
Dance Champêtre no. 2, op. 106, no. 2 Telmanyí, Moore
Auf der Heide, op. 115, no. 1. Ignatius, Makkila
Mazurka, op. 81, no. 1. Ignatius, Makkila
Malinconia, op. 20. Jansen, Werschenskaya
Romance in D flat, op. 24, no. 9. Joyce
    (String Quartet) World Records SH 285(M)

Dance Intermezzo, op. 45, no. 2
Groves–Royal Liverpool Philharmonic Orchestra
    HMV ASD 3287 (Concert no. 2)

The Dryad (Tone Poem), op. 45, no. 1
Barbirolli–Hallé Orchestra
    HMV ASD 2272; US: Seraphim S 60208 (Concert no. 1)
Gibson–Scottish National Orchestra
    RCA RL 25136(2) (Concert no. 7)
Groves–Royal Liverpool Philharmonic Orchestra
    HMV ASD 3287 (Concert no. 2)

Finlandia (Tone Poem), op. 26
Barbirolli–Hallé Orchestra
 HMV ASD 2272; US: Seraphim S 60208 (Concert no. 1)
Beinum–Concertgebouw Orchestra
 (Valse Triste) Philips SABE 2002 (45rpm)
 (Valse Triste; Debussy; Grieg; Tchaikovsky) Philips SABL 102
 (Valse Triste; Berlioz; Debussy; Thomas) US: Epic LC 3477(M)
Boult–London Philharmonic Orchestra
 Pye GGCD 305(2)(M) (Concert no. 6)
Jalas–Hungarian State Symphony Orchestra
 (Kuolema;Scènes Historiques) Decca Ace of Diamonds SDD 489; US:
London 6956
Karajan–Berlin Philharmonic Orchestra
 HMV ASD 3374; US: Angel S 37408 (Concert no. 3)
 (Symphony no. 5) US: Angel S 35922
Sargent–Vienna Philharmonic Orchestra
 CFP CFP 40247 (Concert no. 4)
Schmidt–Hallé Orchestra
 (Violin Concerto, Karelia Suite) CFP CFP 40360
Silvestri–Bournemouth Symphony Orchestra
 (Dukas; Mussorgsky; Ravel; Saint-Saëns; Borodin) HMV ESD 7064
Toscanini–NBC Symphony Orchestra
 (Kodály; Prokofiev) RCA AT 122(M)
Karajan–Berlin Philharmonic Orchestra
 DG 2736 003(6) (Concert no. 10)
Berglund–Philharmonia Orchestra
 (Lemminkäinen's Return; Swan of Tuonela; Valse Triste) HMV ASD
4186

Humoresques (6) for Violin and Orchestra, op. 87b/89
Rosand. Szoke–South West Germany Radio Orchestra
 (Nielsen) UK and US: Turnabout TV 34182S

In Memoriam (Funeral March), op. 59
Beecham–London Philharmonic Orchestra
 (Symphony no. 4; Legend no. 4; The Bard) World Records SH 113(M)
Groves–Royal Liverpool Philharmonic Orchestra
 (Tempest) HMV ASD 2961
Jalas–Hungarian State Symphony Orchestra
 (Legends) Decca Ace of Diamonds SDD 488; US: London 6955

Intrada for organ, op. 111a
Dearnley
 (Dearnley; Alcock; Franck; Nielsen; Gade) Guild GRPS 7011

Karelia Overture, op. 10
Collins–London Symphony Orchestra
    (*Night Ride; Symphony no. 5*) Decca Eclipse ECS 605
Gibson–Scottish National Orchestra
    CFP CFP 40273 (Concert no. 5)

Karelia Suite, op. 11
Gibson–London Symphony Orchestra
    (*Symphony no. 5*) Decca SPA 122; US: London STS 151189
Kamu–Helsinki Radio Orchestra
    (*Legends*) UK and US: DG 2530 656
Maazel–Vienna Philharmonic Orchestra
    (*Symphony no. 1*) Decca Jubilee JB 42; US: London 6375
Sargent–Vienna Philharmonic Orchestra
    CFP CFP 40237 (Concert no. 4)
Iensen–Danish State Radio Orchestra
    (*Symphony no. 5*) Decca Ace of Clubs ACL 72; US: Richmond 19036
Kajanus–London Symphony Orchestra
    World Records SH 173/4(2)(M) (Concert no. 8)
Barbirolli–Hallé Orchestra
    HMV ASD 2272; US: Seraphim S 60208 (Concert no. 1)
Karajan–Berlin Philharmonic Orchestra
    (*Symphony no. 1*) HMV ASD 4097

King Christian II (Suite), op. 27
Gibson–Scottish National Orchestra
    CFP CFP 40273 (Concert no. 5)
Jalas–Hungarian State Symphony Orchestra
    (*Andante festivo; Swanwhite*) Decca Ace of Diamonds SDD 506; US:
    London 7005
Westerberg–Stockholm Radio Symphony Orchestra
    (*Tempest*) Swedish Society LT 33144(M); Westminster XWN
    18529(M)(10") Swedish Society SS 33104

Kullervo Symphony, op. 7
Kostia, Viitanen. Berglund–Bournemouth Symphony Orchestra
    (*Kuolema* exc.; *Swanwhite* exc.) HMV SLS 807(2) US: Angel S 3778(2)
    (*Symphonies nos. 1-7; The Bard; Scènes Historiques Set 1; En Saga*) HMV
    SLS 5129(7)

Kuolema (Incidental Music)
Jalas–Hungarian State Symphony Orchestra
    (*Finlandia; Scènes Historiques*) Decca Ace of Diamonds SDD 489 US:
    London 6956

Kylliki (Three Lyric Pieces), op. 41
Gould
    (Sonatinas) CBS 76674; US: Columbia M 43555

Legends (4), op. 22
Jalas–Hungarian State Symphony Orchestra
    (In Memoriam) Decca Ace of Diamonds SDD 488; US: London 6955
Jensen–Danish State Radio Orchestra
    Decca Eclipse ECS 656
Kamu–Helsinki Radio Orchestra
    (Karelia) UK and US: DG 2530 656
Ormandy–Philadelphia Orchestra
    HMV ASD 3644 US: Angel S 37537
Stein–Suisse Romande Orchestra
    Decca SXL 6973

Luonnotar (Song), op. 70
Valjakka. Berglund–Bournemouth Symphony Orchestra
    (Symphony no. 6; Pohjola's Daughter) HMV ASD 3155
Liukkonen. Schneevoigt–Finnish National Radio Orchestra
    (Symphony no. 4; Oceanides) World Records SH 237(M)
Bryn-Julson. Gibson–Scottish National Orchestra
    RCA RL 25136(2) Concert no. 7)

Music for Violin and Piano
4 Pieces, op. 78; 5 Pieces, op. 81; 4 Pieces, op. 115; 3 Compositions, op.
116
Yaron, Stipelman
    Finlandia FA 301
Sonatina, op. 80; Devotion, op. 77, no. 2; Souvenir, op. 79, no. 1;
Berceuse, op. 79, no. 6
Steiner, Berfield
    (Dohnányi) US: Orion 76244

Night Ride and Sunrise (Tone Poem), op. 55
Boult–London Philharmonic Orchestra
    Pye GGCD 305(2)(M) (Concert no. 6)
Collins–London Symphony Orchestra
    (Karelia Overture; Symphony no. 5) Decca Eclipse ECS 605

Gibson–Scottish National Orchestra
      RCA RL 25136(2) Concert no. 7)
Jochum–Bavarian Radio Orchestra
      (Oceanides; Tempest - Prelude) (10") DG 17075M

The Oceanides (Tone Poem) op. 73
Beecham–Royal Philharmonic Orchestra
      (Pelleas; Tapiola) HMV SXLP 30197
      (Pelleas; Symphony no. 7) US: Angel S 35458
      (Tapiola; Symphony no. 7) HMV SXLP 30290
Berglund–Bournemouth Symphony Orchestra
      (Symphony no. 7; Tapiola) HMV ASD 2874
Boult–London Philharmonic Orchestra
      Pye GGCD 305(2)(M) (Concert no. 6)
Gibson–Scottish National Orchestra
      RCL RL 25136(2) (Concert no. 7)

The Origin of Fire (Cantata), op. 32
Saarits. Johnson O Cincinnati Symphony Orchestra, Helsinki University
Choir
      (Pohjola's Daughter) Varèse Sarabande VS 81041

Pan and Echo (Dance Intermezzo), op. 53
Groves–Royal Liverpool Philharmonic Orchestra
      HMV ASD 3287 (Concert no. 2)

Part Songs, op. 18
Kuuisto–Finnish Radio Choir
      (Rakastava; Brahms; Schumann) Aurora 5058

Pelléas and Mélisande (Incidental Music), op. 46
Berglund–Bournemouth Symphony Orchestra
      (Symphony no. 3) HMV ASD 3629
Stein–Suisse Romande Orchestra
      (Tempest) Decca SXL 6912

Pohjola's Daughter, op. 49
Barbirolli–Hallé Orchestra
      (Symphony no. 5) Pye GSGC 14022
      HMV ASD 2272; US: Seraphim S 60208 (Concert no. 1)
Bernstein–New York Philharmonic Orchestra
      (Symphony no. 5) CBS Classics 61808; US: Columbia MS 6749

Boult–London Philharmonic Orchestra
  Pye GGCD 305(2)(M) (Concert no. 6)
Gibson–Scottish National Orchestra
  RCA RL 25136(2) Concert no. 7)
Kajanus–London Symphony Orchestra
  World Records SH 173/4(2)(M) (Concert no. 8)
Berglund–Bournemouth Symphony Orchestra
  (*Symphony no. 6; Luonnotar*) HMV ASD 3155

Rakastava (Suite) op. 14
Gibson–Scottish National Orchestra
  (*Scènes Historiques; Valse Lyrique*) RCA RL 25051; US: RCA AGL
1-2705
Jones–Little Orchestra of London
  (Grieg; Nielsen) Unicorn UNS 201
Marriner–Academy of St. Martin-in-the-Fields
  (Wirén; Nielsen; Grieg) Argo ZRG 877
Philharmonic Chamber Ensemble
  (J.G. Berwald; Soderlundh; Mozart) Swedish Society SLT 33191
Segerstam–Helsinki Chamber Orchestra
  (*Suite Mignonette; Canzonetta;* Rautavaara; Segerstam) BIS LP 19

Rakastava (Three Part Songs), op. 14
Kuuisto–Finnish Radio Choir
  (*Part Songs;* Brahms; Schumann) Aurora 5058

Romance in C, op. 42
Groves–Royal Liverpool Philharmonic Orchestra
  HMV ASD 3287 (Concert no. 2)

Sacred Music, op. 113
Lehtinen; Raitio
  Decca SDLP 9007

En Saga, op. 9
Beinum–Amsterdam Concertgebouw Orchestra
  (*Tapiola*) Decca Eclipse ECS 655
Berglund–Bournemouth Symphony Orchestra
  (*Symphony no. 5*) HMV ASD 3038
Boult–London Philharmonic Orchestra
  Pye GGCD 305(2)(M) (Concert no. 6)

Karajan–Berlin Philharmonic Orchestra
    (*Symphony no. 5*) HMV ASD 3409; US: Angel S 37490
    HMV ASD 3374; US: Angel S 37408 (Concert no. 3)
Ormandy–Philadelphia Orchestra
    (*Symphony no. 5*) RCA RL 12906; US: RCA ARL 1-2906
Sargent–Vienna Philharmonic Orchestra
    CFP CFP 40247 (Concert no. 4)
Beecham–London Philharmonic Orchestra
    (*Andante festivo; Violin Concerto*) World Records SH 207(M)
Gibson–Scottish National Orchestra
    RCA RL 25136(2) (Concert no. 7)

Scaramouche (Pantomime), op. 71
Jalas–Hungarian State Symphony Orchestra
    (*The Tempest*) Decca Ace of Diamonds SDD 467; US: London 6824

Scènes Historiques, Set 1, op 25
Berglund–Bournemouth Symphony Orchestra
    (*Symphony no. 1*) HMV ASD 3216; US: Seraphim S 60289
Gibson–Scottish National Orchestra
    (*Set 1; Rakastava; Valse Lyrique*) RCA RL 25021; US: RCA AGL
    1-2705
Jalas–Hungarian State Symphony Orchestra
    (*Set 2; Finlandia; Kuolema*) Decca Ace of Diamonds SDD 489; US:
    London 6956

Scènes Historiques, Set 2, op. 66
Gibson–Scottish National Orchestra
    (*Set 1; Rakastava; Valse Lyrique*) RCA RL 25021; US: RCA AGL
    1-2705
Jalas–Hungarian State Symphony Orchestra
    (*Set 1; Finlandia; Kuolema*) Decca Ace of Diamonds SDD 489; US:
    London 6956

Two Serenades for violin and orchestra, op. 69
Haendel. Berglund–Bournemouth Symphony Orchestra
    (*Violin Concerto; Humoresque no. 5*) HMV ASD 3199

Three Sonatinas, op. 67
Gould
(*Kylliki*) CBS 76674; US: Columbia M 34555

Songs
7 Romances
Bjoner, Levin
    (Rangström) HMV NBLP 4(M)(10")

"And I questioned then no further", op. 17, no. 1; "Arioso", op. 3; "Autumn Night", op. 38, no. 1; "Black Roses", op. 36, no. 1; "But my Bird is Long in Homing", op. 36, no. 6; "Come Away Death", op. 60, no. 1; "The Diamond", op. 36, no. 6; "The First Kiss", op. 37, no. 1; "On a Balcony by the Sea", op. 38, no. 2; "Spring is Flying", op. 13, no. 4; "To Evening", op. 17, no. 6; "The Tryst", op. 37, no. 5; "Was it a Dream?", op. 37, no. 4; "Whisper, O Reed", op. 36, no. 4
Flagstad. Fjelstad–London Symphony Orchestra
    Decca Eclipse ECS 794; US: London 33216

"Autumn Night", op. 38, no. 1; "Black Roses", op. 36, no. 1; "The Diamond", op. 36, no. 6; "Spring is Flying", op. 13, no. 4; "The Tryst", op. 37, no. 5; "Was it a Dream?", op. 37, no. 4; "Whisper, O Reed", op. 36, no. 4
Nilsson. Bokstedt–Vienna Opera Orchestra
    (Grieg; Rangström) Decca SXC 6185; US: London 25942

See also Recitals: F 6; S 5

String Quartet in D minor, op. 56, *Voces Intimae*
Budapest Quartet
    (Chamber Works) World Records SH 285(M)
Claremont Quartet
    (Elgar) Nonesuch H 71140
Voces Intimae Quartet
    (Schumann) BIS LP 10
Finlandia Quartet
    HMV 5E 063 34235

Suite Champêtre, op. 98b
Groves–Royal Liverpool Philharmonic Orchestra
    HMV ASD 3287 (Concert no. 2)

Suite Mignonne, op. 98a
Groves–Royal Liverpool Philharmonic Orchestra
    HMV ASD 3287 (Concert no. 2)

Segerstam–Helsinki Chamber Orchestra
　　(*Canzonetta; Rakastava;* Rautavaara; Segerstam) BIS LP 19

Swanwhite (Incidental Music) op. 54
Berglund–Bournemouth Symphony Orchestra
　　(*Kuolema exc.; Kullervo Symphony*) HMV SLS 807(2) US: Angel S
　　3778(2)
Jalas–Hungarian State Symphony Orchestra
　　(*Andante festivo; King Christian*) Decca Ace of Diamonds SDD 506;
　　US: London 7005

Symphony no. 1 in E minor, op. 39
Berglund–Bournemouth Symphony Orchestra
　　(*Scènes Historiques*) HMV ASD 3216; US: Angel S 60289
Collins–London Symphony Orchestra
　　(*Pelleas*) Decca Eclipse ECS 581
Kajanus–Symphony Orchestra
　　(*Symphony no. 2, etc*) World Records SH 191/2 (2, nas)(M)
Maazel–Vienna Philharmonic Orchestra
　　(*Karelia*) Decca Jubilee JB 42; US: London 6375
Garaguly–Dresden Philharmonic Orchestra
　　(*Symphony no. 7*) Philips SFM 23000
Karajan–Berlin Philharmonic Orchestra
　　(*Karelia*) HMV ASD 4097

Symphony no. 2 in D, op. 43
Barbirolli–Royal Philharmonic Orchestra
　　RCA Gold Seal GL 25011; US: Quintessence 7008
Berglund–Bournemouth Symphony Orchestra
　　HMV ASD 3497
Collins–London Symphony Orchestra
　　(*Pohjola*) Decca Eclipse ECS 582
Doráti–Stockholm Philharmonic Orchestra
　　Camden CCV 5029
Hannikainen–London Sinfonia
　　Classics for Pleasure CFP 40315
Schmidt-Isserstedt–Norddeutscherrundfunk Orchestra
　　Parlophone PMC 1054(M); US: Capitol P 18009(M)
Kajanus–Symphony Orchestra
　　(*Symphony no. 1, etc*) World Records SH 191/2(2, nas)(M)
Maazel–Vienna Philharmonic Orchestra
　　Decca Jubilee JB 43; US: London 6408
Szell–Concertgebouw Orchestra
　　UK and US: Philips 6570 084

Davis–Toronto Symphony Orchestra
    CBS D 37801

Symphony no. 3 in C, op. 52
Berglund–Bournemouth Symphony Orchestra
    (Pelleas) HMV ASD 3629
Collins–London Symphony Orchestra
    (Symphony no. 4) Decca Eclipse ECS 604
Maazel–Vienna Philharmonic Orchestra
    (Symphony no. 6) Decca Jubilee JB 44; US: London 6591

Symphony no. 4 in A minor, op. 63
Berglund–Finnish Radio Symphony Orchestra
    (Sallinen) Finlandia FA 312; Decca SXL 6431
Davis–Boston Symphony Orchestra
    (Tapiola) UK and US: Philips 9500 143
Karajan–Berlin Philharmonic Orchestra
    (Swan of Tuonela) UK and US: DG 138974
    (Tapiola) HMV ASD 3485
Maazel–Berlin Philharmonic Orchestra
    (Tapiola) Decca Jubilee JB 45; US: London 6592
Schneevoigt–Finnish National Radio Orchestra
    (Luonnotar; Oceanides) World Records SH 237(M)
Tjeknavorian–Royal Philharmonic Orchestra
    (Symphony no. 5) RCA LRL 1 1534

Symphony no. 5 in E flat, op. 82
Berglund–Bournemouth Symphony Orchestra
    (En Saga) HMV ASD 3038; US: Angel S 37104
    (Symphony no. 3) HMV ESD 7094
Bernstein–New York Philharmonic Orchestra
    (Pohjola) CBS 61808; US: Columbia MS 6749
Collins–London Symphony Orchestra
    (Karelia; Night Ride) Decca Eclipse ECS 605
Davis–Boston Symphony Orchestra
    (Symphony no. 7) UK and US: Philips 6500959
Gibson–London Symphony Orchestra
    (Karelia) Decca SPA 122; US: London STS 15189
Karajan–Berlin Philharmonic Orchestra
    (Valse Triste; Finlandia) UK and US: DG 2542 109
Kajanus–Berlin Philharmonic Orchestra
    (Symphonies nos. 3, 6, 7, etc) World Records SH 173/4 (2, nas)(M)

Ormandy–Philadelphia Orchestra
   (En Saga) RCA RL 12906
Panula–Helsinki Philharmonic Orchestra
   (Rautavaara) Finlandia FA 313; Decca SXL 6433
Tjeknavorian–Royal Philharmonic Orchestra
   (Symphony no. 4) RCA LRL 1 1534

Symphony no. 6 in D minor, op. 104
Berglund–Bournemouth Symphony Orchestra
   (Luonnotar; Pohjola) HMV ASD 3155
Davis–Boston Symphony Orchestra
   (Symphony no. 3) UK and US: Philips 9500 142
Karajan–Berlin Philharmonic Orchestra
   (Symphony no. 7) UK and US: DG 139032
Maazel–Vienna Philharmonic Orchestra
   (Symphony no. 3) Decca Jubilee JB 44; US: London 6591
Schneevoigt–Finnish Symphony Orchestra
   (Symphonies nos. 3, 5, 7, etc) World Records SH 173/4(M)

Symphony no. 7 in C, op. 105
Beecham–Royal Philharmonic Orchestra
   (Tapiola; Oceanides) HMV SXLP 30290; US: Angel S 35458
Berglund–Bournemouth Symphony Orchestra
   (Tapiola; Oceanides) HMV ASD 2874
Collins–London Symphony Orchestra
   (Symphony no. 6) Decca Eclipse ECS 603
Davis–Boston Symphony Orchestra
   (Symphony no. 5) UK and US: Philips 6500 959
Koussevitzky–BBC Symphony Orchestra
   (Symphonies nos. 3, 5, 6, etc) World Records SH 173/4 (2, nas)(M)
Maazel–Vienna Philharmonic Orchestra
   (Symphony no. 5) Decca Jubilee JB 46; US: London 6488
Garaguly–Dresden Philharmonic Orchestra
   (Symphony no. 1) Philips SFM 23000

Tapiola (Symphonic Poem) op. 112
Beecham–Royal Philharmonic Orchestra
   (Oceanides; Symphony no. 7) HMV Concert Classics SXLP 30290;
   (Delius; Dvořák; Grieg; Fauré) US: Seraphim S 60000
Beinum–Amsterdam Concertgebouw Orchestra
   (En Saga) Decca Eclipse ECS 655

Berglund—Bournemouth Symphony Orchestra
    (*Oceanides; Symphony no.* 7) HMV ASD 2874
Berglund—Finnish Radio Symphony Orchestra
    (Kokkonen) Decca SXL 6432; Finlandia FA 311
Boult—London Philharmonic Orchestra
    Pye GGCD 305(2)(M) (Concert No. 6)
Davis—Boston Symphony Orchestra
    (*Symphony no.* 4) UK and US: Philips 9500 143
Gibson—Scottish National Orchestra
    RCA RL 25136(2) (Concert No. 7)
Kajanus—London Symphony Orchestra
    World Records SH 191/2(2)(M) (Concert no. 9)
Karajan—Berlin Philharmonic Orchestra
    HMV ASD 3374; US: Angel S 37408 (Concert no. 3)
    (*Symphony no.* 4) HMV ASD 3485; US: Angel S 37462
Karajan—Berlin Philharmonic Orchestra
    DG 2736 003(6) (Concert no. 10)

The Tempest (Incidental Music), op. 109
Jalas—Hungarian State Symphony Orchestra
    (*Scaramouche*) Decca Ace of Diamonds SDD 467; US: London 6824
Westerberg—Swedish Radio Symphony Orchestra
    (Pettersson) Swedish Society SLT 33203
    (*King Christian*) Swedish Society LT 33144(M); US: Westminster
    XWN 18529(M)

Excerpts:
The Oak Tree; Humoresque; Caliban's Song; Canon; Scene; Berceuse;
Storm; Chorus of the Winds; Intermezzo; Dance of the Nymphs; Prospero;
Song no. 2; Miranda; The Naiads; Dance Episode.
Beecham—Royal Philharmonic Orchestra
    Philips ABR 4045(M)(10")

Valse Lyrique, op. 96, no. 1
Gibson—Scottish National Orchestra
    (*Rakastava; Scènes*) RCA RL 25051; US: RCA AGL 1-2705

Valse Romantique, op. 62b
Groves—Royal Liverpool Philharmonic Orchestra
    HMV ASD 3287 (Concert no. 2)

Vårsång [Spring Song] (Tone Poem), op. 16
Berglund—Bournemouth Symphony Orchestra
    (*Karelia* exc.; *Scènes* exc.; Schalaster; Bull; Glinka; Rimsky-Korsakov;

Halvorsen; Glazunov) HMV ASD 3514
Gibson–Scottish National Orchestra
    RCA RL 25136(2) (Concert no. 7)
Groves–Royal Liverpool Philharmonic Orchestra
    HMV ASD 3287 (Concert no. 2)

Violin Concerto in D minor
Ferras. Karajan–Berlin Philharmonic Orchestra
    (*Finlandia*) UK and US: DG 138961; DG 2736 003(6) (Concert no. 10)
Haendel. Berglund–Bournemouth Symphony Orchestra
    (*Humoresque no. 5; Two Serenades*) HMV ASD 3199
Heifetz. Beecham–London Philharmonic Orchestra
    (*Andante festivo; En Saga*) World Records SH 207(M)
Heifetz. Hendl–Chicago Symphony Orchestra
    (Prokofiev: Violin Concerto no. 2) RCA LSB 4048; LSC 2435
Hudeček. Belohlávek–Prague Radio Orchestra
    (Prokofiev: Violin Concerto no. 2) Panton 11 0544
Kulenkampff. Furtwängler–Berlin Philharmonic Orchestra
    Unicorn UN 1107(M)
Oistrakh. Ormandy–Philadelphia Orchestra
    (*Legend No. 2*) CBS Classics 61041; US: Odyssey Y 30489
Stern. Beecham–Royal Philharmonic Orchestra
    (*Scènes Historiques*) CBS Classics 61876(M)
Stern. Ormandy–Philadelphia Orchestra
    (*Karelia Suite*) US: Columbia M 30068
Sarbu. Schmidt–Hallé Orchestra
    (*Karelia Suite; Finlandia*) CFP CFP 40360

Concert no. 1
Finlandia; Karelia Suite; *Kuolema: Valse triste; Legend* no. 4; *Pohjola's Daughter*
Barbirolli–Hallé Orchestra
    HMV ASD 2272; US: Seraphim S 60208

Concert no. 2
Andante festivo; Canzonetta; Dance Intermezzo; *The Dryads; Pan and Echo;*
Romance; *Suite Champêtre; Suite Mignonne; Valse Romantique; Vårsång*
Groves–Royal Liverpool Philharmonic Orchestra
    HMV ASD 3287

Concert no. 3
En Saga; Finlandia; Legend no. 2; *Tapiola*
Karajan–Berlin Philharmonic Orchestra
    HMV ASD 3374; US: Angel S 37408

Concert no. 4
En Saga; Finlandia; Karelia Suite; Legend no. 2
Sargent–Vienna Philharmonic Orchestra
    CFP CFP 40247

Concert no. 5
The Bard; Karelia Overture; *King Christian* Suite; *Scènes Historiques,* Set 1,
no. 3
Gibson–Scottish National Orchestra
    CFP CFP 40273

Concert no. 6
The Bard; En Saga; Finlandia; Legends nos. 2 and 4; *Night Ride and Sunrise;
Oceanides; Pohjola's Daughter; Tapiola; The Tempest:* Prelude
Boult–London Philharmonic Orchestra
    Pye GGCD 305(2)(M)

Concert no. 7
*The Bard; The Dryad; En Saga; Finlandia; Luonnotar; Night Ride and Sunrise;
Oceanides; Pohjola's Daughter; Tapiola; Vårsång*
Gibson–Scottish National Orchestra
    RCA RL 25136(2)

Concert no. 8
Karelia Suite [1]; *Pohjola's Daughter* [2]; Symphonies nos. 3 [1], 5 [1], 6 [3], and 7 [2]
Kajanus [1]–London Symphony Orchestra
Koussevitzky [2]–BBC Symphony Orchestra
Schneevoigt [3]–Finnish Symphony Orchestra
    World Records SH 173/4(2)(M)

Concert no. 9
Belshazzar's Feast [1]; Symphonies nos. 1 [2] and 2 [2]; *Tapiola* [1]
Kajanus [1]–London Symphony Orchestra [1] and Symphony Orchestra [2]
    World Records SH 191/2(2)(M)

Concert no. 10
The Bard[2]: *Finlandia*[1]; *Legend* no. 2[2]; Symphonies nos. 1[2], 2[3], 4[1], and 5
Tapiola[1]; Violin Concerto[1,4]
Karajan[1]–Berlin Philharmonic Orchestra
Kamu[2]–Finnish Radio Orchestra
Kamu[3]–Berlin Philharmonic
Ferras (violin)[4]
    (with Grieg: Piano Concerto; Peer Gynt) DG 2736 003(6)

SIPILÄ, Eero (1918-72)

See Recitals: F1; F 4

SONNINEN, Ahti (1914-   )

See Recitals: F 3

TULINDBERG, Erik (1761-1814)

String Quartet No. 4
Finnish Quartet
    (Boccherini; Werner) US: Orion 7035

WERNER, Lasse – See SEGERSTAM

Recitals and Concerts of Finnish Music

F 1–Contemporary Finnish Choral Music by Bergman, Johansson, Kokkonen, Rautavaara, Salmenhaara, and Sipilä.
    Andersén–Radion Kamarikuoro
    Philips 839 705 LY

F 2–Finnish Music for Violin and Piano.
A. Merikanto: Prelude; Meriläinen: *Opusculum* for violin solo; Sallinen:
Cadenze for violin solo; Segerstam: Poem
    P. Pohjola, L. Pohjola
    BIS LP 18

F 3–New Finnish Music.
Bashmakov: Quattro Bagatelle
    Bahr, Kuisma
Kokkonen: Wind Quintet
    Helsinki Wind Quintet
Segerstam: A NNNN00000WWW
    Helsinki Wind Quintet
Sonninen: *El Amor Pasa,* op. 40
    Faringer, Bahr. Westerberg–Swedish Radio Symphony Orchestra
    BIS LP 11

F 4–Songs by Finnish Composers. Johansson, Kuusisto, Nummi, Sipilä.
    Lehtinen, Koskimies
    Finnlevy SFX 12

F 5–Songs by Finnish Composers: Kokkonen, Kuusisto, Madetoja, Pylkkänen, Sallinen.
    Valjakka, Gothóni
    BIS LP 89

F 6–Songs by Finnish Composers: Hannikainen, Kilpinen, Kuula, Melartin, Merikanto, Sibelius.
    Antti, Borg, Blomberg, Koskinen, Kuusoja, Kuusisto, Lehtinen
    Rytmi RTLP 7502
(See also Pacius)

Selective Discography
of Swedish Music

AGRELL, Johann, Joachim (1701-65)

Concertos, op. 4, for harpsichord, flute and strings, no. 1 in A; no. 2 in B minor
Nordenfelt, Bengtson. Drottningholm Baroque Ensemble
    Caprice CAP 1130

Harpsichord Sonatas: in B flat; in D
Nordenfelt
    (Roman) US: Orion 74157

Sonatas for flute, harpsichord, and strings: in B flat minor (1753); in A major (1753)
Stig Bengtson, Eva Nordenfelt
    Caprice CAP 1130

Sonata in G minor
Nordenfelt
    (Roman; Johnson; Uttini) HMV 061 35826

Symphony no. 6 in F
Frykberg–Norrköping Symphony Orchestra
    Alfvén; Atterberg; Henneberg; Johanson; Larsson) Sterling S 1003
Nilsen–Örebro Chamber Orchestra
    (Börtz; Carlstedt; Linde) Swedish Society SLT 33246

AHLSTRÖM, Jacob Niklas (1805-57)

See Recitals: S 6

ALFVÉN, Hugo (1872-1960)

Dalarapsodi: Swedish Rhapsody no. 3, op. 48
Alfvén–Stockholm Konsertförening
    (*Symphony no. 3*) HMV 053-34620
Westerberg–Stockholm Philharmonic Orchestra
    (*Festspel; Midsummer Vigil*) Swedish Society SLT 33145

Elegy
Berglund–Bournemouth Symphony Orchestra
    (*Midsummer Vigil:* Grieg; Järnefelt) HMV ASD 2952

En båt med blommor
Saedén. Westerberg–Swedish Radio Orchestra
    (*Midsummer Vigil*) Telestar TRS 11162/3(2)

Festspel, op. 25
Ehrling–Göteborg Symphony Orchestra
    (*Midsummer Vigil;* Nystroem) Lyssna 7
Westerberg–Stockholm Philharmonic Orchestra
    (*Midsummer Vigil; Dalarapsodi*) Swedish Society SLT 33145

Folksongs (arranged for choir)
Stenlung–Uppsala Academic Chamber Choir
    Telestar TRS 11105

Ericson–Swedish Radio Chamber Choir
 HMV C063-29079

Gustav II, Adolf (Suite), op. 49
Westerberg–Swedish Radio Symphony Orchestra
 Swedish Society SLT 33173

The Lost Son (Ballet Suite)
Alfvén–Stockholm Royal Court Orchestra
 (Mountain King) Swedish Society SLT 33182

Midsummer Vigil: Swedish Rhapsody no. 1, op. 19
Alfvén–Stockholm Royal Court Orchestra
 (Festspel; Dalarapsodi) Swedish Society SLT 33145
Berglund–Bournemouth Symphony Orchestra
 (Gustav; Grieg; Järnefelt) HMV ASD 2952
Busch–Malmö Symphony Orchestra
 (En båt med blommor) Telestar TRS 11162/3(2)
Ehrling–Göteborg Symphony Orchestra
 (Festspel; Nystroem) Lyssna 7
Ormandy–Philadelphia Orchestra (Sibelius; Grieg)
 US: Columbia MS 6196

Mountain King (Ballet Suite), op. 37
Alfvén–Stockholm Royal Court Orchestra
 (The Lost Son) Swedish Society SLT 33182

Piano Music
Roos
 Philips 6563 007

Songs
Rodin, Eyron
 (Violin Sonata) HMV E061-34024

Songs for Choir
Orphei Drängar, Ericson
 Swedish Society SLT 33249

Symphony no. 1 in F minor, op. 7
Westerberg–Swedish Radio Symphony Orchestra
 Swedish Society SLT 33161

Symphony no. 2 in D, op. 11
Segerstam–Stockholm Philharmonic Orchestra
Swedish Society SLT 33211

Symphony no. 3, op. 23
Alfvén–Stockholm Konsertförening
(Dalarapsodi) HMV 053-34620
Grevillius–Stockholm Philharmonic Orchestra
Swedish Society SLT 33186

Symphony no. 4, op. 39
Grevillius–Stockholm Philharmonic Orchestra
Swedish Society SLT 33161

Symphony no. 5 in A minor, op. 55 (first part)
Westerberg–Swedish Radio Symphony Ocrhestra
(Tale of the Archipelago) Swedish Society SLT 33174

Tale of the Archipelago (Symphonic Poem), op. 20
Westerberg–Swedish Radio Symphony Orchestra
(Symphony no. 5) Swedish Society SLT 33174

Uppenbarelsekantat, op. 31 - Andante religioso
Frykberg–Norrköping Symphony Orchestra
(Agrell; Atterberg; Henneberg; Johanson; Larsson) Sterling S 1003

Uppsalarapsodi
Rybrant–Berlin Symphony Orchestra
(Atterberg, Eriksson, Lindberg, Smoliansky) Telestar TRS 11180

Violin Sonata in C minor
Saulesco, Solyom
(Songs) HMV E061-34024

See also Recitals: S 1; S 3

ALLDAHL, Per-Gunnar (1943-   )

See Recitals: S 7

ALTHÉN, Ragnar (1883-1961)

See Recitals: S 3

ANONYMOUS

(6) Marches for the Royal Södermanland Regiment (1774)
Musica Camerata Regionalis
(Karkoff; Mozart; Söderlundh) Caprice CAP 1074

ATTERBERG, Kurt (1887-1974)

Aladdin (Overture)
Rybrant—Berlin Symphony Orchestra
(Alfvén; Eriksson; Lindberg; Smoliansky) Telestar TRS 11180

The Foolish Virgins, op. 17
Grevillius—Stockholm Philharmonic Orchestra
(Lindberg) Swedish Society SLT 33192

String Quartet in B minor, op. 11
Saulesco Quartet
(Haydn) Swedish Society SLT 33220

Suite no. 3, op. 19, no. 1
Saulesco, Roehr. Westerberg—Swedish Radio Orchestra
(Frumerie; Wirén) Swedish Society SLT 33167
Liljefors, Koulaksezian. The Stockholm Ensemble
(Haydn) Swedish Society SLT 33248

Symphony no. 2 in F, op. 6
Westerberg—Swedish Radio Symphony Orchestra
Swedish Society SLT 33179

Symphony no. 4, *Piccola*
Frykberg—Norrköping Symphony Orchestra
(Agrell; Alfvén; Henneberg; Johanson; Larsson) Sterling S 1003

AULIN, Tor Bernhard Wilhelm (1866-1914)
4 Akvareller; 3 Dances; Violin Concerto
Tellefsen, Nilson. Segerstam—Swedish Radio Symphony Orchestra
    HMV E061-35157

BÄCK, Sven-Erik (1919-   )

Fågeln (Chamber Opera)
Sivall, Garellick, Näslund.
Bäck—Norrköping Symphony Orchestra
    Swedish Society SLT 33195

Favola, for piano, clarinet and percussion
Instrumental Ensemble
    (Carlstedt; Werle) Caprice CAP 1018(M)

A Game Around a Game
Ehrling—Stockholm Philharmonic Orchestra
    (Larsson; Nystroem) Philips 7325 005 also listed as Philips 6559 004

Motets
Ericson—Swedish Radio Choir
    (Lidholm; Hambraeus) Sveriges Radio RELP 1096

Sonata alla ricercare
Ribera
(Garreta) HMV E061-35136

Tranfjädrarna (Chamber Opera)
Hallin, Ebrelius, Sivall, Saedén, Eric Ericson Barnkör. Chamber
Orchestra. Bäck—Norrköping Symphony Orchestra
    Swedish Society SLT 33183

BELLMAN, Carl Michael (1740-95)

Fredman Epistles and Songs
Sallström, Bengtsson.
    Telefunken TR 11068

Schiøtz
(Brahms; Schubert; Wolf) US: Dyer-Bennet DYBXS 2

Epistles and Songs
Westerberg–Drottningholm's Chamber Orchestra
Swedish Society SLT 33155

BERWALD, Franz Adolf (1796-1868)

Bajadärfesten
Björlin–Royal Philharmonic Orchestra
(Symphonies, Concertos, etc) HMV SLS 5096 (4, nas)
Ehrling–Swedish Radio Symphony Orchestra
(Overtures; Tone Poems) HMV 053-35309; US: Nonesuch H 71218

Estrella di Soria (Overture)
Björlin–Royal Philharmonic Orchestra
(Symphonies, Concertos etc) HMV SLS 5096 (4, nas)
Ehrling–Swedish Radio Symphony Orchestra
(Overtures, Tone Poems) HMV 053-35309; US: Nonesuch H 71218

Memories of the Norwegian Mountains
Björlin–Royal Philharmonic Orchestra
(Symphonies, Concertos, etc) HMV SLS 5096 (4, nas)
Broman–Swedish Radio Symphony Orchestra
(Serious and Joyful Fancies; Broman) Caprice CAP 1029
Ehrling–Swedish Radio Symphony Orchestra
(Overtures, Tone Poems) HMV 053-35309; US: Nonesuch H 71218

Piano Concerto in D
Erikson. Westerberg–Swedish Radio Symphony Orchestra
(Piano pieces) Caprice CAP 1063; US: Genesis 1011
Migdal. Björlin–Royal Philharmonic Orchestra
(Symphonies, Concertos, etc) HMV SLS 5096 (4, nas)

Piano Quintets: no. 1 in C minor, op. 5; no. 2 in A, op. 6
Riefling. Benthian Quartet
Telestar TRS 11039
Vienna Philharmonic Quintet
Decca SDD 448

Piano Trios: no. 1 in E flat; no. 3 in D minor
Berwald Trio
 Telestar TRS 11038

Piano Works
Erikson
 (*Piano Concerto*) Caprice CAP 1063; US: Genesis 1011

Play of the Elves
Björlin–Royal Philharmonic Orchestra
 (*Symphonies, Concertos, etc*) HMV SLS 5096 (4, nas)
Ehrling–Swedish Radio Symphony Orchestra
 (*Overtures, Tone Poems*) HMV 053-35309; US: Nonesuch H 71218

Quartet for Piano and Wind Instruments
Knardahl. Members of the Göteborg Wind Quintet
 BIS LP 44

Queen of Golconda (Overture)
Björlin–Royal Philharmonic Orchestra
 (*Symphonies, Concertos, etc*) HMV SLS 5096 (4, nas)
Ehrling–Swedish Radio Symphony Orchestra
 (*Overtures, Tone Poems*) HMV 053-35309; US: Nonesuch H 71218

Racing
Björlin–Royal Philharmonoc Orchestra
 (*Symphonies, Concertos, etc*) HMV SLS 5096 (4, nas)

Septet in B flat
Hamburg Norddeutscher Rundfunk Orchestra members
 (*String Quartet no. 4*) Telestar TRS 11041
Nash Ensemble
 (Hummel) CRD CRD 1044
Vienna Octet Members
 (Kreutzer) Decca SXL 6462
Uppsala Kammarsolister
 (Spohr) Bluebell BELL 131

Serious and Joyful Fancies
Björlin–Royal Philharmonic Orchestra
 (*Symphonies, Concertos, etc*) HMV SLS 5096 (4, nas)
Broman–Swedish Radio Symphony Orchestra
 (*Memories;* Broman) Caprice CAP 1029

String Quartet no. 1 in G minor
Benthian Quartet
 (*no. 3*) Telestar TRS 11040
Frydén Quartet
 (*no. 4*) Swedish Society SLT 33180
Phoenix Quartet
 (*nos. 3 and 4*) Bärenreiter 1947/8(2); US: Golden Crest 41233(2)

String Quartet no. 3 in E flat
Benthian Quartet
 (*no. 1*) Telestar TRS 11040
Frydén Quartet
 (Roman) Sveriges Radio RELP 5008(M)
Phoenix Quartet
 (*nos. 1 and 4*) Bärenreiter 1947/8(2); US: Golden Crest 41233(2)
Saulesco Quartet
 (Mozart) Swedish Society SLT 33178

String Quartet no. 4 in A minor
Benthian Quartet
 (*Septet*) Telestar TRS 11041
Phoenix Quartet
 (*nos. 1 and 3*) Bärenreiter 1947/8(2); US: Golden Crest 41233(2)
Frydén Quartet
 (*no. 1*) Swedish Society SLT 33180

Symphony no. 1 in G minor, *Sérieuse*
Björlin–Royal Philharmonic Orchestra
 (*Symphonies, Concertos, etc*) HMV SLS 5096 (4, nas)
Ehrling–Swedish Radio Symphony Orchestra
 (Nystroem) Sveriges Radio RELP 1105
Schmidt-Isserstedt–Stockholm Philharmonic Orchestra
 (*no. 3*) Telestar 11037; US: Nonesuch H 71087

Symphony no. 2 in D, *Capricieuse*
Björlin–Royal Philharmonic Orchestra
 (*Symphonies, Concertos, etc*) HMV SLS 5096 (4, nas)
Doráti–Stockholm Philharmonic Orchestra
 (Blomdahl; Rosenberg) RCA Victrola VICS 1319

Symphony no. 3 in C, *Singulière*
Björlin–Royal Philharmonic Orchestra
    (Symphonies, Concertos, etc) HMV SLS 5096 (4, nas)
Ehrling–London Symphony Orchestra
    (no. 4) Decca SXL 6374; Swedish Society SLT 33261
Markevich–Berlin Philharmonic Orchestra
    (no. 4) Heliodor 89717(M)
Schmidt-Isserstedt–Stockholm Philharmonic Orchestra
    (no. 1) Telestar TRS 11037; US: Nonesuch H 71087

Symphony no. 4 in E flat
Björlin–Royal Philharmonic Orchestra
    (Symphonies, Concertos, etc) HMV SLS 5096 (4, nas)
Ehrling–London Symphony Orchestra
    (no. 3) Decca SXL 6374; Swedish Society SLT 33261
Markevich–Berlin Philharmonic Orchestra
    (no. 3) Heliodor 89717(M)

Violin Concerto in C sharp minor, op. 2
Berlin. Krenz–Stockholm Philharmonic Orchestra
    (Debussy) Lyssna 6
Tellefsen. Björlin–Royal Philharmonic Orchestra
    (Symphonies, Overtures, etc) HMV SLS 5096 (4, nas)

BERWALD, Johann Gottfried (1737-*c.* 1814)

Symphony in C
Stockholm Philharmonic Chamber Ensemble
    (Mozart; Sibelius; Söderlundh) Swedish Society SLT 33191

BLOMDAHL, Karl-Birger (1916-68)

Chamber Concerto
Leygraf. Ehrling–London Symphony Orchestra
    (Lidholm; Rosenberg) Decca SXL 6180

Pastoral Suite
Frykberg–Stockholm Radio Symphony Orchestra
 (Larsson; Fernström) London International TW 91091(M)

Praeludium and Allegro
Björlin–Stockholm Philharmonic Orchestra
 (Songs; Spel) HMV SCLP 1063

Forma ferritonans
Comissiona–Stockholm Philharmonic Orchestra
 (Sisyfos) Caprice CAP 1016(M)
  (Kodály) Sveriges Radio RIKS 2(M)

Litet tema med variationes
Baekkelund
 (Tre polyfona; Bäck; Larlid; Larsson; Lidholm) Sonet SLP 2032

Sisyfos (Suite)
Doráti–Stockholm Philharmonic Orchestra
 (Forma) Caprice CAP 1016(M)
  (Berwald; Rosenberg) Caprice CAP 1013; RCA Victrola VICS 1319

(5) Songs
Rosenberg
 (Spel; Praeludium) HMV SCLP 1063

I Speglarnas Sal [In the Hall of the Mirrors]
Hallin, Ericson, Vikström, Näslund, Rundgren. Ehrling–Stockholm
Philharmonic Orchestra, Stockholm Radio Chorus.
 Caprice CAP 1006(M)

Spel för Atta (Ballet Suite)
Björlin–Stockholm Philharmonic Orchestra
 (Songs; Praeludium) HMV SCLP 1063

Suite for cello and piano
Helmerson, Negro
 (Frumerie; Berg; Liszt) Caprice CAP 1019

Symphony no. 2
Doráti–Stockholm Philharmonic Orchestra
 (Pettersson) HMV E061-35142

Symphony no. 3, *Facetter*
Ehrling–Stockholm Philharmonic Orchestra
    (Eklund; Wirén) Swedish Society SLT 33241
    (Rosenberg) Turnabout TV 34318

Tre polyfona stycken
Baekkelund
    (Litet; Bäck; Larlid; Larsson; Lidholm) Sonet SLP 2032
Negro
    (Rosenberg; Brahms) Caprice CAP 1105

See also Recitals: S 8

BÖRTZ, Daniel (1943-   )

Monologhi 2, for bassoon
Samuelsson
    (Monologhi 5; Quartet; Symphony No. 1) Caprice CAP 1128

Monologhi 5, for soprano
Maros
    (Monologhi 2; Quartet; Symphony No. 1) Caprice CAP 1128

Night Clouds
Nilson–Örebro Chamber Orchestra
    (Agrell; Linde; Carlstedt) Swedish Society SLT 33246

Nightflies
Harpans Kraft
    (Eliasson; Hanson; Mellnäs; Sandström) Caprice CAP 1070

Nightwinds
Camerata Homiae
    (Milhaud; Monteverdi; Jannequin; Toch) Caprice CAP 1046

Quartet no. 2
Crafoord Quartet
    (Monologhi 2 and 5; Symphony no. 1) Caprice CAP 1128

Symphony no. 1
Ingebretsen–Stockholm Philharmonic Orchestra
(*Monologhi 2 and 5; Quartet no. 2*) Caprice CAP 1128

Concerto for violin, bassoon, and orchestra
Wedin–Stockholm Sinfonietta
(Larsson; Sibelius) Caprice CAP 1248

BROMAN, Sten (1902-   )

Symphony no. 7
Ehrling–Swedish Radio Orchestra
(Berwald) Caprice CAP 1029

CARLSTEDT, Jan (1926-   )

Sinfonietta for wind quintet
Göteborg Wind Qintet
(Mortensen; Holmboe; Salmenhaara) BIS LP 24

Sonata, op. 15
Dekov
(Linde; Karkoff; Eklund) Swedish Society SLT 33199

String Quartet no. 2
Slovak Quartet
(Bäck; Werle) Caprice CAP 1018(M)

String Quartet no. 3, op. 23
Fresk Quartet
(Shostakovich) Caprice CAP 1052

Symphony no. 2, *Martin Luther King in Memoriam*
Westerberg–Stockholm Philharmonic Orchestra
HMV E055-34424

DÜBEN, Gustav (1628-90)

Suite in G minor, à 5
Drottningholm Baroque Ensemble
(Verdier; Roman) Proprius 7761

Three Dances
Camerata Lutetiensis
(Roman; Buxtehude) Schwann VMS 1004

EKLUND, Hans (1927-   )

(3) Pieces for Organ
Fagius
(Olsson; F. Couperin; Alain) BIS LP 7

String Quartet no. 3
Norrköping Quartet
(Carlstedt; Karkoff; Linde) Swedish Society SLT 33199

Fantasia for cello and string orchestra
Damgaard–Swedish Radio Symphony Orchestra
(Roman, etc) Swedish Society SLT 33245

Music for Orchestra
Westerberg–Swedish Radio Symphony Orchestra
(Blomdahl, Wirén) Swedish Society SLT 33241

EKÖLF, Ejnar (1886-1954)

See Recitals: S 3; S 5

ELIASSON, Anders (1947-   )

Disegno, for solo clarinet
Notturno, for bass clarinet, cello, piano
Ombra, for clarinet and string quartet

Savin String Quartet, Stevensson, Ola Karlsson, Roland Pöntinen
Artemis ARTE 7115

FERNSTRÖM, John (1897-1961)

Concertino for Flute, women's chorus and chamber orchestra, op. 52
Holmstedt. Frykberg–Stockholm Radio Orchestra
(Larsson; Blomdahl) London International TW 91091

FRUMERIE, Gunnar de (1908-   )

Berceuse
Olofsson, Berg
(Roman; Wikmanson; Eklund; Söderlund; Taube) Swedish Society
SLT 33245

Hjärtats sånger
Boström, Negro
(Blomdahl; Berg; Liszt) Caprice CAP 1019

Horn Concerto
Lanzky-Otto. Westerberg–Stockholm Philharmonic Orchestra
(R. Strauss) Caprice CAP 1103

Oboe Concertino
Nilsson. Verde–Musica Sveciae
(Larsson; Roman) Fermat FLPS 10

Pastoral Suite
Marelius. Westerberg–Swedish Radio Orchestra
(Atterberg; Wirén) Swedish Society SLT 33167

Suite no. 1, op. 5a
Rolf Lindblom
(*Chaconne, Lyriskt Intermezzo,* Rosenberg) Proprius 7820

See also Recitals: S 4; S 8

FRYKLÖF, Harald (1882-1919)

Sonata alla leggenda
Mannberg; Kundén
  (Peterson-Berger) Caprice CAP 1120

GEFORS, Hans (1952-   )

See Recitals: S 7

GEIJER, Erik Gustav (1783-1847)

Sonatas for two pianos: in E flat; in F minor
S. and B. Wikman
  Fermat FLPS 4

HAMBRAEUS, Bengt (1928-   )

Electronic Music: *Rota* 2; *Tetragon*
Zetterlund; Schmidt; Bergström
  Caprice CAP 1007

Fresque Sonore
Sjöstrand. Ensemble directed by Bengt Hambraeus (organ, harpsichord
percussion, ring modulator)
  (Transfiguration) Swedish Society SLT 33181

Rencontres for Orchestra
Westerberg–Swedish Radio Symphony Orchestra
  (Larsson) Caprice CAP 1032

Transfiguration
Gielen–Swedish Radio Symphony Orchestra
  (Fresque) Swedish Society SLT 33181

HEDAR, Josef (1894-1960)

See Recitals: S 1

HEDWALL, Lennart (1932-   )

Canzona for strings
Hedwall–Örebro Chamber Orchestra
    (Larsson; Koch; Wirén) Swedish Society SLT 33224

HERMANSON, Åke (1923-   )

Alarme
Lanzky-Otto
    (Larsson; Hindemith) Caprice CAP 1017

Appell I-IV, op. 10
Westerberg–Swedish Radio Symphony Orchestra
    (In nuce; Rosenberg) Swedish Society SLT 33215

In nuce, op. 7
Maderna–South West Radio Symphony Orchestra
    (Appell; Rosenberg) Swedish Society SLT 33215

See also Recitals: S 7

HOLEWA, Hans (1905-   )

Miniature for String Quartet
Frydén Quartet
    (Kallstenius; Stravinsky) Caprice CAP 1008(M)

See also Recitals: S 7

JOHNSEN, Henrik Philip (*c.* 1716-79)

Trio Sonata in E minor
Musica Holmiae
    (Albrici; Roman; Pfleger; Förster; Ritter) HMV E061-35164

Sonata in A minor
Nordenfelt
    (Roman; Agrell; Uttini) HMV 061-35826

Symphony no. 1 in F
Genetay–National Museum Chamber Orchestra
    (Kraus; Roman) HMV 061-35584

JOSEPHSON, Jacob Axel (1818-80)

See Recitals: S 6

KALLSTENIUS, Edvin (1881-1967)

Clarinet Quintet
Westlund. Frydén Quintet
    (Holewa; Stravinsky) Caprice CAP 1008(M)

KARKOFF, Maurice (1927-   )

Figures for Wind and Percussion, op. 118
Musica Camerata Regionalis
    (Söderlundh; Mozart; Anon) Caprice CAP 1074

Symphony no. 4, op. 69
Westerberg–Stockholm Radio Orchestra
    (Larsson) Swedish Society SLT 33164

Ten Japanese Romances
Hallqvist; Karkoff
    (Carlstedt; Eklund; Linde) Swedish Society SLT 33199

See also Recitals: S 8

KOCH, Erland von (1910-   )

Musica malinconica for strings, op. 50
Hedwall–Örebro Chamber Orchestra
    (Hedwall; Larsson; Wirén) Swedish Society SLT 33224

Nordic capriccio, op. 26
Westerberg–Swedish Radio Symphony Orchestra
    (Nystroem) Swedish Society SLT 33136

Oxberg Variations
Westerberg–Stockholm Philharmonic Orchestra
    (Stenhammar) Swedish Society SLT 33227
    (Rosenberg) Swedish Society SLT 43053

Piano Concerto no. 3
Solyon. Wiklander–Stockholm Military Orchestra
    (*String Quartet no. 4*) Caprice CAP 1104

Saxophone Concerto
Rascher. Westerberg–Munich Philharmonic Orchestra
    (*Scandinavian Dances*) HMV E061-34016

Scandinavian Dances nos. 1-6
Westerberg–Munich Philharmonic Orchestra
    (*Saxophone Concerto*) HMV E061-34016

Sonatina no. 2, op. 46
Ibérer
    (Larsson) Polydor 2379 157

String Quartet no. 4, *Concerto Lirico*
Grünfarb Quartet
    (*Piano Concerto*) Caprice CAP 1104

See also Recitals: S 8

KRAUS, Joseph Martin (1756-92)

Fiskarena (Ballet Suite)
Farncombe–Hovkapellet
    (Roman; Naumann) DG 2536 032

Flute Quintet in D
Heidelberg Baroque Ensemble
    (Sonata) Da Camera Magna 92727; UK: Oryx Musica Rara
    MUR 17(M)

Olympie–Overture in D minor
Bonynge–English Chamber Orchestra
    (eighteenth-century overtures) Decca SXL 6531

Sonata in A minor for flute and viola
E. Zukerman; P. Zukerman
    (Beethoven; Telemann) US: Columbia M 32842
Monteux; Trampler
    (eighteenth-century chamber works) US: Music Guild S 47

Sonata in E
Krieger
    (Flute Quintet) Da Camera Magna 92727; UK: Oryx Musica Rara
    MUR 17(M)

String Quartet in A, *Gottinger*
Salzburg Mozarteum Quartet
    (J. and M. Haydn) Amadeo AVRS 6371

Symphony in C minor
Kamu–Stockholm Philharmonic Orchestra
    (Mozart) Lyssna 1
Jenkins–Angelicum Orchestra, Milan
    (Brunetti) UK and US: Nonesuch H 71156
Genetay–National Museum Chamber Orchestra
    (Roman; Johnsen) HMV 061-35584

LARSSON, Lars-Erik (1908-   )

Barococo Suite
Verde–Unga Musiker
    (Lyric Suite; Trumpet Concertino; Pastoral) Proprius Artemis
ARTE 60105

Concertini, op. 45 (solo instrument with string orchestra)

For flute
Bahr. Verde–Musica Sveciae
    (Bassoon Concertino; Beethoven) BIS LP 40
For oboe
Nilsson. Verde–Musica Sveciae
    (Frumerie; Roman;) Fermat FLPS 10
For clarinet
Jansson. Ehrling–Stockholm Philharmonic Orchestra
    (Nystroem; Bäck) Philips 7325 005 (also listed as Philips 6559 004)
For bassoon
Sønstevold. Verdi–Musica Sveciae
    (Flue Concertino; Beethoven) BIS LP 40
Torge. Hedwall–Örebro Chamber Orchestra
    (Hedwall; Koch, Wirén) Swedish Society SLT 33224
For horn
Lanzky-Otto. Philharmonic Chamber Ensemble
    (Hermanson; Hindemith) Caprice CAP 1017
For trumpet
Verde–Unga Musiker
    (Barococo Suite; Lyric Suite; Pastoral) Proprius Artemis ARTE 60105
For trombone
Smith, Kuehefuhs
    (Haydn; Ravel) US: Coronet 1711
Slokar, Angerer–Pforzheim Chamber Orchestra
    (L. Mozart; Albrechtsberger; Angerer) Claves D 707
For violin
Berlin. Westerberg–Stockholm Philharmonic Orchestra
    (Violin Concerto; Vintersaga) Swedish Society SLT 33257
For viola
Andersson. Stockholm Chamber Ensemble
    (Roman; Sallinen; Telemann) BIS LP 46; US: HNH 4011
For cello
Fürst. Malmö Symphony Orchestra
    (Wieslander; Fernström) Caprice CAP 1027

For double bass
Ossoinak. Philharmonic Chamber Ensemble
  (Roman) Swedish Society SLT 33187
For piano
Pålsson. Verde–Musica Sveciae
  (Mozart; Haydn) BIS LP 36

Pastoral Suite, op. 19
Westerberg–Stockholm Philharmonic Orchestra
  (Little March; Wirén) Swedish Society SLT 33176; US: London CS
  6430
Björlin–Stockholm Philharmonic Orchestra
  (Lyric Fantasy; Roman; Uttini) HMV 063-34405

Rejoice in the Lamb
Sjökvist–Storkyrkans kör
  (Missa Brevis) Proprius 7782

Sonatina no. 3
Ibérer
  (Koch) Polydor 2379 157

Symphony no. 3 in C minor, op. 34
Frykberg–Helsingborg Symphony Orchestra
  (Förklädd Gud) BIS LP 96

Variations for Orchestra, op. 50
Ehrling–Stockholm Radio Orchestra
  (Karkoff) Swedish Society SLT 33164

Vintersaga
Westerberg–Stockholm Philharmonic Orchestra
  (Violin Concertino) Swedish Society SLT 33257

Violin Concerto, op. 42
Gertler. Frykberg–Stockholm Radio Orchestra
  (Blomdahl; Fernström) London International TW 91091(M)
Berlin. Westerberg–Stockholm Philharmonic Orchestra
  (Violin Concertino; Vintersaga) Swedish Society SLT 33257

Due Auguri for orchestra
Westerberg–Swedish Radio Symphony Orchestra
   (Hambraeus) Caprice CAP 1032

Förklädd Gud [Disguised God] (Lyric Suite), op. 24
Söderström, Saedén, Ekborg.
Westerberg–Stockholm Radio Orchestra, Martin Lidstams Vokalensemble
   (Grieg) Swedish Society SLT 33146
Sydow, Ligendza, Wixell.
Westerberg–Swedish Radio Symphony Orchestra
   (Rangström) HMV E061-35149
Nordin, Hagegård, Jonsson.
Frykberg–Helsingborg Symphony Orchestra, Helsingborgs Konserthuskör
   (*Symphony no. 3*) BIS LP 96

Little Serenade for strings, op. 12
Stockholm Philharmonic Chamber Ensemble
   (Larsson; Roman) Swedish Society SLT 33187

Lyric Fantasy
Björlin–Stockholm Philharmonic Orchestra
   (*Pastoral Suite;* Roman; Uttini) HMV 063-34405

Lyric Suite
Verde–Unga Musiker
   (*Barococo Suite; Trumpet Concertino; Pastoral*) Proprius Artemis
   ARTE 60105

Missa brevis
Sjökvist–Storkyrkans kör
   (*Rejoice in the Lamb*) Proprius 7782

Pastoral
Verde–Unga Musiker
   (*Barococo Suite; Trumpet Concertino; Lyric Suite*) Proprius Artemis
   ARTE 60105

See also Recitals: S 8; S 9

LIDHOLM, Ingvar (1921-   )

Laudi, for choir
Ericson–Swedish Radio Choir
    (Bäck; Hambraeus) Sveriges Radio RELP 1096

Nausikaa ensam
Söderström. Westerberg–Swedish Radio Symphony Orchestra
    (Pettersson) Caprice CAP 1110
    (Stenhammar; Rosenberg) Caprice CAP 1022; CRD CRD 1004

Poesis for orchestra
Blomstedt–Stockholm Philharmonic Orchestra
    (Rosenberg) Swedish Society SLT 33160

Riter [Rites]
Ehrling–London Symphony Orchestra
    (Blomdahl; Rosenberg) Decca SXL 6180

LILJEFORS, Ruben (1871-1936)

See Recitals: S 8

LINDBERG, Nils (1933-   )

7 *Dalmålningar* (Variations on Folktunes)
Lindberg. Swedish Symphony Orchestra
    Swedish Society SLT 33217

Lapponian Suite
Wickman. Sjökvist–Norrköping Symphony Orchestra
    (Concerto Grosso in Dalecarlian Form) Bluebell BELL 140

Concerto Grosso in Dalecarlian Form
Sjökvist–Norrköping Symphony Orchestra
    (Lapponian Suite) Bluebell BELL 140

LINDBERG, Oskar (1887-1955)

Leksandssvit
Grevillius–Stockholm Philharmonic Orchestra
(Atterberg) Swedish Society SLT 33192

See also Recitals: S 1

LINDBLAD, Adolf Fredrik (1801-78)

See Recitals: S 1; S 6

LINDE, Bo (1933-70)

(2) Songs
Hallqvist; Linde
(Eklund; Carlstedt; Karkoff) Swedish Society SLT 33199

LUNDQUIST, Torbjörn (1920-   )

Symphony no. 3, *Dolorosa*
Maag–Stockholm Philharmonic Orchestra
Artemis ART 50-104

Landscape for Tuba & Strings
Lind. Westerberg–Swedish Radio Symphony Orchestra
(Nilsson, Vaughan Williams) Caprice CAP 1143

LUNDVIK, Hildor (1885-1951)

See Recitals: S 1

MALMFORS, Åke (1918-51)

See Recitals: S 1

MELLNÄS, Arne (1933-   )

Cabrillo
Harpans Kraft
    (Börtz; Sandström; Hanson, Eliasson) Caprice CAP 1070

NAUMANN, Johann Gottlieb (1741-1801)

Gustav Vasa (Overture)
Farncombe–Hovkapellet
    (Roman; Kraus) DG 2536 032

Pas de deux; Pas de quatre
Björlin–Drottningholm Theatre Chamber Orchestra
    (Roman; Uttini) HMV 063-34404; US: Nonesuch H 71213

Quartet in C for glass harmonica, flute, viola, cello
Hoffman and instrumental ensemble
    (Mozart) UK and US: Turnabout TV 34452

Sonatas: in D minor; G minor; E major
Ribbing
    (Piano recital) Sveriges Radio RELP 1079

NILSSON, Bo (1937-   )

Brief an Gösta Oswald
Dorow. Travis–Berlin Radio Symphony Orchestra, Günther Arndt Choir
    Suecia PS 3

Frequenzen; Szene III
Travis–Maderna Ensemble
    (Clementi; Kotónski; Schoenberg; Takahashi; Xenakis) US: Mainstream 5008

NYSTROEM, Gösta (1890-1966)

Concertino ricercante
Lareti. Ehrling–Stockholm Philharmonic Orchestra
(Bäck; Larsson) Philips 7325 005 (also listed as Philips 6559 004)

The Merchant of Venice (Theatre Suite no. 4)
Ehrling–Swedish Radio Symphony Orchestra
(Berwald) Sveriges Radio RELP 1105

Sinfonia Concertante
Bengtsson. Westerberg–Swedish Radio Symphony Orchestra
(Koch) Swedish Society SLT 33136

Songs of the Sea
Finnilä, Parsons
(Elgar) BIS LP 38

Symphony no. 1, *Breve*
Ehrling–Göteborg Symphony Orchestra
Caprice CAP 1116

Symphony no. 2, *Espressiva*
Ehrling–Göteborg Symphony Orchestra
(Alfvén) Lyssna 7

Symphony no. 3, *Del Mare*
Eskell. Mann–Stockholm Radio Symphony Orchestra
Metronome CLP 504
Söderström. Westerberg–Swedish Radio Symphony Orchestra
Swedish Society SLT 33207

See also Recitals: S 4

OLSSON, Otto (1879-1964)

Adagio
Lundkvist
(*Prelude and Fugue;* Vierne; Lundkvist; Sköld; Bach) Proprius 7750

3 Etudes
Fagius
> *(Sonata; Variations)* BIS LP 85

Holy Spirit Visit Us, (Advent)
Levén–Stockholm Philharmonic Orchestra, Gustav Vasa Chorus
> *(Psalm; Te Deum)* Swedish Society SLT 33169

Prelude and Fugue no. 3
Lundkvist
> *(Adagio;* Vierne; Lundkvist; Sköld; Bach) Proprius 7750

Prelude and Fugue in D sharp minor, op. 56
Fagius
> (Eklund; F. Couperin; Alan) BIS LP 7

Psalm no. 121
Levén–Stockholm Philharmonic Orchestra, Gustav Vasa Choir
> *(Holy Spirit; Te Deum)* Swedish Society SLT 33169

Sonata in E
Fagius
> *(3 Etudes; Variations)* BIS LP 85

Te Deum
Levén–Stockholm Philhramonic Orchestra, Gustav Vasa Choir
> *(Holy Spirit; Psalm)* Swedish Society SLT 33169

Variations on *Ave Maris Stella*
Fagius
> *(Etudes; Sonata)* BIS LP 85

PERGAMENT, Moses (1893-1977)

Den judiska sången
Nordin; Eliasson. Priest–Stockholm Philharmonic Orchestra and Choir
> Caprice CAP 2003

Krelantems och Eldeling (Ballet Suite)
Westerberg–Swedish Radio Symphony Orchestra
> (Pettersson) Caprice CAP 1126

See also Recitals: S 7

PETERSON-BERGER, Wilhelm (1867-1942)

Arnljot (Excerpts from the opera)
Hagegård; Thallaug; Langebo; Asker; Jehrlander. Kamu–Stockholm
Philharmonic Orchestra
  HMV E061-34925

Frösöblomster nos. 1 to 3 (complete)
Ribbing
  I: HMV E055-34351
  II: HMV E055-34352
  III: HMV E055-34353

Frösöblomster (Arr. Lundqvist)
Mats Olssons Orkester; Egon Kjerrmans Orkester
  Electra YSJL 1-540

Romance for Violin and Orchestra
Pierrou. Westerberg–Swedish Radio Symphony Orchestra
  (Violin Concerto) HMV CSDS 1083

Romances and Songs
Jonth; Brillioth; Alin
  BIS LP 42

(8) Songs for mixed choir
Stenlund–Uppsala Academic Chamber Choir
  (Swedish Choruses) Telestar TRS 11105

Songs to texts by E. A. Karlfeldt
Brilioth; Hagegård; Eyron
  HMV E161-34197/8

Suite for violin and piano, op. 15
Lysell; Bodin
  (Frösöblomster) Bluebell BELL 125

Symphony no. 1, op. 9
Doráti–Stockholm Philharmonic Orchestra
  (Utopia) Caprice CAP 1206

Symphony no. 2 in E flat, *Journey South*
Westerberg–Swedish Radio Symphony Orchestra
    HMV 061 35455

Symphony no. 3 in F minor, *Same Ätnam*
Frykberg–Swedish Radio Symphony Orchestra
    Sveriges Radio RELP 5001(M)

Ur Fridolins lustgård
Hagegård; Ahlmark
    (Rangström; Stenhammar) Fabo SLP 33106

Utopia per orchestra, op. 20
Segerstam–Stockholm Radio Symphony Orchestra
    (Symphony no. 1) Caprice CAP 1206

Violin Concerto
Pierrou. Westerberg–Swedish Radio Symphony Orchestra
    (Romance) HMV CSDS 1083

Violin Sonata no. 2
Mannberg; Lundén
    (Fryklöf) Caprice CAP 1120

See also Recitals: S 3

PETTERSSON, Allan (1911-   )

Barefoot Songs
(24): Rodin; Saedén; Ostman
    Swedish Society SLT 33230
(13): Sjunnesson; Larsson; Hemberg
    (Violin Sonatas) Caprice CAP 1028
(8, orch. Doráti): Saedén. Doráti–Stockholm Philharmonic Orchestra
    (Mahler) US: HNH 4003/4(2)

Concerto no. 1 for strings
Westerberg–Swedish Radio Symphony Orchestra
    (Lidholm) Caprice CAP 1110, (Pergament) Caprice CAP 1126

Mostly for strings
Westerberg–Swedish Radio Symphony Orchestra
(Sibelius) Swedish Society SLT 33203

Symphony no. 2
Westerberg–Swedish Radio Symphony Orchestra
Decca SXL 6265; Swedish Society SLT 33219

Symphony no. 6
Kamu–Norrköping Symphony Orchestra
UK: CBS 76553

Symphony no. 7
Doráti–Stockholm Philharmonic Orchestra
Swedish Society SLT 33194; Caprice CAP 1015; UK: Decca SXL
6538; US: London 6740

Symphony no. 8
Comissiona–Baltimore Symphony Orchestra
Polar POLS 289; DG 2531 176

Symphony no. 9
Comissiona–Göteborg Symphony Orchestra
Phonogram (in prep)

Symphony no. 10
Doráti–Swedish Radio Symphony Orchestra
(Blomdahl) HMV E061-35142

Symphony no. 12, *De döda på torget*
Larsson–Stockholm Philharmonic Orchestra and Choir, Uppsala Academy
Chamber Choir
Caprice CAP 1127

Symphony no. 14
Comissiona–Stockholm Philharmonic Orchestra
Phono Suecia PS 12

2-Violin Sonatas nos. 3 and 7
Grünfarb; Mannberg
(Barefoot Songs) Caprice CAP 1028

2-Violin Sonatas nos. 1, 3, 6, and 7
Röhn; Hamann
    Sverige Radio RELP 1119(M)

Vox Humana
Mellnäs; Rödin; Alexandersson; Hagegård. Westerberg–Swedish Radio
Chorus and Symphony Orchestra
    BIS LP 55

RANGSTRÖM, Ture (1884-1947)

Divertimento Elegiaco
Westerberg–Royal Court Orchestra
    (*Ur Kung Eriks visor*) Telefunken TR 11130

Songs
R. Leanderson; H. Leanderson
    (Stenhammar) RCA Victrola VICS 1603
(4): Nilsson. Bokstedt–Vienna Opera Orchestra
    (Sibelius; Grieg) UK: Decca SXL 6185; US: London 25942
(3):Ligendza. Westerberg–Swedish Radio Symphony Orchestra
    (Larsson) HMV E061-35149
(15):Söderström; Ronnlund
    (Nystroem; Ives) HMV C053-35162
18 Songs
Hagegård; Scheja
    Caprice CAP 1208

String Quartet
Crafoord Quartet
    (Ravel; Mendelssohn) Swedish Society SLT 33225

Symphony no. 1 in C sharp minor, *August Strindberg in memoriam*
Mann– Stockholm Concerts Association
    Decca LXT 2665(M)

Ur Kung Eriks visor [King Eric's Songs]
Hagegård; Ahlmark
    (Stenhammar; Peterson-Berger) Fabo SLP 33106

Söderström; Saedén; Westerberg
(*Divertimento*) Telestar TR 11130
Brilioth; Carlsen
(Sjögren; Stenhammar; Schubert; Schumann) HMV E155-35211/2
(2, nas)

See also Recitals: S 2; S 4; S 5; S 9

ROMAN, Johan Helmich (1694-1758)

Drottningholm Music, B. 2
(nos. 1, 3, 19, 7, 10, 11, 13, 14, 16, 17, 20, 23): Westerberg–Drottningholm Chamber Orchestra
(*Symphonies in D and E minor*) Swedish Society SLT 33140
(nos. 1, 3, 4, 5, 7, 8, 9, 10, 11, 19, 20, 23): Farncombe–Hovkapellet
(Kraus; Naumann) DG 2536 032
(nos. 1, 4, 12, 17, 7, 9, 10, 13, 15, 16, 18, 22, 23): Björlin–Drottningholm Chamber Orchestra
(Naumann; Uttini) HMV 063-34404 (old no. SCLP 1054); US:
Nonesuch H 71213

Oboe Concerto in B flat, B. 46
Gillblad. Björlin–Stockholm Baroque Ensemble
(Larsson; Uttini) HMV 063-34405

Oboe d'amore Concerto in D
Nilsson. Verde–Musica Sveciae
(Larsson; Frumerie) Fermat FLPS 10

Organ Concertos in B flat and G
Arnér
(Koch) Proprius 7761

Overture in G minor, B. 42
Musica Holmiae
(*Symphonies in D and E*) Taglietti; Bononcini; Galuppi. Sveriges
Radio RELP 1178

Sonatas in C and D minor
Nordenfelt
(Agrell) US: Orion 74157

Sonata à tre in F minor
Musica Holmiae
(Albrici; Johnsen; Pfleger; Förster; Ritter) HMV E061-35164

Suite in D minor (1Bn no. 6)
Genetay–National Museum Chamber Orchestra
(Kraus; Johnsen) HMV 061 35584

Suite in C; Suite in D; *Sicilienne*
Ribbing
(Recital) Sveriges Radio RELP 1078

Suite in D
Nordenfelt
(Agrell; Johnsen; Uttini) HMV 061 35826

Swedish Mass
Wolf; Olsson; Aruhn
Hemberg–Norrköping Symphony Orchestra; Stockholm University Choir
US: Peters PLE 053

Symphony in E, B. 3 (Suite)
Musica Holmiae
(*Symphony in D; Overture in G minor;* Taglietti; Bononcini; Galuppi)
Sveriges Radio RELP 1178

Symphony in G, B. 9
Liljefors–Stockholm Ensemble
(Bach; Zellbell) Aurora ARS 7107

Symphony in B flat, B. 11
Philharmonic Chamber Ensemble
(*Violin Concerto;* Larsson) Swedish Society SLT 33187

Symphony in E minor, B. 22
Drottningholm Chamber Orchestra
(*Symphony in D; Drottningholm Music)* Swedish Society SLT 33140
Stockholm Chamber Ensemble
(Larsson; Sallinen; Telemann) BIS LP 46; US: HNH 4011

Symphony in D, B. 23
Drottningholm Chamber Orchestra
(*Symphony in E minor; Drottningholm Music)* Swedish Society SLT
33140

Symphony in D, B. 24
Musica Holmiae
   (*Symphony in E; Overture in G minor;* Taglietti; Bononcini; Galuppi)
   Sveriges Radio RELP 1178

Violin Concerto in D minor, B. 49
Berlin. Philharmonic Chamber Ensemble
   (*Symphony in B flat;* Larsson) Swedish Society SLT 33187

ROSELL, Lars-Erik (1944-   )

See Recitals: S 7

ROSENBERG, Hilding (1892-   )

Christmas Oratorio
Ericson–Swedish Radio Choir and Orchestra
   Sveriges Radio RELP 5007

Concertino no. 3, *Louisville* Concerto
Westerberg–Swedish Radio Symphony Orchestra
   (Hermanson) Swedish Society SLT 33215

Journey to America (Excerpts)
Doráti–Stockholm Philharmonic Orchestra
   (Berwald; Blomdahl) Caprice CAP 1013; UK and US: RCA Victrola
   VICS 1319

Marionetter (Overture)
Ehrling–London Symphony Orchestra
   (Blomdahl; Lidholm) Decca SXL 6180

Orfeus i Stan [Orpheus in Town] (Dance Suite)
Westerberg-Swedish Radio Symphony Orchestra
   (Lidholm; Stenhammar) Caprice CAP 1022; CRD CRD 1004

Sonata no. 2
Negro
   (Blomdahl; Brahms) Caprice CAP 1105

String Quartet no. 4
Fresk Quartet
   (Bartók) Caprice CAP 1051

String Quartet no. 6
The Gotland Quartet
   (Beethoven) Caprice CAP 1237

String Quartet no. 12
Copenhagen Quartet
   (Bentzon) Caprice CAP 1100

Symphony no. 2, *Grave*
Blomstedt–Stockholm Philharmonic Orchestra
   (Wirén) Turnabout TV 34436
   (Lidholm) Swedish Society SLT 33160

Symphony no. 3
Blomstedt–Stockholm Philharmonic Orchestra
   HMV CSDS 1071

Symphony no. 6
Westerberg–Stockholm Philharmonic Orchestra
   (Koch) Swedish Society SLT 43053
   (Blomdahl) Turnabout TV 34318

(3) Violin Sonatas
Berlin; Barter; Spierer
   Caprice CAP 1010(M)

SANDSTRÖM, Sven-David (1942-   )

(5) Duets
Harpans Kraft
   (Börtz; Mellnäs; Hanson; Eliasson) Caprice CAP 1070

In the Meantime
Naumann–Musica Nova
   (Webern; Naumann; Kotónski; Nilsson, etc) Caprice CAP 1034

See also Recitals: S 7

SJÖBERG, Birger (1885-1929)

10 Songs from *Fridas Book*
Sällstrom, Bengtsson
Telestar TR 11058

See also Recitals: S 3

SJÖGREN, Emil (1883-1918)

Violin Sonata no. 1 in G minor, op. 19
Berlin, Erikson
(Sibelius; Schumann) Swedish Society SLT 33201

See also Recitals: S 2; S 3

SÖDERLUNDH, Lille Bror (1912-57)

Oboe Concertino
Nilsson. Philharmonic Chamber Ensemble
(J.G. Berwald; Sibelius; Mozart) Swedish Society SLT 33191

Suite from *The Land o' Bells*
Byström. Musica Camerata Regionalis
(Karkoff; Mozart; Anon) Caprice CAP 1074

SÖDERMAN, August (1832-76)

7 Sacred Songs for Choir and Organ
Ericson. Swedish Radio Choir
(Olsson) Sveriges Radio RELP 1092

See also Recitals: S 5

STENHAMMAR, Wilhelm (1871-1927)

Chitra (Incidental Music)
Blomstedt–Stockholm Philharmonic Orchestra
(*Sången;* Lidholm) HMV CSDS 1072

(3) Choruses, à cappella
Ericson–Swedish Radio Chamber Choir
(Swedish Choral Music) HMV C063-29079

(3) Fantasias
Hjort
(*Violin Sonata*) HMV CSLP 1058

Florez och Blanzeflor
Wixell. Westerberg–Swedish Radio Symphony Orchestra
(*Serenade*) HMV E061-35148

Piano Concerto no. 1 in B minor
Mannheimer. Dutoit–Göteborg Symphony Orchestra
Sterling S 1004

Piano Concerto no. 2 in D minor
Solyom. Westerberg–Munich Philharmonic Orchestra
(Liszt) HMV E063-34284

Sången, Mellanspel
Blomstedt–Stockholm Philharmonic Orchestra
(*Chitra;* Lidholm) HMV CSDS 1072

Sensommarnätter
Roos
(Eklund; Mozart, Liszt; Hindemith) Caprice CAP 1020

(2) Sentimental Romances
Tellefsen. Westerberg–Swedish Radio Symphony Orchestra
(Rosenberg; Lidholm) Caprice CAP 1022

Serenade in F, op. 31
Kubelik–Stockholm Philharmonic Orchestra
(Koch) Swedish Society SLT 33227 (2 sides) UK: Helidor 89622
Westerberg–Swedish Radio Symphony Orchestra
(*Florez och Blanzeflor*) HMV E061-35148

Sonata in A minor, op 19
Saulesco, Solyom
  (3 Fantasias) HMV SCLP 1058

Songs
R. Leanderson; H. Leanderson
  RCA Victrola VICS 1603
Seadén, Ribera
  (String Quartet No. 6) HMV E053-35116

String Quartet no. 2
Kyndel Quartet
  Sveriges Radio RELP 1038(M)

String Quartet no. 4
Vlach Quartet
  DG 2530 396

String Quartet no. 6
Frydén Quartet
  (Songs) HMV E053-35116

Symphony no. 1 in F
Järvi–Gothenburg Symphony Orchestra
  BIS LP 219

Symphony no. 2 in G minor, op. 34
Mann–Stockholm Philharmonic Orchestra
  Swedish Society SLT 33198; US: RCA LSC 9854
Westerberg–Stockholm Philharmonic Orchestra
  Caprice CAP 1151

See also Recitals: S 2; S 3; S 4; S 5; S 9

UTTINI, Francesco (1723-95)

Les Chinois (Ballet Suite)
Björlin–Stockholm Baroque Ensemble
  (Larsson; Roman) HMV 063-34405

Fiskarena (Ballet Suite)
Farncombe–Hovpakellet
 (Roman; Naumann) DG 2536 032

Il Rè Pastore (Overture)
Björlin–Drottningholm Theatre Chamber Orchestra
 (Naumann; Roman) HMV 063-34404; US: Nonesuch H 71213

Sonata no. 4 in A
Nordenfelt
 (Roman, Agrell, Johnsen) HMV 061 35826

WELIN, Karl-Erik (1934-   )

String Quartet no. 2, *PC-132*
Saulesco Quartet
 (Shostakovich; Wirén) Caprice CAP 1024

WERLE, Lars Johan (1926-   )

The Dream of Thérèse (Scenes from the opera)
Hallin; Saedén; Malmborg; Jehrlander; Jonsson; Stättegård; Höiseth;
Nåslund; Tyrén. Gielen–Medlemmer Royal Court Orchestra
 Swedish Society SLT 33177

Nautical Preludes for Choir
Ericson–Swedish Radio Choir
 (Penderecki; Ligeti; Castiglioni) Electrola C063-29075

Pentagram
Kyndel Quartet
 (Carlstedt; Bäck) Caprice CAP 1018(M)

Die Reise (Excerpts from the opera)
Ludwig–Hamburg Opera Orchestra
 Electrola C195-29107/9(3)

WIKLUND, Adolf (1879-1950)

Piano Concerto no. 2 in B flat
Erikson. Westerberg–Swedish Radio Orchestra
(*Three pieces for strings and harp; Sång till våren*) Caprice CAP 1165

Three Pieces for strings and harp (1924)
Westerberg–Swedish Radio Orchestra
(Piano Concerto no. 2; Sång till våren) Caprice CAP 1165

WIKMANSON, Johan (1754-1800)

Piano Pieces
Ribbing
(Naumann; Kraus) Sveriges Radio RELP 1079

String Quartet in B flat, op. 1, no. 1
Kyndel Quartet
(Beethoven) Caprice CAP 3014

String Quartet in E minor, op. 1, no. 2
Chilingirian Quartet
(Berwald) CRD CRD 1061
Saulesco Quartet
(Verdi) Caprice CAP 1065
(Wirén) HMV SCLP 1069

String Quartet in B flat, op. 1, no. 3
Saulesco Quartet
Caprice CAP 1133

WIRÉN, Dag (1905-   )

Music for Strings
Hedwall–Örebro Chamber Orchestra
(Hedwall; Koch; Larsson) Swedish Society SLT 33224

Serenade for Strings, op. 11
Montgomery–Bournemouth Sinfonietta
   (Dvořák; Grieg; Nielsen; Tchaikovsky) HMV ESD 7001
Somary–English Camber Orchestra
   (Grieg) US: Vanguard C 10067
Westerberg–Stockholm Philharmonic Orchestra
   (Larsson) Swedish Society SLT 33176; US: London CS 6430

Sinfonietta in C, op. 7A
Westerberg–Radio Orchestra
   (Atterberg; Frumerie) Swedish Society SLT 33167

String Quartet no. 2
Saulesco Quartet
   (Wikmanson) HMV SCLP 1069

String Quartet no. 5
Saulesco Quartet
   (Shostakovich; Welin) Caprice CAP 1024

Symphony no. 4
Ehrling–Swedish Radio Symphony Orchestra
   (Blomdahl) Swedish Society SLT 33147
   (Blomdahl; Eklund) Swedish Society SLT 33241
   (Rosenberg) Turnabout TV 34436

See also Recitals: S 9

ZELLBELL, Ferdinand (1719-80)

Flute Concerto in G
Adorján. Liljefors–Stockholm Ensemble
   (Bach; Roman) Aurora ARS 7101

Recitals and Concerts of Swedish Music

S 1–Choruses by Alfvén, Hedar, Lindberg, Lindblad, Lundvik, and Malmfors.
    Eyron. Ericson–Swedish Radio Chorus
    Swedish Society SLT 33188

S 2–Songs by Rangström, Sjögren, and Stenhammar
    Brilioth, Carlson
    (Schubert, Schumann) HMV E155-35211/2 (2, nas)

S 3–Songs by Alfvén, Althén, Ekölf, Peterson-Berger, Sjöberg, Sjögren, and Stenhammar
    Gedda. Grevillius–Stockholm Philharmonic Orchestra
    RCA LSC 10034

S 4–Songs by Frumerie, Nystroem, Rangström, and Stenhammar
    Meyer; Söderström; Eyron
    Swedish Society SLT 33171

S 5–Songs and Romances by Eklöf, Rangström, Söderman, Stenhammar
    Rautavaara; S. Björling; J. Berglund; Alfer; Schymberg; G. Björling
    (Sibelius) Telestar TR 11148

S 6–Elisabeth Soderström sings Jenny Lind Songs (by Ahlström, Josephson, Lindblad, Benedict, Berg, Jeffreys, Mendelssohn and Schumann)
    Söderström, Eyron
    Swedish Society SLT 33209

S 7–Swedish Chamber Music
Alldahl: *Stem the Blood-Flow*
    Sitar. Bohlin–Lund University Male Choir
Gefors: Four Songs about Trusting
    Leanderson, Rörby
Hermanson: *Suoni d'un Flauto; Flauto d'inverno*
    Bahr
Holewa: Concertino no. 3
    Instrumental Ensemble
Pergament: Sonatina

Bahr. Westerberg-Musica Sveciae
Rosell: *Poem in the Dark*
Raccuja. Westerberg—Instrumental Ensemble
Sandström: *Close to ...*
 Stevensson, Persson
 BIS LP 32

S 8—Swedish Composers play their own Music
Blomdahl: Six Small Pieces without Pedal
Frumerie: Chaconne
Karkoff: *Oriental Pictures,* op. 66
Koch: Rhythmic Bagatelles
Larsson: *Espressivo,* op. 36
Liljefors: Three Studies, nos. 2 and 3
 Swedish Society SLT 33184

S 9—Swedish Piano Music
Larsson: Sonatina no. 1, op. 16
Rangström: *Legends of Mälaren Lake*
Stenhammar: Three Fantasies, op. 11
Wirén: *Ironical Miniatures,* op. 19
 Scheja
 RCA LSC 3119

Bibliography

List of Works Cited

Cnattingius, Claes M. *Contemporary Swedish Music.* Stockholm: The Swedish Institute, 1973

Eckman, Karl. *Jean Sibelius; his Life and Personality.* Helsinki: Holger Schildts, 1935; translation London: Alan Wilmer, 1936.

Gray, Cecil. *Sibelius the Symphonies.* London: Oxford University Press, 1935

Horton, John. *Scandinavian Music.* London: Faber and Faber, 1963.

Kalevala translation W.F. Kirby. London: J.M. Dent, 1907

Layton, Robert. *Sibelius.* London: J. M. Dent & Sons, 1965; revised 1978.

Musikrevy Stockholm. *Swedish Music Past and Present.* Stockholm: Musikrevy, 1966.

Parmet, Simon. *The Symphonies of Sibelius.* Helsinki: Soderström, 1955; translation London: Cassell, 1959.

Sermilä, Jarmo. *Finland's Composers.* Helsinki: Ministry for Foreign Affairs, 1976.

Simpson, Robert. *Sibelius and Nielsen.* London: BBC Publications, 1965

Index